》》》》》》》》》》 《《《《《《《《《《

Honoré de Balzac The Bureau-crats

EDITED AND WITH AN INTRODUCTION BY MARCO DIANI

TRANSLATED BY CHARLES FOULKES

NORTHWESTERN UNIVERSITY PRESS

EVANSTON, ILLINOIS

》》》》》》》》》》 《《《《《《《《《《

Northwestern University Press
Evanston, Illinois 60208

ISBN CLOTH 0-8101-0973-5
PAPER 0-8101-0987-5

The Bureaucrats

»»» CONTENTS «««

Introduction: The Letters of Bureaucracy   vii

Note on the Text   xxx

PART I. BETWEEN TWO WOMEN

I. The Rabourdin Household   5

II. Monsieur des Lupeaulx   29

III. The Teredos Navalis, Otherwise Known as Shipworm   46

PART II. THE BUREAUS

IV. Three-Quarter-Length Portraits of Certain Civil Servants   73

V. The Machine in Motion   114

VI. The Worms at Work   151

PART III. TO WHOM THE PLACE?

VII. Scenes from the Home Front   173

VIII. Enter Madame Rabourdin   189

IX. Forward, Mollusks!   204

X. The Resignation   222

The Letters of Bureaucracy
by Marco Diani

For M and M

"Bureaucracy" is a term that is still up-to-date after more than two centuries and shows no sign of going out of fashion. On the contrary, with the passage of time, as modern societies become more complex and more fragmented, so grows the equivocal, evocative power of the concept of bureaucracy: it has profound resonance, often provoking a disturbing unease. The philosopher Claude Lefort is correct in observing that "fallen onto the common ground between Political Sociology, Theory of History, and Theory of Public Opinion, fully sanctioned by the success it has been granted, the concept of Bureaucracy nevertheless remains so imprecise in its application that we continue to inquire, with good reason, into the identity of the phenomenon that it presumes to designate."[1]

From the very beginning of the "bureaucratic phenomenon" and the discourse it has generated, the path has been laid and the signs posted to help us combine various methods in order to comprehend it in all its social, political, and psychological ramifications. Baron Grimm wrote to Diderot in July 1964: "We are obsessed with the idea of regulation and our *Maîtres de requêtes* refuse to understand that there is an infinity of things in a great nation with which the government should not occupy itself. The late Mr. Gournay had the habit of saying that 'in France we have a national malady: Buromania.'"[2] The "ideal/typical" territory to be studied is already delineated here, and a year later, in another letter, Grimm specified that "the true spirit of the Law, in France, is the Bureaucracy. The offices, the clerks, the secretaries, the inspectors, the superintendents, are not employed for the benefit of the public interest. Rather, in practice, it seems that the public interest is instituted so that these offices may exist."[3]

The genealogy and the very identity of a concept destined for such a remarkable career are characterized from the beginning by close contact between literature and politics, between art and social science—a trademark that lasts into our own day. After Grimm and Diderot came Honoré de Balzac and Karl Marx, and, in this century, Max Weber, Franz Kafka, and Robert Musil—to name only a few sublime examples of the literature on bureaucracy. And why should it not be so? The anguish of any society can be found in its literature, often earlier and more clearly revealed than in its social sciences. It is not the goal of this essay to determine whether the literary fortune of the concept of bureaucracy, inaugurated with such distinction by Balzac, is a reflection, to borrow a term from Lukács and the Marxist critics—or rather, to use a more literary expression, a prophetic anticipation—of a new social reality. It is in fact precisely in the difference and the radical distance between literature and social science—in their respective methods, language, and aims—that, paradoxically, in their attempts to comprehend the bureaucratic phenomenon, their common interest is revealed. Scientific analyses, political imagination, harrowing doubts that remain unanswered, individual behavior and collective passions, all measure themselves on the same ground: the reaction of people to the new way of living called the "modern." Thanks to and through his exploration of the terra incognita of the bureaucracy, we are able to discover a new dimension in Honoré de Balzac.

For more than a century after his death, Balzac's work on political theory was for the most part undervalued, misunderstood, or simply ignored. This lack of interest contributed in no little measure to the almost total loss of some of his most brilliant and profound discoveries. These insights reveal themselves today, more than two centuries after the French and American revolutions and the rise of the "centralized" states, as genuine "scientific" prophecies.[4] Like his contemporary Alexis de Tocqueville, that other great but misunderstood figure, Balzac has received new recognition as the model of the "democratic," and the "mass" society that both writers so prophetically analyzed has taken on shape and definition.

The evolution of the concept of bureaucracy is intimately intertwined with that of democracy; it is in fact democracy's other face, and as such appears quite early among Balzac's reflections. Notwithstanding the multiplicity of his themes and interests, Balzac was a thinker who continuously rewrote the same single book, pivoting constantly around his leitmotif, amplifying it finally into the gigantic, heroic proportions of *La Comédie humaine*.[5] He himself was quite aware of the anachronistic modernity of his ideas and scientific methods. Unconcerned about his own personal lack of success, he wrote without embarrassment to his most faithful friends and admirers:

I don't really believe, in this day and age, in the error of the reading public's opinion. I am therefore committed to discover where *I* have gone wrong. I think the problem I'm looking for lies in the nature of the book itself, which treats something obscure and problematic that doesn't grab the imagination of the public. If I had spoken about democratic society only in the United States, it would have been easily understood. If I had spoken about democratic society only in France as it exists today, again, it would all have been easily comprehended. Starting from the ideas that both the French and the American societies furnish, however, I wished to illustrate the general characteristics of democratic society, which still lacks a comprehensive model. That's where the spirit of the typical reader escapes me.[6]

This letter already contains the entire program of the research Balzac would attempt to complete, particularly in his last decade, in working on his analysis of the Revolution.

The Career of "The Bureaucrats"

With *The Bureaucrats*, Balzac wrote the great novel of the bureaucracy, paradoxically managing to create at one stroke both a new literary type and its uncontested masterpiece. In so doing he inspired all those who followed him, from Flaubert and Melville to Kafka, and not only these novelists but all the great reformers and idealists of modernity up to Max Weber and C. Wright Mills.

Balzac did not invent a new genre. We have seen how the "common base of the bureaucratic stereotype" had existed in France for some time and was deeply rooted in the collective consciousness of his society. Rather, Balzac's innovation was in overcoming the banalization of the bureaucratic stereotype by giving a more adventurous, dramatic, and mock-heroic stamp to the preexisting verbal and narrative material. Balzac himself alerted us to this, in case it were not sufficiently clear. He was not writing a novel, but an analysis of a new form of power that would dominate modern societies: the mediocracy, marked by the end of individuality, the disappearance of traditional values, and the rise of mass society.[7] Balzac the social scientist witnessed what was being built on the ruins of premodern society, a harmony between two new aspects of social being: one having to do with the subjectivity of the individual actor and his passion for power; the other concerning the objective inscription of the sign of money—the gold that blinds and consumes. "Desire burns us and Power destroys us, but Knowledge leaves our system in a perpetual state of calm," says one of his characters.[8]

Knowledge/Power, Nascent State

Knowledge, therefore, remains. In modern literature, Balzac represents one of the extreme examples of intellectual power in its nascent form. Bequeathed a prophetic vision in which the motif of money, the tragic isolation of the modern individual, and the absolute rift between values and "things" assume extraordinary importance, Balzac wrote almost as though to define modernity as an epoch of transition—as, in fact, the transitional epoch par excellence. The visionary power of his intellectuality must be stressed, because visionary knowledge can exist only in the realm of the immeasurable, the ineffable, the immaterial, whose elements encompass all of Balzac's novels, to paraphrase the apt expression of Stefan Zweig. The accumulation of capital and the concentration of finance, political revolution, the birth of the social state and the rise of the bureaucracy, the emergence of completely unprecedented personal and collective relations—Balzac treats these themes, always anchoring his thought in the novel, thus obligating his readers to reenact his own process of analysis and definition of the problem.[9]

This is, in fact, the very paradox of the prophetic modernity of Balzac. We can call him our contemporary, not in virtue of some kind of "rediscovery" of his work, nor because of some real backward "reflection" of our time to his, but because only now have modern societies finally taken on the forms he prophesied, explored, and analyzed. This is so, above all, politically, because instead of manifesting nostalgia for the past, Balzac never missed the chance to exalt the figure of Napoleon as a brilliant organizer, an astute populist revolutionary, and a fervid model of an entirely modern form of efficiency and audacity.

Since 1789, the state, nation, or *patrie* if you like, has replaced the prince. Instead of looking directly to the chief political magistrate, the clerks have become, in spite of our fine patriotic ideas, the employees of the government, and their superiors are buffeted by the winds of a power called minister, who does not know from day to day whether he will be in office tomorrow. Since the routine of business must go on, a certain number of indispensable clerks survive; indispensable but at the mercy of the administration, they want to keep their positions. Bureaucracy, a giant power set in motion by dwarfs, is thus born. If, by subordinating all things and all men to his will, Napoleon for a time put off the influence of bureaucracy (that mighty veil between the task at hand and the man who can get it done), it was permanently organized under the constitutional government, which was, inevitably, the friend of all mediocrities, the lover of authentic documents and accounts, and as meddlesome as a petit bourgeois.[10]

The paradoxical scenario that for years cast Balzac as a monarcho-clerical legitimist, political reactionary, and artistic progressive should be discredited once and for all. The legend was born—other than from contradictory statements, as ambiguous as they are innumerable, made by Balzac himself—in the letters of Marx and Engels, from which Marxist scholars have since constructed analytic telescopes so reductive as to eliminate the possibility of any other vision. For example, Engels wrote to Miss Harkness:

> Certainly, Balzac was a political legitimist; his great work is a continuous elegy of the inevitable ruin of decent society. All his sympathies are for the class condemned to fade into the dusk. Nevertheless, his satire is never so pungent, his irony never so bitter, as when he puts into play the very men and women with whom he so profoundly sympathizes—that is, the nobles. And the only men of whom he always speaks with frank admiration are their most resolute political adversaries. . . . That Balzac therefore was compelled to act against his own class sympathies and political prejudices, that he saw the necessity for the sun to set on his beloved nobles and that he describes them as men who merit no better destiny, that he saw the true men of the future in the place they were to be found in that era—all this I consider one of the triumphs of realism, and one of the greatest qualities of dear old Balzac.[11]

This reading willingly acknowledges the analytical "progressivism" in Balzac's work, while simultaneously pointing out the limitations of his conclusions, drawn in an era of theoretical immaturity—which is to say, before the scientific explanation of capitalist society as presented by Marx. Thus, what results is a curious oscillation of the criticism between a progressive and a reactionary Balzac, carried to the point of caricature when the author and his work are turned into a battlefield between "Right" and "Left." The critics seem unaware of the involuntary irony of their acting out scenarios already foreseen, down to the smallest detail, by Balzac himself.[12] By a still greater irony and paradox, both such opposed readings manage to perceive the double valences, the multiplicity, in the infinite and sublime Balzac: the "progressive"—conscious of the fundamental importance of the "economic" outlook, analyst of the liquidation of values that comes with industrial development, forerunner and prophet of Marx and "materialism"—goes hand in hand with Balzac the literary genius, who lays the foundation for a scientific analysis of society, in that revolution takes place in the forms of things.

THE REVOLUTION IN FORM[13]

Balzac constantly sought to weave together these two threads that would seem to be impossible to join, to understand how the impulse to power is congeni(t)ally linked to the capitalist circulation of money. These perpetual and incessant movements, which require the virtuosity of a true "political Paganini," form the continuum of *La Comédie humaine*; they are the ontological essence of the new leaders, the shining god of the new society represented by and amplified in the bureaucracy.

Even if the reactionary/progressive view of Balzac happened to be accurate—and it most certainly is not, no matter how many critics, Marxist and not, have bogged themselves down in it for a century—it could never be applied to *The Bureaucrats*. Who loses this match? Certainly the reformer Rabourdin, betrayed by a conspiracy among his own followers; the fiery republican Fleury,[14] who gets fired; the delicate and pathetic Minard, fashioning paper flowers with his wife, who quits. Even the opportunist par excellence, the "vaudevillian" Bixiou, wicked, lazy, and fantastical, finds that it does not pay to cretinize himself in the halls of a power with no center. But these are not in fact the losers: their escape from the ministry explicitly signals their entry into the history, the political relations, and the economy of modernity.

Contrary to what "dear old" Engels might imagine, Balzac has an extremely clear political vision, as well as a theory of modern political relations, which appears in *The Bureaucrats* in all its power. It is a theory whose actors call themselves Napoleon, a theory born of the epic moment of the Convention, a model of energy, consisting for the most part of young people, of which

no sovereign can ever forget that it was able to raise fourteen armies against all of Europe. Its policy, fatal in the eyes of those who cling to so-called absolute power, was nevertheless dictated by strictly monarchical principles, for it acted essentially like one great king.

After ten or twelve years of parliamentary struggle, having pondered politics to the point of wearing himself out, this minister was actually enthroned by his party, which saw him as their man for business. Happily for him, he was closer to sixty than fifty; if he had retained even a vestige of youth's vigor he would have quickly been broken. But, used to being broken, to retreating and returning to take charge, he would let himself be struck again and again—by his party, by the Opposition, by the Court, by the clergy—by running up against inertia with a substance at once soft and consistent; and so he reaped the fruits of his misfortune.[15]

The Bureaucrats is not a "historical novel," but rather a *theoreti-*

cal novel. And thoroughly to topple the reading of Engels, we must say that Balzac confronts the problems of the state, economy, and money not only *en poète*—that is, without really knowing what he is doing—but, on the contrary, with extreme refinement and theoretical cognizance, as a "doctor of social science" from the 1840s on. It is a remarkable coincidence that the years during which he threw himself entirely into *La Comédie humaine* are the same during which Marx and Engels first elaborated their theories, and when Tocqueville was already famous for having written *Democracy in America*.[16] All these authors have in common not only an era but, even more, a will to analyze its structural principles, composed of elements invisible to "vulgar" observers up to that time. Thus, after many years of "blindness," we render to Balzac that which is rightfully his, even if the work of the others enjoys the primacy accorded their privileged "form of discourse"—that is, the "scientific"—in addition, of course, to their immense political influence. We shall reverse the traditional roles; we shall regard the novelist as a social theorist; we shall ask the poet to give us the very essentials for the comprehension of his society. Furthermore, we shall start from the central ideas of Balzac's sociology to arrive, ultimately, at a rereading of the role played by the bureaucracy in Marx. After all, it is terribly banal to apply standard Marxism to Balzac; that is the canon. Perhaps we shall discover that it is more interesting to proceed in the opposite direction, to pass through Balzac on the way to Marx.[17]

Instead of limiting himself to the story of a single protagonist or the study of a single character, in *The Bureaucrats* Balzac managed to write the "novel of a social class," just as he would do again later (and certainly not by chance) with *Paysans*, which can be considered the other face of *The Bureaucrats*. Although Balzac proceeds decisively toward this break with the "novelistic pact" dominant in his time, his choice was not an easy one, and turned out to be even more difficult for his public: Balzac had overdone it, had moved too rapidly, and had left no way back. The numerous palimpsests, the complicated editorial history, the various editions, and the transformations in the body of the novel itself all testify to the birth and growth of this brilliant, extremely modern, and extremely risky intuition in Balzac. In 1838 a first version appeared entitled *La Femme supérieure*, centering on the character of Célestine Rabourdin, one of the many masterpieces of feminine beauty and perspicacity that populate *La Comédie humaine*. The publication had appeared serially in feuilleton the previous year. "Yesterday," Balzac wrote to his beloved Madame Hanska, "after Heine, I met Rothschild on the boulevard, which is to say all the intelligence and all the money of the Jews. Rothschild couldn't resist saying, 'What have you done now?' *La Femme supérieure* had been flooding La Presse for fourteen days."[18]

That Balzac was not satisfied with his work seems clear from the insistence with which he justified himself to his *etrangère* in a letter some days earlier:

You will read in a few days *La Femme supérieure*, and if I have ever needed serious and sincere advice on a composition, I need it now. Every day twenty letters of reproof arrive at the newspaper, from people canceling their subscriptions, etc., saying there could be nothing more boring, that the chatter is insipid; and they send me these letters. There is one, among all the others, that claims to be a great admirer of mine and cannot comprehend the stupidity of such a composition. If that's the way it is, then I must have made a grave mistake.[19]

But rather than confessing to a mistake he did not make and accepting the public's verdict of his own failure, Balzac, knowing that

nomen est omen, realized that with the development of the bureaucracy we stand before a new, unprecedented, and colossal stage de-
sign that will provide a setting for the representation of the drama
of the world born of the French Revolution. It will be a drama
without main characters, dominated by a new temporal unity em-
bracing a long period of Western history.[20] The protagonist of the
new drama must be at once collective and anonymous, and the
shoulders of the lovely Rabourdin cannot support the weight. "*La
Femme supérieure*," Balzac wrote later, "no longer expresses the
subject of my study, as the heroine, though decidedly a superior
woman, is by now no more than an accessory instead of the principal character."[21] But the principal character of the novel no longer
has a single name or a recognizable face; it is a "machine in motion"
where we find "the worms at work," in the words of two chapter titles. But how to write a novel about "nothingness"? How to render comprehensible what happens in the "compartmentalized civilization of the Administration" where a person lives on twenty-two
sous a day, in perpetual struggle with the tailor and the shoemaker,
without becoming anything but a cretin?

Writing a precise and minute study of a French ministerial division through the public life and private habits of its doorkeepers,
clerks, chiefs, directors, general secretaries, and ministers, without
leaving out the role of their families, wives, and lovers, as well as
journalists and other extras—this describes *The Bureaucrats* exactly. These are the true protagonists, the clerks of a state from which
one does not know quite what one wants or where this humiliated
and degraded humanity, left perennially suspended, is. It hangs
somewhere between classes that history, within its own temporali-
ty, called, in professional slang, the "career." To achieve this,
Balzac the physiologist followed the advice that Cuvier gave to
Stendhal: "If you wish to overcome the repulsion certain disgusting
creatures inspire, study their loves, their intimacy, the hidden and

unexpected sides of their character." Balzac recognized how great, in society as in nature, is the strength "of the worm that topples an elm by tunneling itself a path through its bark." In his writing he renders visible the microscopic view that enlarges and delineates the worms whose faces resemble Mitral, Gigonnet, Baudoyer, Saillard, Gaudron, Falleix, Transon, Godard, and Company—that is, the clerks. Having found a way to speak about the worms who swarm in the offices, he must now uncover the object of their restless avidity and endless activity.

In *The Bureaucrats*, it is no longer a question of portraying only the great stereotypical "Balzacian" characters who build and destroy colossal fortunes and destinies, such as Grandet or Birotteau. Here we do not find the strokes of genius of the usurer Gobsek or the supreme intelligence of the banker Nucingen. Instead we stand before a boundless vision of an "armed bureaucracy" that never existed under the monarchy—in fact, never at all before the *aurea mediocritas* of the clerks, before the mystery of the bureaucracy that, after Balzac and his reformer hero Xavier Rabourdin, was to preoccupy all social thought.

Deeply troubled by the misery he witnessed in the lives of the civil servants, Xavier Rabourdin considered the cause of their growing discontent. He looked to its causes and found them in those petty partial revolutions—the eddies, as it were, of the storm of 1789—which the historians of great social movements fail to inquire into, although as a matter of fact it is they that have made our manners and customs what they now are.[22]

Laid out here, in a single sentence, is Balzac's theoretical program: to be able to show, to extract from the invisible, microscopic revolutions, the causes of the great social movements and, above all, of the changes in social behavior. At center stage can no longer be the great "characters," but rather the classes, with their history and the collective psychology and mentality that constitutes one of the highest achievements of Balzac's art.

The new foundations of power and the new hierarchies lie elsewhere, however. Power cannot be found where it is sought; it always remains somewhere just beyond. Ambiguously hidden beneath everything is gold—money, the measure of value of all things. Probably no one has felt and described more forcefully than Balzac the collective torments exacted by the passage to capitalist society and bourgeois values, and the profound spiritual and moral degradation that always accompanies this evolution at every level of society. This "ambiguity of the times" is the ambiguity of capitalist society under construction: progressive in its triumph of modern methods of production and organization, but terrifyingly inhuman because it places the destiny of enormous masses of the population in the hands of a few. Through its fundamental and systematic annulment of social differences, its rejections of particularities and localisms, the French Revolution, in the name of "universal" equality, of industrialization and its "hidden" consequences, established money as the only possible means of equalization.

The rhetoric of money and liberty, of power, will, and desire, developed with Balzac into a narrative of modern society compounded of ambivalence, hidden dimensions, brutal changes, and unexpected consequences. This binary code, moral as well as political and intellectual, reveals itself fully in *The Bureaucrats*. It was to become entirely typical of other of his works, especially when the analysis focused on the "ambiguous oppositions" between modern and premodern, aristocracy and equality, industry and liberty, and democracy and revolution. This universal revolution, the groundwork for which was laid by all the social and judicial turmoil, cannot be fully understood without a constant awareness of its other aspect: the emergence of an absolute passion for power rendered possible by a new incarnation of forces and social currents within the bosom of the new "financial" society.

And that is power. But where is the power? The bureaucracy, Balzac says, "a gigantic force driven by dwarfs," constantly annuls itself through continuous restaging and excessively theatrical performances. It is a power smashed to bits by the waves of revolution, or rather, by the erasure of mundane reality, its reduction to the world of mounds of paperwork, dust, impersonality, total alienation. *The Bureaucrats* deals with reality; but it is not (as, for that matter, is no other of Balzac's novels) a realistic novel. From beginning to end it has the atmosphere of a fantastic world, Hoffmanian, with strokes of Calembour absurdity, manias, tics of every type and sort, senseless hierarchies, a modern emporium of the right of the state. Herein lies the very solitude of modernity, in which light, locations, spaces, and volumes are "dematerialized," and appear as signs and symbols of a power that is only microscopically visible but extremely oppressive, in which one battles an implacable, invisible enemy. Enough to make you lose your mind. Or perhaps it would be better to say un/reason.

THE UN/REASON OF THE STATE
The bureaucracy is an authority that vacillates despite its continual expansion in numbers and importance, propped up at every level of the hierarchy by myriad insignificant objects that signify the meaninglessness of the activity taking place there.

Paved like the corridor and hung with shabby paper, the room where the office boy is stationed is furnished with a stove, a large black table with inkstand, pens, and paper, and benches without mats for the general public's feet; but the boy, seated in a good armchair, has a rug to put his up on. The office of the employees is a large room, more or less well-lighted, usually without a wooden floor. Wooden floors and fireplaces are specially set apart for bureau and division chiefs, as are the armoires, tables, and desks of mahogany, red or green morocco leather armchairs, sofas, silk curtains, and other articles of administrative luxury. The office of the employees has a stove, the pipe of which feeds into a blocked-off chimney, if there even is a chimney. The wallpaper is plain and one color, green or brown. The tables are of black wood. The ingenuity of the employees is demonstrated by the ways they sit at their desks: one who is cold has a wooden footstool under his feet; the man with a hot temperament only has a little something Spartan; the sluggard who dreads the opening and closing of doors, as well as other causes of fluctuations in temperature, constructs a little windbreak out of boxes. There is a wardrobe where everyone keeps his work coat with linen sleeves, glasses, caps, skullcaps, and other tools of the trade. Nearly every day the fireplace is full of bottles of water, glasses, and leftovers from lunch. In some out-of-the-way areas there are lamps. The door of the deputy chief's office is always open so that he can keep an eye on the employees, prevent them from chatting too much, or come out and talk with them if something big is up. The furnishings of the offices indicate to the observer the caliber of those who inhabit them. The drapes are white or of some colored cloth, either cotton or silk; the chairs are cherry or mahogany, trimmed with straw, leather, or cloth; the wallpaper is more or less new. Yet, to whichever administration all of these public possessions belong, as soon as it changes, there is nothing quite so uncanny as all of this furniture that has seen so many masters and so many administrations, that has weathered so many disasters. . . . all sorts of unimaginable tools with which France is administered—all have a horrible appearance. It all looks like a combination of theater props and acrobatic equipment. Even on the obelisks you find traces of intelligence and ghosts of writing that trouble the imagination, like anything we see without understanding its purpose![23]

This is comedy played by actors unaware of being in a performance whose meaning cannot be understood because it represents a world whose inhabitants are anonymous, in which writing itself begins to fatigue: "They did nothing but their work and represented the perfect type of pure-bred clerk, haggard from paperwork and long years in offices. Chazelle often fell asleep while working, and his pen, which he still hung on to, would mark out his breathing with little dots."[24] Writing, like modern life itself, becomes petty and monotonous, drowsing in a regular, unvarying somnolence, slouching in offices, surrounded by things—words, objects, people—without meaning, or rather, with a meaning that has no dimension to it. The power residing in the offices, on the desks, those enormous bric-a-bracs, functions exclusively thanks to a continual effort of *bricolage* that extends itself even into our lives and minds, somewhat resembling the character of Godard, who "collected minerals and shells, knew how to stuff birds, stored in his bedroom a host of odd things bought at a good price: landscaping stones, models of palaces made out of cork, petrified relics from the Saint-Allyre spring at Clermont (Auvergne), and so on. He hoarded phials and perfume bottles for his barium oxide samples, his sulfates, salts, magnesia, corals, etc. He collected butterflies in shadow boxes and pinned the walls with Chinese parasols—in fact dried fish skins."[25]

The public reacts against the new actor bursting onto the scene of the novel, but Balzac anticipates and warns his readers:

> The author expects to be accused of immorality, but he has already clearly explained that his idée fixe is to describe society as a whole and as it really is; in its virtues, its greatness, its honor, and its shame, with the collapse of its tangled hierarchies, in the confusion of its principles, its new needs and old contradictions. He still lacks the courage to declare himself more historian than novelist; the more so because the critics would accuse him of glorifying himself. He can only add that in a time such as this, in which everything is analyzed and examined, when there is faith neither in the priest nor the poet, when we abjure today what we extolled yesterday, poetry is impossible.

"The author," Balzac concludes, "therefore believes that there still exists only one marvelous thing to do: to describe the great social disease, and this could not be described except by society, because the afflicted victim is himself the affliction."[26]

But what is this affliction? Where is the sick body? How to describe something that can be experienced but not defined?

It is a matter of conducting an interrogation of extreme immediacy, opening still unsurpassed theoretical perspectives from which to understand the dynamics of postrevolutionary society. Several years later, Tocqueville was to ask the same questions that Balzac here attempts to answer:

> Where does this new race come from? Who produced it? Who made it so efficient? Who makes it last? Why do we always find ourselves facing the same men, even though the cir-

cumstances vary, who have rooted themselves throughout the civilized world? My spirit burns to conceive a precise notion of this object and to find the means to describe it well. Separate from all that is explained by the French Revolution remains something still unexplained in its spirit and its actions. I can sense where the unknown object is, but despite all my labor I still cannot manage to lift the veil that covers it. I poke at it as though at a strange body that somehow keeps me both from really touching it and really seeing it.[27]

Balzac, like his contemporaries Marx and Tocqueville, was to spend his life searching obsessively for an answer to that idée fixe. The nearly hundred novels that comprise the pieces of the mosaic of *La Comédie humaine* are parts of a body that we can see fully only much later—only today, in fact—because the world has revolved toward the image of the "doctor of social science" that prefigured it.

Notes

This essay takes up and develops some of the topics treated during my course on literary bureaucracies offered at Northwestern University during the 1988–89 academic year. I extend thanks to all those who helped me with comments and suggestions during the development of this essay: my "Balzacian" colleagues, Mariolina Bongiovanni-Bertini and Gerald Mead, Martha Pollak, Nicole Savy, Michela Nacci, Scipione Guarracino, Giorgio Rebuffa, and Daniel Vidal. To Bruno Bongiovanni, whose writings on Marx have been so useful and intellectually stimulating, I am especially indebted for his encouraging me to make a close comparison be-

tween the two authors from an unusual point of view. I should like
to explain the source for the title of this essay: it is freely inspired
by the following passage from *Sarrasine*: "Passing from the landed
monarchy to the industrial monarchy, society changed its reading
matter, from the nobility's letter to the number."

Unless otherwise specified, translations are mine. Also, I naturally
assume total responsibility for anything written in these pages.

1. Claude Lefort, *Eléments d'une théorie de la bureaucratie* (Paris: Gallimard, 1977), p. 23.

2. Grimm-Diderot, *Correspondance littéraire, philosophique et critique
(1753–1769)* (Paris, 1878), 6:30.

3. Ibid., p. 98.

4. On this point see the writings of those who have sustained the vital-
ity and actuality of "theoretical" perspectives on Balzac: A. M. Bijaoui-
Baron, "La Bureaucratie Balzacienne: Aux sources d'un thème et de ses
personnages," *L'Année Balzacienne* 3 (1982): 166–79, and "La Bureaucratie et ses images," *L'Année Balzacienne* 1 (1977): 91–110; J.-H. Don-
nard, *Balzac: Les réalities économiques et sociales dans "La Comédie humaine"* (Paris: A. Colin, 1961); A. Wurmser, *La Comédie inhumaine* (Paris:
Gallimard, 1965); P. Barbéris, *Balzac et le mal du siècle*, 2 vols. (Paris: Gallimard, 1968).

5. Observing his last works, his method of rethinking the same topics
over and over, and approaching them from the perspective of different
times and places, becomes clear. Such diversity contributes to modifying
the dimensions of the topic described. See the essential reflections of P.
Nykrog, *La Pensée de Balzac dans "La Comédie humaine": Esquisse de
quelques concepts clés* (Copenhagen: Munksgaard, 1965).

6. Balzac, *Lettres á Madame Hanska*, ed. Roger Pierrot, vol. 1 (Paris,
1971), p. 369. Compare this with Tocqueville's letter to J. S. Mill, December 18, 1840, in *Oeuvres Complètes*, ed. G. de Beaumont, vol. 11 (Paris:
Michel Lévy, 1866), p. 329.

7. See the recent work by J. Grange, *Balzac* (Paris: La Différence, 1990).

8. *Le peau de chagrin*, in *La Comédie humaine*, vol. 3, "Bibliothèque de la Pléiade," 1976–81, p. 436. Volume 1 contains a very valuable introduction by Professor Castex entitled "L'Univers de la *Comédie humaine*," pp. ix–lxxvi.

9. Sainte-Beuve, a hostile but acute critic of Balzac, managed to penetrate in part the "pact" that so extraordinarily linked Balzac with his readers: "Balzac especially forged a common cause with the half of the public it is essential to conquer, and he won their complicity by artfully stroking certain sensitive points of which only he is aware." C. A. de Sainte-Beuve, "M. de Balzac, 1834," in *Portraits contemporains* (Paris: Calman Lévy, 1870), 2:341.

10. *The Bureaucrats*, p. 14–15.

11. In Peter Riazanov, ed., *Kark Marx. Homme, penseur et révolutionnaire. Articles, discours, souvenirs* (Paris: Anthropos, 1968), p. 79.

12. I am referring to the following dialogue:

Bixiou (returning). "Chazelle is crazy. Where does he see a thousand sovereigns? . . . In his own pocket by any chance?"

Chazelle. "Shall we add them up? Four hundred over there at the end of the Pont de la Concorde (so called because it leads to the scene of perpetual discord between the Right and Left of the Chamber); three hundred more at the end of the Rue de Tournon. The Court, which ought to count for three hundred, has to have seven hundred times the power of the emperor to get *one* of its protégés any post whatsoever. . . . "

Fleury. "All of which means that, in a country where there are three powers, you can bet a thousand to one that a single bureaucrat who is protégé to none but himself will never get ahead." *The Bureaucrats*, pp. 127–28.

13. See the dialogue by Balzac in *Les Comédiens sans le savoir*: "'C'est

une révolution!' lui dit Bixiou en faisant l'enthusiaste. 'Oui, radicale, car il faut changer la forme.'" See also Marco Diani, "La Révolution dans la forme. Société immaterielle et inscription de l'argent chez Balzac," *Stanford French Review*, vol. 15, no. 3 (Fall–Winter 1991): 373–92, for further analysis on this point.

14. "In the Rabourdin bureau, there was yet another employee, a man of seeming courage who professed Left-Center opinions and rebelled against the tyrannies of Baudoyer for the sake of the miserable slaves of that bureau. This lad, named Fleury, boldly subscribed to an Opposition newspaper, wore a gray hat with a broad brim, red stripes on his blue trousers, a blue waistcoat with gilt buttons, and a double-breasted overcoat like that of a quartermaster of the gendarmerie. Though unyielding in his opinions, he continued on as an employee in the bureau, but he foretold a disastrous future for the government if it persisted in mixing with religion. He openly expressed his support for Napoleon, now that the death of that great man put an end to the laws against 'the partisans of the usurper.'" (*The Bureaucrats*, p. 109)

15. Ibid., p. 138.

16. The first two volumes of *Democracy in America* are dated 1835; the second two, 1840; Marx's first writings on his theory of the state and the bureaucracy are from 1841–42; *The Communist Manifesto*, by Marx and Engels, is from 1847. Balzac wrote the foreword to *La Comédie humaine* in 1842.

17. See Marco Diani, "La 'République prêtre': Marx, Balzac et la Bureaucratie," *Milieux*, no. 32 (1988): 28–37.

18. Balzac to Hanska, Wednesday, July 19, 1837, in *Lettres á Madame Hanska*, p. 521. Thus Balzac expressed himself immediately after the publication of the volume with which he had begun his great comparative analysis of the modern world's different "models of bureaucracy," a study that was to continue until his last days.

19. Ibid., p. 517.

20. Within this framework the destiny of Balzac's work seems still more paradoxical, considering that it still has not received the attention it deserves, despite the fact that it offers one of the principal theories of revolu-

tion from an era dominated by revolutions.

21. From the introduction to the 1838 *Employés*.

22. *The Bureaucrats*, p. 14.

23. Ibid., pp. 74–75.

24. Ibid., p. 106.

25. Ibid., p. 85. Gustave Flaubert, in *Bouvard et Pécuchet*, would amplify to the point of neurosis and paroxysm these characteristics so implacably sketched by Balzac.

26. From the introduction to the 1838 *Employés*.

27. Letter from Tocqueville to Kergorlay, May 16, 1858, *Oeuvres complètes*, 7 vols., vol. 5: Tocqueville-Kergorlay Correspondence (Paris: Gallimard, 1951–), 5:231.

Note on the Text

Les Employés/The Bureaucrats was first published in 1838, as a feuilleton entitled *La Femme supérieure*. It is this text which is followed in modern critical French editions and which has been translated here. The divisions into chapters with titles, and some of the divisions into parts and paragraphs, were omitted in the 1842–43 publication of *La Comédie humaine* in order to save space, but they have been reintroduced here for the greater convenience of the reader.

The Bureaucrats

»»» PART I «««

Between Two Women

The Rabourdin Household

In Paris, where men of thought and study bear a certain likeness to one another, living as they do in a common center, you must have met some like Monsieur Rabourdin, whose acquaintance we are about to make when he was bureau chief in one of our most important ministries. At this time he was forty years old, with gray hair of so pleasing a shade that women liked it just as it was, softening a rather melancholy-looking face; blue eyes full of fire; skin that was still fair, though rather ruddy and marked here and there with bright red blotches; a forehead and nose à la Louis XV; a serious mouth; a tall figure, thin, or perhaps wasted, like that of a man just recovering from an illness; and finally, a gait conveying an attitude midway between the carefree air of one on a stroll and the gravity of a busy man deep in thought. If this portrait serves to depict a character, a sketch of the man's dress will perhaps bring it further into relief. Rabourdin habitually wore a blue redingote, a white cravat, a waistcoat crossed à la Robespierre, black trousers without stirrups, gray silk stockings, and low shoes. Well shaven, and with his stomach warmed by a cup of coffee by eight in the morning, he left home with the regularity of clockwork, always passing along the same streets on his way to the ministry: so neat was he, so formal, so impeccable, that he could have been taken for an Englishman on the way to his embassy.

From these basic features you can readily recognize a family man, harassed by vexations in his own household, frustrated by worries at the ministry, yet philosophical enough to take life as it came; an honest man, who loved his country and served it, not hiding from the obstacles placed in the way of those who seek to do right; prudent because he understood people; extraordinarily courteous to women, because he expected nothing of them; a man full of accomplishments, gracious toward his inferiors, holding his equals at a distance, and dignified toward his superiors. At the time we took up this study, you would notice in him the coolly resigned air of one who has buried the illusions of youth, has renounced every secret ambition; you would have seen a discouraged but not disgusted man, one who was clinging to his original intentions more to the purpose of using his talents than in the hope of a would-be success. He was not decorated with any order and always accused himself of weakness for having worn that of the *Lys* in the early days of the Restoration.

The life of this man was marked by some rather mysterious details. He had never known his father. His mother, a woman for whom luxury was everything, was always elegantly dressed and bent solely on pleasure, and whose beauty in retrospect seemed miraculous to him even though he seldom saw her, left him little at her death; but she had given him that incomplete and all too common education which produces so much ambition and so little ability. At sixteen, a few days before his mother's death, he left the Lycée Napoléon to enter as a supernumerary into the bureaus, where an unknown benefactor had promptly had him appointed. At age twenty-two, Rabourdin became deputy chief; at twenty-five, bureau chief. From that day on, the hand that guided the young man's life was never again felt save for one single instance; it led him, poor fellow, to the house of a Monsieur Leprince, former auctioneer and widower, said to be extremely rich, and the father of an only daughter. Xavier Rabourdin fell desperately in love with Mademoiselle Célestine Leprince, then seventeen years old and supposedly endowed with a dowry of two hundred thousand francs. Carefully raised by an artistic mother who passed her own talents on to her daughter, this young lady was groomed to attract the most highly positioned suitors. Tall, handsome, and well figured, she spoke several languages and knew something of science— a dangerous advantage that obliges a woman to carefully avoid all appearance of pedantry. Blinded by misguided tenderness, the mother gave the daughter inflated ideas about her probable future; to the maternal eye, a duke or an ambassador, a marshal of France or a minister of state alone could give her Célestine her due place in society. The young lady, moreover, had the manners, language, and graces of grand society. She dressed more richly and elegantly than was appropriate for an unmarried girl; a husband could give her nothing more, except happiness. And yet, all these indulgences, the foolish spoiling of the mother, who died a year after the girl's marriage, made love's task all the more difficult. What coolness and composure of mind were needed to master such a woman! Bourgeois suitors held back in fear. An orphan without fortune aside from his position as bureau chief, Xavier was proposed to Célestine by Monsieur Leprince. Mademoiselle Leprince had no objection to his proposal—he was young, handsome, and in love— but she shrank from being called Madame Rabourdin. The father told his daughter that Rabourdin was of the stock of which statesmen are made. Célestine replied that a man named Rabourdin would never be anything under the rule of the Bourbons, etc., etc. Driven back to his entrenchments, the father committed the grave indiscretion of telling his daughter that her future husband would be Rabourdin *de something or other* before he reached the age for admission to the Chamber. Xavier would soon be appointed Master of Petitions and secretary-general in his ministry. From these two rungs the young man would surely rise to the higher ranks of the Administration, be endowed with a fortune and given a name bequeathed to him in a certain testament of which he, Monsieur Leprince, was aware. The marriage took place.

Rabourdin and his wife believed in the mysterious benefactor referred to by the old auctioneer. Swept away by the hopes and those natural, carefree feelings which young love preaches to newlyweds, Monsieur and Madame Rabourdin in five years squandered nearly one hundred thousand francs of their capital. Justly alarmed at not seeing her husband advance, Célestine insisted on investing the remaining hundred thousand francs of her dowry in real estate—an investment that did not generate much income. But one day the inheritance from Monsieur Leprince would compensate prudent sacrifices with the fruits of the good life. When the former auctioneer saw his son-in-law deprived of his good fortune, he tried, for love of his daughter, to make up the loss by risking part of his estate in a speculation with promising chances of a good return. But the poor man, hit by one of the liquidations of the House of Nucingen, died of grief, leaving behind nothing but a dozen fine pictures, which adorned his daughter's salon, and a few old-fashioned pieces of furniture, which she put in the attic.

Eight years of vain expectation finally made Madame Rabourdin realize that her husband's paternal benefactor must have died, and that his testament had been suppressed or lost. Two years prior to Monsieur Leprince's death, the vacant position of division chief had been given to a certain Monsieur de La Billardière, who was related to a deputy of the Right made minister in 1823. It was enough to make one want to change careers. But could Rabourdin give up his salary of eight thousand francs plus perquisites when his family had grown accustomed to spending it, when that made up three-quarters of his income? Besides, if he had the patience to stick it out for a few more years, was he not entitled to a pension? What a disaster this was for a woman whose high expectations at the outset of life were more or less legitimate, and who passed as a superior woman!

Madame Rabourdin fulfilled the expectations formed by Mademoiselle Leprince; she possessed the elements of that apparent superiority which pleases society; her broad education enabled her to speak to everyone in his or her own language; her talents were genuine; she demonstrated independent and higher thought; her conversation charmed as much by its variety and ease as by the oddness and originality of her ideas. Such qualities, useful and appropriate in a sovereign or an ambassadress, were of little use in a household bound to the basics of life. Those who have the gift of fine speech desire an audience; they like to talk, and at times can be trying. To satisfy her intellectual cravings, Madame Rabourdin received once a week and often went out to socialize so as to savor the pleasures her vanity craved. Those who know Parisian life will readily understand how a woman of her caliber suffered and was martyred at heart by the impoverished state of her pecuniary means. No matter what foolish declarations people make about money, they one and all, if they live in Paris, must grovel before accounts, do homage to figures, and kiss the forked hoof of the golden calf. What problems!—twelve thousand livres a year to defray the costs of a household consisting of father, mother, two children, a chambermaid, and a cook, all living on the second floor of a house in the rue Duphot, in an apartment costing a hundred louis a year. Deduct for clothes and carriages for Madame even before you figure the great expenses of the household, because "clothes" come before everything else; then see what is left for the education of the children (a girl of seven and a boy of nine, whose expenses, in spite of a full scholarship, were already two thousand francs), and you will find that Madame Rabourdin could barely afford to give her husband thirty francs a month. Almost all the husbands in Paris are in the same position, lest they be accused of being monsters.

This woman who thought herself destined to shine in the world, to dominate it, saw herself in fact condemned to engage her mind and wits in an unexpected, sordid struggle—hand-to-hand combat with an account book. What a terrible sacrifice of pride! She had dismissed her manservant after the death of her father. Most women grow weary of this daily struggle; they complain and end up by giving in to fate. But instead of giving in, Célestine's ambition only grew; and, finding herself unable to conquer it, she sought to eliminate it. In her eyes, this complicated tangle of life's affairs was like a Gordian knot, impossible to untie and through which genius must cut. Far from accepting the pettiness of a bourgeois existence, she grew angry at the delays that kept the great things of life from her grasp, blaming fate as deceptive. Célestine sincerely believed herself to be a superior woman. Perhaps she was right: perhaps she would have been great in great circumstances; perhaps she was out of place. Let us recognize the fact that differences do exist in women as in men, all of whom society molds to meet its needs. And, in the social order, as in the natural order, there are more young shoots than trees, more spawn than full-grown fish, and much of the potential, the Athanase Gransons, must die withered, like seeds fallen on stony ground.

Without a doubt, there are housewives, accomplished women, ornamental women, women who are exclusively wives or mothers or sweethearts, women purely spiritual or purely material, just as there are artists, soldiers, artisans, mathematicians, poets, merchants, men who understand only money, or agriculture, or government. Add to this the fact that life's strange twists and turns lead to contradictions: Many Are Called and Few Are Chosen is the law of Earth, as of Heaven. Madame Rabourdin considered herself fully capable of lighting the way for a statesman, inspiring an artist, furthering the interests of an inventor and helping him through his struggles, of devoting herself to the financial politics of a Nucingen, of brilliantly representing a large fortune. Perhaps she was only trying to justify to herself her hatred of the laundry list, the food bills, having to cut corners, and the cares of a small household. She was superior only in those things in which it gave her pleasure to be so. Feeling as keenly as she did the thorns of a position which can only be likened to that of Saint Lawrence on his gridiron, did she not at times have to cry out? In her paroxysms of thwarted ambition, in the moments when her wounded vanity gave her terrible throbbing pains, Célestine attacked Xavier Rabourdin. Was it not her husband's duty to give her a suitable position in the world? If she were a man, she would have had the means to make a quick fortune for the sake of making an adored wife happy! She reproached him for being too good. From the mouth of some women this accusation is utter nonsense. She presented him with brilliant plans in which she took no account of the obstacles imposed by men and circumstance; then, like all women under the influence of violent emotion, she became in thought more Machiavellian than a Gondreville, more cunning than Maxime de Trailles. Célestine's mind conceived everything in this way, and she saw herself in the full scope of all her ideas.

When these lovely ideas first began, Rabourdin, who saw the practical side, remained cold. Célestine, upset, thought her husband narrow-minded, timid, not understanding; and she acquired, insensibly, the most erroneous opinion of her lifelong companion. First, she was always outshining him through the brilliance of her rhetoric; then, as her ideas came to her in flashes, she would cut him short when he began an explanation, because she did not want the slightest scintilla of her own brilliance to be lost. From the very first days of their marriage, feeling herself loved and admired by her husband, Célestine took him for granted; she placed herself above all conjugal laws and the rules of intimate courtesies by expecting love to pardon all her little wrong-doings; and, as she never changed her habits, she always had her way. In such a situation a man finds himself in relation to his wife like a teacher before a child when he cannot, or will not, recognize that the child he was once superior to has grown up. Like Madame de Staël, who exclaimed in a roomful of people, when addressing, we may say, a greater man than herself, "Do you know, you have really said something very profound!" so Madame Rabourdin said of her husband, "He certainly has a good deal of sense at times." Gradually, her domination of Xavier, almost imperceptibly, could be read in her look. Her attitude and mannerisms expressed lack of respect. Without being aware of it, she belittled her husband in the eyes of others; for all over the world, society, before making up its mind about a man, listens to what his wife thinks of him, and thus obtains from her what the Genevese call a *préavis*, pronounced in Genevese "*préavisse.*"

By the time Rabourdin became aware of the mistakes love had led him to commit, the groove had been cut; he suffered and was silent. Like other men in whom feelings and ideas are of equal strength, in whom a noble soul concurrently meets with a well-balanced mind, he was his wife's before the tribunal of his own judgment. He told himself that nature had doomed her to a disappointed life through his fault, *his;* she was like a thoroughbred English horse, a racer harnessed to a cartload of stones. She suffered, and he blamed himself. His wife, through constant repetition, had indoctrinated him with her own belief in herself. Ideas are contagious in a household; the Ninth Thermidor, like so many other portentous events, was the result of female influence. Thus, goaded by Célestine's ambitions, Rabourdin had long wondered how to satisfy her; but he kept his dreams from her so as to spare her any anguish. This fine man was resolved to make it in the Administration by carving out a place for himself. He intended to bring about one of those revolutions which send a man to the head of either one party or another in society; but being incapable of causing a shake-up for his personal interest, he merely pondered useful thoughts and dreamt of triumphs won for his country by noble means. This was at once generous and ambitious, and few bureaucrats have not thought of it at some time. Yet among bureaucrats as among artists, there are more miscarriages than births, which is tantamount to Buffon's saying that "Genius is patience."

Placed in a position where he could study French administration and observe its mechanism, Rabourdin worked in an environment where chance sparked his imagination, which, parenthetically, is the secret of much human accomplishment; and he ended up by inventing a new system of civil administration. Knowing the people he had to deal with, he left the then operating machine working, as it still works and will continue to work for a long time to come, because everybody is always afraid of recasting it; but no one, according to Rabourdin, should be unwilling to simplify it. The problem to be resolved consisted in a better use of existing resources. In its simplest form, his plan was to revise taxation in such a way as to lower taxes without diminishing the revenues of the state and, from a budget equal to one now arousing frantic discussions, to obtain double the current results. Long practical experience had taught Rabourdin that, in all things, perfection is brought about by changes made in favor of simplicity. To economize is to simplify. To simplify is to eliminate unnecessary machinery: thus cuts must be made. Furthermore, his system rested upon a weeding-out process and the establishment of a new administrative order. Perhaps out of this arises the hatred that reformers incur. Cuts required by this perfecting process, always poorly understood, threaten the existence of those who do not take well to change. What made Rabourdin really remarkable was that he was able to restrain the enthusiasm that takes hold of all reformers and patiently seek out a mechanism for all changes in order to avoid shocks, leaving it to time and experience to prove the excellence of each reform. The great scope of the results would lead one to doubt their feasibility if one were to lose sight of the goal in a brief overview of the system. Therefore it is essential to indicate the point of view, gathered through his personal musings, imperfect though they were, from which he viewed the administrative horizon. Moreover, this account, which is at the very heart of the intrigue, may perhaps even explain some of the evils of present social customs.

Deeply troubled by the misery he witnessed in the lives of the civil servants, Xavier Rabourdin considered the cause of their growing discontent. He looked to its causes and found them in those petty partial revolutions—the eddies, as it were, of the storm of 1789—which the historians of great social movements fail to inquire into, although as a matter of fact it is they that have made our manners and customs what they now are.

Formerly, under the monarchy, the bureaucratic armies did not exist. Few in number, the clerks were under the orders of a prime minister who was always in touch with the sovereign; thus they directly served the king. The superiors of these zealous servants were simply called "first clerks." In those branches of administration which the king did not direct himself, such as the *fermes* (public domains throughout the country on which a revenue was levied), the clerks were to their superior what the clerks of a business are to their employer; they learned a science that would one day lead them to prosperity. Thus, all points of the circle were linked to the center and drew their life from it. The result was devotion and confidence. Since 1789, the state, nation, or *patrie* if you like, has replaced the prince. Instead of looking directly to the chief political magistrate, the clerks have become, in spite of our fine patriotic ideas, the employees of the government, and their superiors are buffeted by the winds of a power called *minister*, who does not know from day to day whether he will be in office tomorrow. Since the routine of business must go on, a certain number of indispensable clerks survive; indispensable but at the mercy of the administration, they want to keep their positions. Bureaucracy, a gigantic power set in motion by dwarfs, is thus born. If, by subordinating all things and all men to his will, Napoleon for a time put off the influence of bureaucracy (that weighty veil between the task at hand and the man who can get it done), it was permanently organized under the constitutional government, which was, inevitably, the friend of all mediocrities, the lover of authentic documents and accounts, and as meddlesome as a petit bourgeois. Delighted to see the various ministers constantly at odds with four hundred petty minds, with their ten or twelve ambitious and dishonest leaders, the various government offices hastened to make themselves indispensable by substituting real work for written work. Thus they created a power of inertia named "the Report." Let us explain the Report.

When the kings of France had ministers, which only first happened under Louis XV, they made them submit reports on all important matters instead of, as formerly, holding grand councils of state with the nobles. Imperceptibly, the ministers of the various departments were led by their bureaus to imitate this kingly practice. Their time being taken up in defending themselves before the two Chambers and the courts, they let themselves be influenced by the findings of the Report. Nothing important was ever brought before the government without a minister saying, even when the case was urgent, "I have called for a Report." The Report thus became, both as to the matter concerned and for the minister himself, the same as the report to the Chamber of Deputies on a question of laws—namely, a consideration of the pros and cons stated with more or less partiality. The minister, like the Chamber, is just as close to a decision before as after the Report is given. Any sort of decision is reached in an instant. Do what we will, the moment comes when the decision must be made. The more reasons for and against, the less sound the judgment will be. The finest things of which France can boast were accomplished when Reports did not exist and when decisions were spontaneous. The reigning law of a statesman is to apply precise formulas to all circumstances, as judges and physicians do.

Rabourdin, who said to himself, "A minister is minister in order to make decisions, to know public affairs and manage them," saw "the Report" rampant throughout France, from the colonel to the marshal, from the police commissioner to the king, from the prefects to the ministers of State, from the Chamber to the courts. After 1818 everything was discussed, compared, and weighed, orally and in writing; everything had to be written down. France was going to ruin in spite of this lovely array of documents; dissertations in place of action: a million Reports were written every year! Records, statistics, documents, without which France would have been lost, circumlocution, without which she could not function, increased, multiplied, and grew majestic. Bureaucracy, from that day forth, used for its own ends the mistrust between receipts and expenditures; it degraded the administration for the benefit of the administrators. In short, it spun those Lilliputian threads which have chained France to Parisian centralization—as if from 1500 to 1800 France had undertaken nothing for want of thirty thousand clerks. In attaching themselves to public offices, like a mistletoe on a pear tree, these officials indemnified themselves completely, and this is how.

Obliged to obey the princes or the Chambers who impose upon them the distribution of the public monies, thus forcing them to maintain a staff, the ministers lowered salaries and increased the number of workers, believing that the more people employed by the government the stronger the government would be. In fact, the opposite is the law of the universe: efficiency is inversely proportional to the number of active principals. In July 1830 events proved the error of the ministerialism of the Restoration. To plant a government in the heart of a nation, it is necessary to bind *interests* to it, not *men*. Led to despise the government that had lowered both their importance and their salaries, the bureaucrats treated it as a courtesan treats an old lover: it received work for money, a state of affairs as intolerable for the Administration as for the employees, had either party bothered to take the other's pulse, or had the higher-paid not succeeded in stifling the voices of the lower-paid. Thus, wholly and solely occupied in retaining his position, drawing his pay, and securing a pension, the government employee felt free to do anything in order to attain this great goal. This state of things led to servility on the part of the clerks and to endless intrigues within the various departments, where the poorer clerks struggled vainly against degenerate members of the aristocracy, who sought positions for their ruined sons in bourgeois territory.

Superior men could scarcely bring themselves to tread these tortuous ways, to stoop, cringe, wade through the mire of these gutters where the presence of a fine mind only alarmed others. The ambitious man of genius grows old striving for the Triple Crown; he does not follow in the steps of Sixtus V merely to become bureau chief. No one comes to or stays in the government offices but idlers, incompetents, or fools. Thus the mediocrity of French administration has slowly come about. Made up entirely of petty minds, the bureaucracy has stood as an obstacle to the prosperity of the nation, has delayed for seven years by its machinery a canal project that would have stimulated the production of a province, is afraid of everything, prolongs procrastination, and perpetuates the abuses which in turn perpetuate and consolidate its very existence. The bureaucracy holds everything in its control: even the minister is in its web; finally, it stifles men of talent who are bold enough to be independent of it or to expose its follies. The pension list had just been issued, and on it Rabourdin saw the name of an office boy slated for a larger pension than the old colonel maimed and wounded for his country. In that fact lay the entire story of the bureaucracy.

Another evil, brought about by modern customs, which Rabourdin counted among the causes of this secret demoralization, was the fact that there is no real subordination in the Administration in Paris; complete equality reigns between the chief of an important division and the humblest copy clerk: one is as important as the other in an arena in which things are lorded over others as a lowly employee is made of a poet or a businessman. Does not education, equally distributed among the masses, bring the son of a porter into a position to decide the fate of a man of merit or of some landed proprietor whose doorbell his father may have answered? The Johnny-come-lately can thus challenge the oldest veteran. A wealthy supernumerary splashes his superior as he drives his tilbury to Longchamps with his pretty wife beside him, pointing out with his crop the poor father of a family and remarking, "That's my boss." The Liberals call this state of affairs PROGRESS; Rabourdin thought it ANARCHY at the very heart of authority. He saw how it resulted in restless intrigues, like those between eunuchs and women and imbecile sultans in a harem, or the petty troubles of nuns full of underhanded vexations, or college tyrannies, or diplomatic maneuverings fit to terrify an ambassador, all put in motion to obtain a fee or an increase in salary; it was like the hopping of fleas harnessed to pasteboard cars, the spitefulness of slaves visited on the minister himself. Thus, the really useful men, the workers, were victims of such parasites; men sincerely devoted to their country, who stood out boldly from the mass of incompetency, succumbed to ignoble trickeries.

All the higher offices being gained through parliamentary influence and royalty no longer having anything to do with them, the clerks sooner or later found themselves to be merely the running-gears of a machine, the most important consideration for them being to keep the wheels well greased. This fatal conviction, having already taken its toll on some of the best minds, smothered many conscientiously written memoranda on the secret evils of the nation, lowered the courage of many hearts, and corrupted sterling honesty, weary of injustice and won to indifference by poisoned worries. A single agent of the Rothschilds corresponds with all of England; one single government worker could by the same token communicate with all the prefects. But, whereas the one learns the way to make his fortune, the other wastes time and health and life to no avail. Out of this grows the evil. Certainly a nation does not seem threatened with immediate dissolution because an able bureaucrat is sent away and a middling sort of man replaces him. Unfortunately for nations, no single man seems essential to their existence. But, over time, when all has wound itself down, nations disappear. Everyone who seeks instruction on this point can look to Venice, Madrid, Amsterdam, Stockholm, and Rome—all places that were formerly resplendent with mighty power and today have been destroyed by the infiltrating littleness that gradually attained the highest eminence. When the day to fight came, all being found rotten, the state succumbed to a weak attack. To worship the fool who succeeds and not grieve over the fall of an able man is the result of our sorry education, our manners and customs, which drive men of intellect to disgust and genius to despair.

What a difficult undertaking is the rehabilitation of the civil service at a time when liberalism cries out in her newspapers that the salaries of clerks are a standing theft, calls the items of the budget a cluster of leeches, and every year asks why the nation should be saddled with a billion in taxes. In Monsieur Rabourdin's eyes, the bureaucrat in relation to the budget was very much what the gambler is to the game: the one he wins he plays again. All remuneration implies some good provided. To pay a man a thousand francs a year and to demand all of his time was surely to organize theft and poverty; a galley slave costs nearly as much and does less. But to expect a man whom the state remunerated with twelve thousand francs a year to devote himself to his country would be a profitable contract for both sides, fit to tempt all who were able.

These reflections had led Rabourdin to a reorganization of personnel. To employ fewer men, to double or triple salaries and do away with pensions, to choose only young employees (as had Napoleon, Louis XIV, Richelieu, and Ximenes), but to keep them long and train them for the higher offices and highest honors— these were the principal features of a reform as beneficial to the state as to its employees themselves. It is difficult to recount in detail, chapter by chapter, a plan that embraced the whole budget and continued down through to the minutest details of administration in order to synthesize the whole; but perhaps a slight sketch of the principal reforms will suffice for those who understand such matters, as well as for those who are wholly ignorant of the administrative system. Although the historian's position is rather hazardous in reproducing a plan that may be considered the politics of a chimney-corner, it is nevertheless necessary to sketch it so as to explain the man by his own handiwork. Were the explanation of his efforts omitted, the reader would not believe the narrator if he merely lauded the talent and the courage of this official.

Rabourdin's plan divided the government into three ministries, or departments. He thought that if in former days France possessed brains enough to incorporate both foreign and domestic affairs into one office, the France of today was not likely to be without its Mazarin, its Suger, its Sully, its de Choiseul, or its Colbert to direct even vast administrative departments. Besides, constitutionally speaking, three ministers will agree better than seven; and furthermore, there is less chance for wrong decisions. Moreover, perhaps the kingdom might escape those perpetual ministerial oscillations which obstructed all foreign-policy plans and prevented any domestic improvements. In Austria, where many diverse united nations present so many conflicting interests to be conciliated and carried out under one crown, two statesmen alone bear the burden of public affairs and are not overwhelmed by it. Was France less well endowed than Germany in political potential? The rather silly game of what are called constitutional institutions, carried beyond bounds, has ended, as everybody knows, in requiring a great many offices to satisfy the multiple ambitions of the bourgeoisie. In the first place, it seemed to him natural to join the Ministry of War with the Ministry of the Navy. To him, the navy was one of the current expenses of the War Department, like the artillery, cavalry, infantry, and commissariat. Surely it was absurd to give separate administrations to admirals and marshals when both were employed to a common end—namely, the defense of national possessions. The Ministry of the Interior ought in like manner to combine the departments of commerce, police, and finances, or else belie its own name. To the Ministry of Foreign Affairs belonged the administration of justice, the household of the king, and all that concerned arts, sciences, and belles lettres. All patronage ought to flow directly from the sovereign. This ministry implied the supremacy of the Council. Each of the three ministries contributed no more than two hundred bureaucrats to his central administration, whereas Rabourdin believed they should be housed, as in former days, under the monarchy. Allowing on average the sum of twelve thousand francs a head, he figured seven million for the cost of the whole body, which actually stood at twenty in the budget.

By thus reducing the ministers to three heads, he eliminated entire departments that had become useless, along with the enormous costs of their maintenance in Paris. He proved that an arrondissement could be managed by ten men, a prefecture by twelve at most, which thus figured the entire civil-service force throughout France at five thousand employees, excluding the departments of war and justice. Under this plan, the clerks of the courts were charged with the system of loans, whereas the Ministry of the Interior was responsible for registration and management of domains. Rabourdin united in one center all divisions that were similar. Thus mortgage, inheritance, and registration did not pass outside of their relevant domains and only required three supernumeraries per tribunal and three per royal court. The steady application of this principle brought Rabourdin to reforms in the fiscal system. He merged the collection of revenue into one channel, taxing mass consumption instead of property. According to him, consumption was the sole thing properly taxable in times of peace. Land taxes should always be held in reserve in case of war; only then could the state justly demand sacrifices from the soil, since then it was a matter of defending it. But in times of peace it was a serious political fault to burden it beyond a certain limit; otherwise it could never be depended upon in great emergencies. *Loans* in peacetime should be put on the market, for at such times it could be placed at par, instead of at fifty percent loss, as in bad times; then, in wartime, resort should be made to *mandatory contributions*.

"The invasions of 1814 and 1815," Rabourdin would say to his friends, "founded in France and demonstrated an institution that neither law nor Napoleon had been able to establish—*Credit*."

Unfortunately, Xavier considered the true principles of this admirable machine to be very little understood at the time when he began his work in 1821. Rabourdin levied a tax on consumption by means of direct taxation, eliminating the machinery of indirect taxation. The levying of the tax was simplified by a single classification made up of various articles. This did away with the more harassing customs at the gates of the cities, from which were obtained greater revenues, by actually simplifying them, thus lowering the great expense of collecting them. To lessen the burden of taxation is not, in matters of finance, to cut the taxes, but to assess them better; if they are lightened, you increase the volume of business by giving it freer play; the individual pays less and the state receives more. This reform, which may seem immense, relies on a very simple mechanism. Rabourdin regarded personal and estate tax as the best representative of general consumption. Individual fortunes are usually revealed in France by rentals, by the number of servants, horses, and luxury carriages, all of which are of interest to fiscal policy. Houses and what is in them vary little and are not liable to disappear. After indicating the means of making an assessment list more impartial than the current one, Rabourdin estimated the sums to be brought into the treasury by *indirect* taxes as a *set percent* of each individual share. A tax is a levy of money on things or persons under disguises that are more or less specious; have not these disguises, excellent when the object is to extort money, become ridiculous in an age when the class on which the taxes weigh knows why the state imposes them and by what machinery they are given back? In fact, the budget is not a strongbox to hold what is put into it, but a watering can: the more it takes in and the more it pours out, the more a nation prospers. Therefore, supposing there are six million *well-to-do* taxpayers (Rabourdin proved their existence, including the *rich*), is it not better to have them pay a duty on the consumption of wine, which would not be any more offensive than that on doors and windows and would return a hundred million, rather than harass them by taxing the thing itself? By this rationalization of taxation, each individual would in fact pay less, the state would receive more, and consumers would profit by a vast reduction in the price of goods that the state would no longer subject to its never-ending interference. Rabourdin retained cultivation rights on vineyards to protect that industry from a flood of its own products. Then, to reach the consumption of the poor taxpayers, the licenses of retailers were taxed according to the population of the neighborhoods in which they lived.

Thus, in three ways: the duty on wine, cultivation, and licenses, the Treasury would raise enormous revenues without the current expense or annoyance that weighs on the consumer and the state. Taxation would weigh upon the rich without overburdening the poor. To give another example: assume a share assessed on each individual of one or two francs for the consumption of salt, and you raise ten or twelve million, the modern *gabelle* disappears, the poor breathe easier, agriculture is relieved, the state receives as much, and no one complains. Everyone, whether industry or proprietor, would see at once the benefits of a tax so assessed, observing that life improved in rural areas and that commerce expanded. In short, from year to year the state would see the number of her *well-to-do* increasing. By doing away with the means of indirect taxation, which is very costly (a state, as it were, within the state), the Treasury and the individual taxpayer are greatly benefited, even considering only the savings in the costs of collection. Tobacco and snuff came under state control, an overseeing body. The system regarding these two goods, developed by persons other than Rabourdin since the renewal of the law on tobacco products, was so convincing that this law would hardly have passed in a chamber that was not asked to take it or leave it, as the minister in fact did. The whole issue was thus less a question of finance than a question of government. The state no longer possessed anything of its own— forests, mines, or public works. In Rabourdin's eyes, the state as owner of domains constituted an administrative contradiction. The state cannot make a profit and deprive itself of tax revenue: it loses two goods at once. As for government factories, it is the same nonsense as in the sphere of industry. The state obtains products at a higher cost than those of commerce, produces them more slowly, and loses its tax on the industry, the support of which is in turn diminished. Can manufacturing instead of promoting manufacture be seen as governing a country? Owning property instead of creating all the more diverse possessions? Under this system, the state would exact no financial security. Rabourdin only allowed mortgage securities. This is why: either the state actually holds on to the security, which hinders the transfer of monies; or it invests it at a higher rate than it itself gives, which is contemptible robbery; or else it loses on the transaction, which is foolish; or, finally, if one day it disposes of a mass of these securities, it gives rise in certain instances to terrible bankruptcy.

The territorial tax did not entirely disappear in Rabourdin's plan: he kept a minute portion of it as a resource in case of war; obviously farm products were freed, and industry, finding raw material at a low price, could compete abroad without the deceptive aid of customs duties. The rich carried on the administration of the departments without any compensation other than that of receiving a peerage under certain conditions. Magistrates, learned bodies, and officers of the lower ranks found their services honorably rewarded. There was no employed man who failed to obtain great consideration as merited by the value of his labors and the excellence of his salary; each one looked to his own future, and France was delivered from the cancer of pensions. As a result, Rabourdin figured seven hundred million in expenditures and twelve hundred million in receipts. A saving of five hundred million annually had far more virtue than the accumulation of a sinking fund whose dangers were plainly to be seen. In this, according to him, the state became a stockholder, just as it persisted in being a landholder and a manufacturer. Finally, to bring about his reform without upheavals or incurring a Saint Bartholomew of bureaucrats, Rabourdin needed twenty years.

Such were the ideas this man had been hatching ever since his promised place had been given to Monsieur de La Billardière, a man of sheer incompetence. This plan—so vast in appearance, so simple in fact—which did away with so many large staffs and equally useless little offices, required continuous calculations, precise statistics, and self-evident proof. Rabourdin had long studied the budget under its double aspect of ways and means and of expenditure. He had also been at it many nights, unbeknownst to his wife. But so far he had only dared to conceive the plan and to superimpose it on the administrative cadaver; now he had to gain the ear of a minister capable of appreciating his ideas. Rabourdin's success depended on a tranquil political environment, currently very unsettled. He did not consider the government as definitely secure until three hundred deputies had the courage to form a majority pact, systematically ministerial. An administration founded on that basis had come into power since Rabourdin had finished his plans. At that time, the luxury of peace under the Bourbons had eclipsed the warlike luxury of the days when France shone like a vast encampment, prodigal and magnificent because it was victorious. After the Spanish campaign, the ministry seemed to enter an era of tranquillity in which some good might be accomplished, and three months before the opening of our story, a new reign had begun without any apparent opposition, for the Liberals of the Left had welcomed Charles X with as much enthusiasm as the Right. Even clear-sighted and suspicious persons were misled. The moment seemed propitious for Rabourdin. What could better attest to the stability of an administration than to propose and carry out a reform whose results were to be so far-reaching?

Never had this man seemed so anxious, so preoccupied in the morning as he walked the streets to the ministry and at half-past four in the afternoon when he returned. For her part, Madame

Rabourdin, devastated over her wasted life, weary of secretly toiling to obtain a few luxuries of dress, had never appeared so bitterly discontented as now. But, like any wife who is really attached to her husband, she considered it unworthy of a superior woman to stoop to the shameful devices by which the wives of some bureaucrats make up for the insufficiency of their means. This feeling made her refuse all contact with Madame Colleville, then very intimate with François Keller, whose parties overshadowed those of the rue Duphot. She mistook the quietude of the political thinker and the preoccupation of the intrepid worker for the apathetic torpor of an official broken by the dullness of routine, vanquished by that most hated of all miseries, the mediocrity that simply ekes out a living; and she groaned at being married to a man without energy.

Furthermore, it was at about this time that she resolved to take the making of her husband's fortune upon herself, to thrust him at any price into a higher sphere, and to hide from him the secret springs of her machinations. She brought to all her plans the independence of ideas that characterized her, and was proud to think that she could rise above other women by sharing none of their petty prejudices and by keeping herself untrammeled by the restraints society imposes. In her anger, she resolved to fight fools with their own weapons and to make a fool of herself if need be. She at last saw the big picture. The time was right. Monsieur de La Billardière, attacked by a mortal illness, was likely to die in a matter of days. If Rabourdin succeeded him, his talents (for Célestine did credit him with administrative talents) would be so thoroughly appreciated that the office of Master of Petitions, formerly promised, would be given to him; she fancied him as King's Commissioner, defending bills in the Chambers: she would help him! She would even be his secretary, if necessary; she would sit up all night to do the work! All this to drive in the Bois de Boulogne in a charming carriage, to equal Madame Delphine de Nucingen, to raise her salon to the level of Madame Colleville's, to be invited to the great ministerial solemnities, to win listeners and make them talk of her as "Madame *de something or other*" (she had not yet determined of which estate), just as they did of Madame Firmiani, Madame d'Espard, Madame d'Aiglemont, Madame de Carigliano, and thus forever efface the odious name of Rabourdin.

These secret schemes brought about some changes in the household. Madame Rabourdin began to walk with a firm step in the path of *Debt*. She took up a manservant again, dressed him in ordinary livery of brown cloth with red piping. She renovated parts of her furniture, hung new papers on the walls, adorned her salon with plants and flowers, always fresh, cluttered it with trendy knick-knacks; then she, who had always shown scruples with regard to her personal expenses, did not hesitate to elevate her dress in keeping with the rank to which she aspired, to the benefit of several shops where she equipped herself for war. To make her "Wednesdays" fashionable, she gave a dinner on Fridays, the guests being expected to pay their return visit and take a cup of tea on the following Wednesday. She chose her guests cleverly from among influential deputies or other persons of note who, sooner or later, might advance her interests. In short, she gathered an agreeable and befitting circle about her. People amused themselves at her house; they said so at least, which in Paris is quite enough to attract society. Rabourdin was so absorbed in completing his great and serious work that he did not notice the sudden reappearance of luxury in the bosom of his family.

Thus the wife and the husband were besieging the same fortress, working along parallel lines, each without the other's knowledge.

Monsieur des Lupeaulx

At the ministry flourishes, as secretary-general, a certain Monsieur Clément Chardin des Lupeaulx, one of those men whom the tide of political events brings to the surface for a few years, then washes away in a storm, but whom you find again on a distant shore, tossed up like the wreck of a small ship that nevertheless still looks like something. A passerby asks himself if this wreck might have contained some precious cargo or had an important mission, cooperated in some defense, carried a royal train, or even borne away the corpse of a monarch. At this moment Clément des Lupeaulx (the "Lupeaulx" absorbed the "Chardin") had reached his apogee. In the most prominent lives, as in the most obscure, in animals as in secretary-generals, is there not a zenith and a nadir, a period when the look is magnificent, the fortune dazzling? In the ontology created by the fabulists, des Lupeaulx belonged to the genus Bertrand, and was always in search of Ratons, and as one of the principal actors in this drama, he deserves a description all the more precise, as the revolution of July has eliminated this position so eminently useful to a constitutional ministry.

Moralists usually use their energies against outright abominations. For them, crimes belong in the courts or the police correctionals, yet socially finessed ones escape them; the sleights of hand that triumph under the banner of the Code are either above them or beneath them; they have neither microscope nor telescope; they want good, hard crimes, easily visible ones. Always preoccupied with the carnivores, they pay no attention to the reptiles; and, luckily for the comedy writers, the nuances that color a Chardin des Lupeaulx are left to them. Egotistical and vain, supple and proud, libertine and gourmand, greedy because of his debts, discreet as a tomb from which no visible sign contradicts the epitaph intended for the passerby's eye, intrepid and fearless when soliciting, good-natured and witty in every sense of the word, a timely jester, full of tact, knowing how to compromise others by a glance or a nudge, shrinking from no mudhole but gracefully leaping over it, intrepid Voltairian, and attending mass at Saint Thomas Aquinas if fashionable company were to be found, this secretary-general resembled all the mediocrities that form the kernel of the political world. Knowledgeable in the science of human nature, he assumed the role of listener; and none was ever more attentive. So as not to arouse suspicion, he was fawning ad nauseam, insinuating as a perfume, and flattering as a woman. He was in his late forties. His youth had long been a source of despair, for he felt that making his political career depended on becoming a deputy.

How had he reached his present position may be asked. Quite simply: a political Bonneau, des Lupeaulx took charge of certain delicate missions that can be given neither to a man of self-respect nor to a man lacking in self-respect, but are confided to grave and enigmatic individuals who can be acknowledged or disavowed at will. His business was that of being always compromised; but he got ahead as much by defeat as by success. He well understood that, under the Restoration, a period of continual transactions between men, between things, between accomplished facts and other facts looming on the horizon, the establishment could use a cleaning lady. Once inside a home, the old gal who knows how to make and unmake the beds, where to sweep away the filth, where to toss and put away the soiled linens, how to appease the creditors, which persons should be let in and who must be kept out of the house—this creature, even if she has vices, is dirty, decrepit, or toothless, or plays the lottery and steals thirty sous a day for her stake—heads of the household like out of habit; they talk and consult in her presence, even about the most critical matters; she is just there, suggests resources, gets on the trail of secrets, brings the rouge or the shawl at the right moment, lets herself be scolded, pushed downstairs, and the next morning reappears smiling with an excellent consommé. No matter how high a statesman may stand, he needs a housekeeper before whom he can be weak, undecided, argumentative with his own fate, self-questioning, self-doubting, and self-reassured for the fight. Is it not like the soft wood of savages, which, when rubbed against hard wood, strikes fire? Many great geniuses spark themselves in this way. Napoleon lived with Berthier, Richlieu with Père Joseph.

Des Lupeaulx was at home with everybody. He remained friends with fallen ministers and made himself their intermediary with the newly arrived, thus diffusing both the perfume of the last flattery and the fragrance of the first compliment. Moreover, he understood all the little matters a statesman has no time to think about: he understood necessities as they arose and took orders well. He redeemed his baseness by being the first to make fun of it so as to play it to the hilt, and among the services he rendered always chose the one that would not be forgotten. Thus, when it was necessary to cross the rift between the Empire and the Restoration, when everyone was looking for planks to bridge the gap, at a time when the curs of the empire were howling their devotion right and left, des Lupeaulx made it across by borrowing large sums from usurers. Risking all to win all, he bought up Louis XVIII's most pressing debts and in this manner was first to liquidate nearly three million at twenty percent, for he was lucky enough to be backed in 1814 and 1815. The profits were swallowed up by Gobseck, Werbrust, and

Gigonnet, the croupiers of the project; but des Lupeaulx had promised they should have them. He was not playing for a stake; he challenged the bank, as it were, knowing very well that Louis XVIII was not a man to forget this cleanup of his. Des Lupeaulx was appointed Master of Petitions, Knight of the Order of Saint Louis, and officer of the Legion of Honor. Once in, the shrewd man sought out the means to maintain his foothold, for, in the fortified city into which he had wormed himself, generals do not long keep useless mouths. To his general profession of housekeeper and go-between he added that of gratuitous consultant on the ills of power.

After discovering in the so-called higher-ups of the Restoration a substantial inferiority relative to the issues at hand, he taxed their political mediocrity by giving them—selling them—in the midst of a crisis, the right words, which men of genuine talent listen for in forethought. Do not think he came up with this himself; if he had, he would have been a genius, when in fact he was only shrewd. This Bertrand went everywhere, gathered opinions, sounded out consciences, and caught all the tones echoed back. He gathered knowledge like a true and relentless political bee. This living Bayle dictionary did not act, however, like that famous lexicon: he did not report all opinions without drawing conclusions; he had the talent of a fly that lands plumb on the best piece of meat in the middle of a kitchen. Also, he passed for an indispensable aid to statesmen. This belief had taken such deep root in people's minds that the more ambitious public men felt it necessary to neutralize des Lupeaulx in order to keep him from moving up; they compensated him for his lack of public importance with secret trusts.

Nevertheless, feeling everyone leaning on him, this fisher of ideas exacted his dues. Salaried by the staff of the National Guard, in which he held a sinecure paid for by the city of Paris, a government commissioner to a secret society, he was also a superintendent in the Royal Household. His two official and appropriated posts were those of secretary-general to his ministry and Master of Petitions. Now he wanted to be made commander of the Legion of Honor, Gentleman of the Bedchamber, count, and deputy. To be a deputy, it was necessary to pay a thousand francs in fees, and the miserable shack of des Lupeaulx was valued at barely five hundred. Where could he get money to build a château, to surround it with several respectable properties, all in order to throw dust in the eyes of everyone in the arrondissement? Although he dined in town every day, had been put up for the last nine years at the cost of the state, and was chauffeured about by the ministry, des Lupeaulx possessed absolutely nothing at the time our story opens but thirty thousand francs of debt, which no one disputed. A marriage might float this careerist and pump the waters of debt out of his bilge, but a good marriage depended on his advancement, and his advancement, on being a deputy. Searching about for the means of breaking this vicious circle, he could only think of rendering some great service or making some sort of deal. But, alas! conspiracies were out of date and the Bourbons had seemingly overcome party politics. And, unfortunately, for the last few years the government had been so thoroughly exposed by the ridiculous debates of the Left, which was attempting to make government of any kind impossible in France, that no good business deals could be made: the last ones were tried in Spain, and what an outcry they roused!

On top of all this, des Lupeaulx complicated matters by believing in the friendship of his minister, to whom he had had the imprudence to express the desire to sit on the ministerial benches. The ministers guessed the real meaning behind the desire: des Lupeaulx wanted to consolidate a precarious position and no longer be their dependent. The jackrabbit was turning against the hunter. The ministers gave him several lashes with the whip and stroked him in turn; but des Lupeaulx behaved like an adroit courtesan with new arrivals: he laid traps, they fell in, and he quickly got even. The more he felt himself threatened, the more he longed for a tenured position; yet he had to play carefully. In a second he could lose everything. One stroke of a pen could lop off his civilian colonel epaulettes, his place at court, his sinecure in the anonymous society, his two offices and their advantages—in all, six salaries retained under the legal fire governing concurrent salary draws. Often he threatened his minister as a mistress threatens her lover, telling him he was about to marry a rich widow; the minister then cajoled the dear little des Lupeaulx. After one of these reconciliations, he received the formal promise of a place in the Academy of Belles Lettres on the first vacancy. "It would pay," he said, "the keep of a horse." In his fine position, Clément Chardin was like a tree planted in good soil. He could satisfy his vices, his fancies, his virtues, and his faults.

Here are the toils of his life: from among five or six daily invitations, he had to choose the house where he could be sure of the best dinner. He went every morning to amuse the minister and his wife at the morning reception; he petted the children and played with them. Then he worked for an hour or two—that is, he lay back in a comfortable chair to read the newspapers, dictated the contents of a letter, received when the minister was not in, explained the work in a general way, caught or shed a few drops of the holy water of the court, glanced over the petitions with the stroke of a lorgnette, or wrote his name in the margin—a signature that meant, "I couldn't care less; do as you like." Everybody knew that when des Lupeaulx was interested in someone or something, he meddled in the matter personally. He let the higher-ranking bureaucrats chat candidly over delicate affairs, and he listened to their gossip. From time to time he went to the château to get his cue. And he always waited for the minister returning from the chamber, when in session, to hear if any maneuvers needed to be arranged or directed. This official sybarite dressed, dined, and visited twelve or fifteen salons between eight and three in the morning. At the opera, he chatted with journalists, for he stood high in their favor; a perpetual exchange of little services went on between them: he poured into their ears misleading news and gobbled up theirs; he prevented them from attacking this or that minister on such and such a matter, on the plea that it would cause real hardship to their wives or mistresses.

"Say that his bill is worth nothing, and prove it if you can, but do not say that Mariette danced poorly. Slander our affections for our loved ones in petticoats, but do not dig up the skeletons of our youth. What the devil! We have all pulled our vaudevilles, and we do not know what time will make of us. You yourself may become a minister, you who today feed dirt to that rag the *Constitutional* . . . ."

In return, he helped the editors out, clearing the way for the performance of a scene, giving gratuities or a good dinner at the right moment, or promised his services to wrap up some affair. Moreover, he liked literature and protected the arts: he collected autographs, obtained splendid albums gratis, sketches, and paintings. He did artists a great deal of good by not maligning them but supporting them in certain circumstances when their egos wanted some cheap gratification. He was also well liked in the world of actors, journalists, and artists. For one thing, they had the same vices and indolence as himself; furthermore, they all couldn't care less about the differences between two wines or two *danseuses*! What ways to ruin friendships! If des Lupeaulx had not been secretary-general, he would have been a journalist. Thus, in that fifteen-year struggle in which the battering of the epigram opened the breach through which insurrection would enter, des Lupeaulx never received so much as a scratch.

Watching this man playing at bowls with Monseigneur's children in the gardens of the ministry, the small fry of the civil service racked their brains to guess the secret of his influence and the nature of his work, while the aristocratic ministers looked upon him as the most dangerous Mephistopheles, courted him, and paid him back with interest the flatteries he bestowed in the higher sphere. Indecipherable as a hieroglyphic inscription to the little ones, the usefulness of the secretary-general was as plain as the rule of three to the self-interested. Responsible for gathering advice, ideas, and making oral reports, this little prince of Wagram of Napoleonic ministerialism knew all the secrets of parliamentary politics: he dragged in the lukewarm; fetched, carried, and buried propositions; said the *yea* or the *nay* that no minister dared utter. Made to receive the first fire and first blows of disappointment or anger, he moaned or laughed with the minister. A mysterious link by which many interests were in some way connected with the château, and discreet as a confessor, he sometimes knew everything and sometimes nothing; and he said for the minister that which a minister cannot say for himself. In short, with this political Hephaestion, the minister dared to be himself: to take off his wig and his false teeth, to lay aside his scruples and put on his slippers, to let down his guard and give way to his conscience.

However, it was not all a bed of roses for des Lupeaulx: he flattered and advised his master, was forced to flatter in order to advise, to advise while flattering, and to disguise flattery with advice. All politicians in this trade have bilious faces. Their constant habit of nodding to affirm what is being said, or seeming to do so, gives a certain peculiar turn to their heads. They agree indifferently with whatever is said in front of them. Their talk is full of "buts," "notwithstandings," "for myself, I should," "were I in your position" (they say "in your position" a lot)—all phrases that set up contradictions.

In person, Clément des Lupeaulx was the remains of a handsome man; five feet, four inches tall, tolerably stout, with a complexion flushed from good living, a worn look, a powdered wig, delicate spectacles; naturally fair-skinned, as indicated by a hand plump as an old woman's, a little too square, with short nails and the hand of a satrap. His foot lacked no distinction. After five o'clock, des Lupeaulx was always in silk stockings, shoes, black trousers, a cashmere waistcoat, an unscented cambric handkerchief, a gold chain, a royal-blue coat with brass buttons and his row of orders. In the morning he wore creaking boots and gray trousers, and the short fitted topcoat of an "intriguer." His appearance resembled that of a sharp lawyer rather than a ministerial officer. His eyes, glazed by the constant use of spectacles, made him plainer than he really was when by misfortune he removed them. To keen judges and upright men who are only at ease with honest natures, des Lupeaulx was intolerable. To them, his gracious manners only draped his lies; his tired courtesies, always new to fools, looked too worn. Any shrewd man saw in him a rotten plank on which no step could be trusted.

No sooner had the beautiful Madame Rabourdin decided to see to her husband's administrative fortune than she fathomed Clément des Lupeaulx's true character, and studied him thoughtfully to discover whether in this acrobat there were pliable fibers strong enough to let her lightly trip over the bureau to the division, from eight thousand to twelve thousand francs. The superior woman believed she could play this political roué. Monsieur des Lupeaulx was thus partly the reason for the extraordinary expenditures that were made and sustained in the Rabourdin household.

The rue Duphot, built up under the Empire, was remarkable for several houses with elegant exteriors and in which the apartments were generally well laid out. That of Madame Rabourdin was particularly well arranged, an advantage that counts a lot in the private lives of the noble. A nice and rather large antechamber, lighted from the courtyard, led to the grand salon, the windows of which looked onto the street. To the right of the salon were Rabourdin's study and bedroom, behind which was the dining room, entered from the antechamber; to the left was Madame's bedroom and dressing room, and behind them her daughter's little bedroom. On reception days, the door of Rabourdin's study and that of his wife's bedroom remained open. The space was enough to receive a select company without the absurdity that attends many bourgeois soirées where luxury is improvised at the expense of daily comfort, and consequently seems to be an exception. The salon had lately been rehung in yellow silk with touches of carmine. Madame's bedroom was draped in *genuine chintz* fabric and furnished in a rococo style. Rabourdin's study had inherited the late hangings of the salon, carefully cleaned, and was adorned by the fine pictures left by Monsieur Leprince. The daughter of the auctioneer used in her dining room certain exquisite Turkish rugs, a bargain grabbed by her father, and had them framed in old ebony, the price of which had become exorbitant. Elegant buffets made by Boulle, also purchased by the late auctioneer, furnished the sides of this room, in the center of which sparkled the brass arabesques inlaid in tortoise shell of one of the first base clocks that reappeared to reclaim honor for the masterpieces of the seventeenth century. Flowers perfumed this apartment so full of good taste and exquisite things, where each detail was a work of art well placed and well complemented, where Madame Rabourdin, dressed with that natural simplicity which artists attain, gave the impression of a woman accustomed to such elegances, never speaking of them and leaving to the charms of her wit the completion of the effect produced upon her guests by this ensemble. Thanks to her father, as soon as rococo was in style, Célestine was the talk of the town.

Accustomed as he was to false as well as real magnificence in all its stages, des Lupeaulx was nevertheless surprised at Madame Rabourdin's. The charm it exercised over this Parisian Asmodeus can be explained by an analogy: a traveler wearied by the thousands of rich aspects of Italy, Brazil, or India, who returns to his homeland and finds on his way a delightful little lake, like Lake Orta at the foot of Monte Rose, with an island resting on the calm waters, bewitching and simple; wild and yet cultivated; solitary but well adorned, with regal clusters of trees and statues of fine effect. The surroundings are both wild and cultivated: the panorama with its tumult outside; inside, the proportions all human. The world the traveler has seen is here in miniature, modest and pure; his soul, refreshed, bids him remain here, since a charm, poetic and melodious in all its harmony, awakens fresh ideas in his mind. It is at once a Chartreuse and real life.

A few days earlier the beautiful Madame Firmiani, one of the most ravishing women of the Faubourg Saint-Germain who visited and received Madame Rabourdin, had said to des Lupeaulx (invited expressly to hear the remark), "Why do you not call on Madame?" She made a motion toward Célestine. "Madame gives delightful parties, and her dinners, above all, are better than mine." Des Lupeaulx allowed himself to be drawn into an engagement by the lovely Madame Rabourdin who, for the first time, raised her eyes to him as she spoke. He had gone to the rue Duphot; does that not tell all? Woman has but one ruse, cries Figaro, but it is infallible. After dining at the house of this simple bureau chief, des Lupeaulx made up his mind to dine there once in a while. Thanks to the perfectly proper and becoming advances of the beautiful woman, whom her rival, Madame Colleville, called the "Célimène of the rue Duphot," he had dined there every Friday for the last month, and returned of his own accord for a cup of tea on Wednesdays. Within a few days, having watched him narrowly and knowingly, Madame Rabourdin believed she had found on this ministerial plank the spot where she might tread. She no longer doubted success. Her inner joy can be understood only in the families of government officials where one has for three or four years counted on prosperity through some hoped, nurtured, and longed-for appointment. How much grief relieved! How many entreaties and pledges proffered to the ministerial divinities! How many visits of self-interest paid! At last, thanks to her boldness, Madame Rabourdin heard the hour strike when she was to have twenty thousand francs a year instead of eight thousand.

"And I shall have managed well," she said to herself. "I have had to make a small outlay; but these are not times when one goes looking for hidden talents; rather, by putting oneself in the limelight, being seen in society, cultivating relationships and building new ones—that is how one succeeds. After all, ministers and their friends interest themselves only in the people they see, and Rabourdin knows nothing of society! If I had not cajoled those three deputies, they might have wanted La Billardière's place: whereas, now received by me, shame strikes them and they will become our supporters instead of rivals. I have rather played the coquette but am glad that the first nonsense with which one fools a man sufficed. . . . "

The day on which a serious and unlooked-for struggle over this appointment began, after a ministerial dinner that preceded one of those receptions which ministers regard as public, des Lupeaulx was standing beside the fireplace near the minister's wife. Taking his coffee, he once again included Madame Rabourdin among the seven or eight truly superior women in Paris. Several times already he had staked out Madame Rabourdin very much as Corporal Trim staked his cap.

"Don't say that too often, my dear friend, or you will do her wrong," said the minister's wife to him, half laughing.

No woman likes to hear other women praised; they all keep silent in that circumstance, so as to sour the effect.

"Poor La Billardière is dying," remarked His Excellency the Minister. "That place falls to Rabourdin, one of our ablest men, and one toward whom our predecessors did not act kindly at all, even though one of them actually owed his position in the prefecture of police under the Empire to a certain person paid to interest himself in Rabourdin. Frankly, my dear friend, you are still young enough to be loved for yourself. . . . "

"If La Billardière's place is given to Rabourdin, I may be believed when I praise the superiority of his wife," replied des Lupeaulx, piqued by the minister's irony. "But if Madame la Comtesse would be willing to judge for herself. . . . "

"You want me to invite her to my next ball, don't you? Your clever woman would arrive when I had women here who had come to make fun of us, hearing announced: 'Madame Rabourdin.'"

"But Madame Firmiani is announced at the Foreign Affairs parties?"

"Ah, but she is a born Cadignan!" said the newly created count, casting a savage glance at his secretary-general, for neither he nor his wife was noble.

The persons present thought important matters were being discussed, so the solicitors of favors remained at bay. When des Lupeaulx left, the countess said to her husband, "I think des Lupeaulx is in love."

"It would be the first time in his life, then," he replied, shrugging his shoulders as if to inform his wife that des Lupeaulx did not concern himself with such nonsense.

The minister saw a deputy of the Center-Right enter the room, and he left his wife to cajole an undecided vote. But under the blow of a sudden and unexpected disaster, this deputy wanted to be assured of protection and had come to announce privately that in a few days he would be compelled to resign. Thus forewarned, the minister would be able to open his batteries for the new election before those of the Opposition.

The minister, that is to say des Lupeaulx, had invited to dinner one of those irremovable officials found in every ministry, embarrassed by his appearance and who, in his desire to look dignified, stood rigidly planted, his two legs together, rather like an Egyptian herma. This functionary lingered near the fireplace to thank the secretary-general, whose abrupt and unexpected departure took him by surprise at the very moment he was about to pay a compliment. This was, purely and simply, the cashier of the Ministry, the only civil servant who did not tremble when the government changed hands.

At the time of which we write, the Chamber did not meddle shabbily with the budget, as it does in the deplorable days in which we now live; it did not contemptibly reduce ministerial emoluments, nor save, as they say in the kitchen, the candle ends; it granted to each minister in charge of a public department an indemnity, called a "stipend." It costs, alas, as much to enter a ministry as it does to retire from it, and entrance involves expenses of all kinds, which are quite impossible to list. This indemnity amounted to the pretty little sum of twenty-five thousand francs. The appointment appeared in *The Monitor*, while the greater or lesser officials hovering around stoves or before fireplaces, rocked by the storm around them, asked themselves: "What will he do? Will he increase the number of employees? Will he dismiss two to make room for three?" The calm cashier took out twenty-five clean bank notes, clipped them together, and wore the satisfied expression of a Swiss Catholic. He mounted the private staircase and had himself introduced to Monseigneur, as he rose, by people who blend everything into one single power, the contents and the container, the idea and the form. The cashier caught the ministerial pair in the dawn of official delight, when a statesman is benign and affable. To the "What do you want?" of the minister, he replied with the bank notes, informing His Excellency that he did not tarry to pay the customary indemnity; he explained the matter to the surprised yet pleased minister's wife, who was never without some want, usually for everything: a stipend is a household affair. The cashier then turned his compliment and slid in a few political phrases to Monseigneur: "If His Excellency would deign to retain him; if, satisfied with his purely mechanical services, he would, etc. . . . " As a man who brings twenty-five thousand francs is always a worthy employee, the cashier was sure not to leave without his confirmation of the post from which he had seen a succession of ministers come and go during a period of twenty-five years. Then he put himself at the command of Madame: monthly he brought thirteen thousand francs at the right moment; he advanced or delayed the payment as requested; and thus managed to obtain, as they say in the monasteries, a voice in the chapter.

Formerly bookkeeper at the Treasury when the Treasury kept its books by double entry, the 'Sieur Saillard had been compensated for the loss of that position by his appointment as cashier of a ministry. He was a bulky, fat man, very strong in the matter of bookkeeping and very poor at everything else; round as a round *o*, simple as a how-do-you-do, he stomped to his office with the measured steps of an elephant and returned with the same measured tread to the Place Royale, where he lived on the ground floor of an old mansion belonging to him. He usually had a companion in the person of Monsieur Isidore Baudoyer, bureau chief in Monsieur de La Billardière's division and consequently one of Rabourdin's colleagues, who had married Elisabeth Saillard, his only daughter, and naturally took the apartment above his own. No one at the Ministry had the slightest doubt that Saillard was a blockhead, but neither had anyone ever found out the extent of his stupidity; it was too trite even to be considered, too shallow to be questioned; it did not even ring hollow: it absorbed everything and echoed nothing. Bixiou (an employee of whom more later) had caricatured the cashier by drawing a head in a wig at the top of an egg and two little legs at the other end, with this caption: "Born to pay out and take in without blundering. A little less luck, and he might have been son to the Bank of France; a little more ambition, and he could have been honorably discharged."

At this time, the minister regarded his cashier as we would regard a coat hook or a cliff, without supposing that either could hear conversation or fathom secret thoughts.

"I am all the more anxious that we should settle everything with the prefect in the most hushed manner because des Lupeaulx had ambitions," said the minister, continuing his chat with the deputy. "His paltry little estate is in your arrondissement; we don't want anything to do with him."

"He has neither rents nor the years to be eligible," said the deputy.

"Yes, but you know how it was decided for Casimir Périer regarding age. As for worldly possessions, des Lupeaulx does possess something, which is not worth much. But the law does not take into account growth, which he may very well obtain. Commissions have wide margins for the deputies of the Center, you know, and we cannot openly oppose the goodwill that is shown this dear friend."

"But where could he get the money?"

"How did Manuel manage to become the owner of a house in Paris?" cried the minister.

The cashier listened and heard, but reluctantly and against his will. These rapid remarks, though murmured, landed in Saillard's ear by way of one of those acoustic reverberations that are very little understood. Do you know what he felt when he heard these political confidences? A burning terror. He was one of those simple-minded beings who are shocked to hear anything they are not intended to hear, or to enter where they are not invited, and, seeming bold when they are really timid, appear inquisitive while they are truly discreet. The cashier accordingly began to glide along the carpet to edge himself away, so that the minister only saw him at a distance when he first noticed him. Saillard was a ministerial henchman absolutely incapable of indiscretion; even if the minister had thought he had overheard his secret, he had only to say, "Mum's the word." The cashier got into a carriage from his neighborhood, hired by the hour for these costly entertainments, and returned to his home at the Place Royale.

The Teredos Navalis
Otherwise Known as Shipworm

While old Saillard traveled across Paris, his son-in-law and his dear Elisabeth were busy with Abbé Gaudron, their mentor, at a virtuous round of Boston in the company of a few neighbors and a certain Martin Falleix, a brass founder from the Faubourg Saint-Antoine, to whom Saillard had loaned the funds needed to establish a profitable business. This Falleix, a respectable Auvergnat come to Paris with his smelting pot on his back, had been immediately employed by Brézacs, scavengers of châteaux. About twenty-seven years old, spoiled like others by success, Martin Falleix had the good fortune of being a partner with Monsieur Saillard in the development of a smelting discovery (patent and gold medal granted at the Exposition of 1825). Madame Baudoyer, whose only daughter was walking—to use an expression of old Saillard's—on the tail of her twelve years, had her heart set on Falleix, a stocky fellow, swarthy, active, of strong integrity, whom she was educating. According to her, this education consisted of teaching him to play Boston, to hold his cards properly, not to let others see his hand; to shave himself before he came over, to wash his hands with good cleansing soap; not to swear, to speak their kind of French; to wear boots instead of shoes, cotton shirts instead of burlap, to brush his hair up instead of plastering it down flat. Eight days before, Elisabeth had succeeded in persuading Falleix to remove from his ears two enormous flat rings that resembled hoops.

"You go too far, Madame Baudoyer," he said, seeing her satisfied at this sacrifice. "You order me around too much: you make me clean my teeth, which loosens them; shortly you will make me brush my nails and curl my hair, which won't do at all in our business; we don't like dandies."

Elisabeth Baudoyer, born Saillard, is one of those persons who escape portraiture through their utter repulsiveness, yet who ought nevertheless to be sketched because they are specimens of that Parisian petite bourgeoisie, situated above the wealthy artisans and below the upper classes, whose virtues are nearly vices, whose defects have nothing agreeable about them, but whose mores, though insipid, are not without originality. Elisabeth had something wretched about her that made her an eyesore. Scarcely over four feet tall, she was so thin that her waist hardly measured twenty inches. Her small features, pudgy around the nose, gave her face the vague look of a weasel's snout. Past thirty years, she looked only sixteen or seventeen. Her eyes of Wedgwood blue, dominated by heavy eyelids joined in the arch of the eyebrows, did not sparkle much. Everything about her was shabby: her hair, a shade of blond verging on white, her flat forehead, from which the light did not reflect, and her complexion of a gray, almost leaden hue. The lower portion of her face, more triangular than oval, irregularly ended the otherwise irregular outline of her face. Finally, her voice had a rather pretty range of intonation, from sharp to sweet. Elisabeth was a perfect specimen of the petite bourgeoisie, nagging her husband in the evening, without the least credit for her virtues, ambitious without ulterior motive, and that only through the development of her domestic selfishness: in the country she would have liked to round out her estate; in administration she wanted to get ahead.

In telling the story of her father and mother, we will tell hers too, by painting a picture of the little girl's childhood.

Monsieur Saillard had married the daughter of a furniture sales-
man who kept shop under the arcades of Les Halles. Limited
means had from the start compelled Monsieur and Madame Saillard
to bear constant privation. After thirty-three years of marriage and
twenty-nine years of toil in a government office, the estate of "the
Saillards"—their circle of acquaintances called them such—consisted of sixty thousand francs entrusted to Falleix, the house in the
Place Royale, bought for forty thousand francs in 1804, and thirty-
six thousand francs given in dowry to their daughter. Out of this capital, the inheritance of the Bidault widow, mother of Madame Saillard, came to a sum of about fifty thousand francs. Saillard's salary
had always been four thousand, five hundred francs, since his position was a dead end which for a long time interested no one. These
ninety thousand francs, gathered sou by sou, were derived from
sordid economies very unintelligently invested. In fact, the Saillards
did not know any other way to manage their funds than to carry them,
five thousand francs at a time, to their notary, Monsieur Sorbier, Cardot's predecessor, and let him invest it at five percent in first mortgages, with the wife's rights reserved in case the borrower was married! In 1804, Madame Saillard obtained a government office for the
sale of stamped papers, a situation that brought a servant into the
house. At this time, the house, which was worth more than a hundred thousand francs, brought in eight thousand a year. Falleix
paid seven percent for his sixty-thousand share, in addition to an equal
share in the profits. The Saillards were therefore enjoying an income
of at least seventeen thousand francs a year. The whole ambition of
the good man now centered on obtaining the cross of the Legion upon
retirement.

Elisabeth's youth was one constant chore in a family whose
habits were very harsh and ideas very narrow. There was a debate
over a new hat for Saillard; one estimated how many years a coat had
lasted; umbrellas were carefully hung up on brass hooks. Since

1804, no repairs of any kind had been made to the house. The Saill-lards kept the ground floor in precisely the state in which their predecessor had left it: the gilding of the full-length mirror worn off, the paint on the door frames hardly to be seen for the layers of dust that time had deposited. They kept, in the fine, large rooms, sculptured marble by the mantel, work worthy of Versailles on the ceiling, the old furniture found in the Bidault widow's home. It consisted of a curious mixture of walnut armchairs, disjointed and covered with tapestry, rosewood bureaus, round pedestal tables with brass railings and cracked marble tops, one superb Boulle secretary, the value of whose style had not yet been recognized—in short, a hodgepodge of bargains picked up by the haggler at Les Halles stalls: pictures bought for the sake of nice frames, mixed china services—that is, a magnificent set of dessert plates and all the rest porcelains of all kinds—unmatched silver, old crystal, fine damask, and a four-poster bedstead hung with curtains and garnished with plumes.

Amid all these relics, Madame Saillard lived on a sofa of modern mahogany, her feet up on a small stove burned out at every hole, near the mantel on which stood a clock, some antique bronzes, and a candelabra with flowers but no candles: the room was lit by a brass candlestick caked with old wax. Madame Saillard had a face upon which, despite its wrinkles, were portrayed obstinacy and severity, narrow ideas, a square sort of uprightness, religion without piety, simple avarice, and the peace of a quiet conscience. In certain Flemish paintings you see the wives of burgomasters cut out by nature in the same manner and wonderfully reproduced on canvas; but they wear fine robes of velvet and precious cloth, whereas Madame Saillard possessed no robes, only that venerable garment called, in Touraine and Picardie, *cottes*, or more generally known in France as petticoats, a sort of skirt pleated behind and on each side, with other skirts hanging over it. Her bust was enclosed in what was called a *casaquin*, another fashion from an age gone by! She continued to wear a bonnet with starched wings and shoes with high heels. Although she was fifty-seven, and her lifetime of vigorous housework would now enable her to rest, she knitted her husband's stockings and her own, and those of an uncle, just as her countrywomen knit them—walking, talking, strolling in the garden, or on her way to see what was going on in her kitchen.

Originally born of necessity, the avarice of the Saillards had become second nature. When the cashier got back from the office, he laid aside his coat; he worked the beautiful garden himself, shut off from the courtyard by an iron grill and which the family kept to itself. For years Elisabeth had gone to market in the morning with her mother, and the two did all the housework. The mother cooked a good duck with turnips; but according to the old Saillard, Elisabeth had no equal for her leftover mutton with onions. "You might eat your boots with those onions and not even know it." As soon as Elisabeth could hold a needle, her mother made her mend the household linen and her father's clothes. Forever at work like a servant, she never went out alone. Though living a couple of steps from the boulevard du Temple, where Franconi, La Gaîté, and l'Ambigu-Comique were, and, a little farther on, the Porte Saint-Martin, Elisabeth had never seen a play. When she took a fancy to "see what it was like," with the Abbé Gaudron's permission of course, Monsieur Baudoyer took her—for the thrill of it, and of course to expose her to the finest of all performances—to the Opéra, where the "The Chinese Laborer" was playing. Elisabeth found "the theater" as boring as flies and never wanted to go back. On Sundays, after walking up and down four times from the Place Royale and Saint-Paul's Church, for her mother made her practice the precepts and duties of religion, her father and mother took her to the Café Turc, where they sat on chairs placed between a railing and the wall. The Saillards always hurried to reach the spot early so as to get the right seats and entertained themselves watching the passersby. In those days the yard of the Café Turc was the rendezvous of fashionable society from the Marais, the Faubourg Saint-Antoine, and the surrounding area.

Elisabeth never wore anything but cotton dresses in the summer, merino in the winter; and she made them herself. Her mother only gave her twenty francs a month for her expenses, but her father, who was very fond of her, tempered this harsh treatment with a few gifts. She never read what the Abbé Gaudron, vicar of Saint-Paul's and the family mentor, called profane books. This discipline had borne fruit. Forced to direct her feelings to some other passion, Elisabeth became eager for gain. Although she was not lacking in sense or wit, religious theories and her ignorance had confined all her abilities in an iron band; they were exercised only on the most banal things of life; but, not being at all spread thin, she went full-force to the task at hand. Repressed by devotion, her natural intelligence had to develop within the limits demarcated by her conscience, which formed a store of subtleties from which self-interest selected its outlets. Like those saintly characters in whom religion did not stifle ambition, she was able to get others to do the dirty work so that she might reap the rewards; under the right circumstances, she would be as implacable as they for her due, crafty in all ways. Once offended, she would watch her adversaries with the perfidious patience of a cat, and would be capable of wreaking some cold and complete vengeance, laying it all in the hands of the dear Lord.

Until Elisabeth's marriage, the Saillards lived without company other than that of the Abbé Gaudron, a priest from Auvergne appointed vicar of Saint-Paul's after the restoration of Catholic worship. Besides this ecclesiastic, who was a friend of the late Madame Bidault, there was the paternal uncle of Madame Saillard, an old paper dealer retired from business ever since Year II of the Republic, now sixty-nine years old, who came to see them only on Sundays, because no business was transacted on that day.

This little old man, with a greenish complexion blazoned by the red nose of a tippler and lighted by two gleaming vulture eyes, kept his gray hair under a three-cornered hat, wore breeches with stirrups that extended beyond the buckles, cotton stockings of mottled thread knitted by his niece, whom he always called "the little Saillard," heavy shoes with silver buckles, and a multicolored overcoat. He looked very much like those little village sacristan–beadle–bell-ringer–grave-digging–parish clerks, whom we take to be caricatures until we see them in action. On the present occasion he had come on foot to dine and would return by way of the same rue Greneta, where he lived on a third floor. His business was discounting commercial paper in the Quartier Saint-Martin, where he was known by the nickname of "Gigonnet," for the nervous, convulsive movement with which he lifted his leg when walking. Monsieur Bidault began this business in the Year II with a Dutchman named Werbrust, a friend of Gobseck.

Some time later, at the council of the Fabrique de Saint-Paul, Saillard made the acquaintance of Monsieur and Madame Transon, wholesale dealers in pottery with a shop in the rue de Lesdiguière, who took an interest in Elisabeth and who, with the intention of marrying her off, showed up at the Saillards with young Isidore Baudoyer. The match of Monsieur and Madame Baudoyer with the Saillards was reinforced by the approval of Gigonnet, who, for quite some time, had employed a certain Monsieur Mitral, a civil servant, brother of Madame Baudoyer the mother, the one who wanted to retire to a nice home at L'Isle-Adam. Monsieur and Madame Baudoyer, father and mother of Isidore, highly respectable leather-dressers in the rue Censier, had slowly amassed a moderate fortune out of a small trade. After marrying off their only son, to whom they gave fifty thousand francs, they decided to live in the country, and chose the area of L'Isle-Adam, where they were joined by Mitral. But they frequently came to Paris, where they kept a small flat in the house in the rue Censier given in dowry to Isidore. The Baudoyers still enjoyed a thousand ecus in pension after having established their son.

Mitral, a man with a sinister-looking wig, a face the color of Seine water in which sparkled a pair of Spanish-tobacco-colored eyes, cold as a well-rope, always smelling a rat, guarded the secret of his success but probably worked his territory just as Gigonnet worked the Quartier Saint-Martin.

Although the circle of this family's acquaintances grew, neither their ideas nor their mores changed. The saints' days of father, mother, daughter, son-in-law, and grandchild were observed, as were the anniversaries of birth and marriage, Easter, Christmas, New Year's, and Epiphany. These celebrations were occasions for great house cleaning and the full clearing-out of the house, which added an element of usefulness to these family ceremonies. Then, the presents were offered with much pomp and were accompanied by flowers, and practical gifts, too: silk stockings or a fur cap for Saillard; gold earrings and a silver platter for Elisabeth or her husband, for whom, little by little, the parents were accumulating a whole silver service; silk petticoats for Madame Saillard, who never even put them together. As for these gifts, they tried to give them to one another sitting in an armchair and after a while asking, "Guess what we have for you?" Then came a splendid dinner lasting at least five hours, to which were invited the Abbé Gaudron, Falleix, Rabourdin, Monsieur Godard, former deputy chief to Monsieur Baudoyer, and Monsieur Bataille, captain of the company to which Saillard and his son-in-law belonged. Monsieur Cardot, born popular, did as Rabourdin did—namely, accepted one invitation out of six. They sang at dessert, shook hands, and embraced with enthusiasm, wishing each other all manner of happiness; and they displayed the presents, asking the guests' opinions of them. The day the fur cap was given, Saillard wore it during the dessert, to the satisfaction of all. At night, mere acquaintances came by and there was a dance. For a long time they used to dance to just a violin; but for the last six years Monsieur Godard, who was a great flute player, contributed the piercing tones of a flageolet. The cook and Madame Baudoyer's maid, old Catherine, Madame Saillard's woman servant, and the porter or his wife, stood looking on at the door to the salon. The servants always received a sum of three livres on these occasions, to buy themselves wine and coffee.

This company considered Saillard and Baudoyer to be transcendent beings: they were employed by the government; they had risen on their own merits; they worked, it was said, with the minister himself; they owed their success to their talents; they were politicians. But Baudoyer passed for the more able; his position as head of a bureau implied more complicated tasks, more arduous than those of a cashier. Moreover, although the son of a leatherdresser in the rue Censier, Isidore had had the genius to study, the audacity to cast aside his father's business and find a career in the Administration, which had led to a distinguished post. In short, though not very talkative, he was looked upon as a deep thinker; and perhaps, said the admiring circle, he would someday become deputy of the eighth arrondissement. Listening to such remarks, Gigonnet pursed his already pinched lips closer together and cast a glance at his great-niece Elisabeth.

Physically, Isidore was thirty-seven, tall and stout, perspired freely, and had a head resembling that of a hydrocephalic. This enormous head, covered with closely cropped chestnut hair, was joined to his neck by rolls of flesh that overhung his coat collar. He had the arms of Hercules, the hands of Domitian, and a stomach that sobriety held within the limits of the majestic, to use a saying of Brillat-Savarin. His face was a good deal like that of the Emperor Alexander. The Tartar type was to be seen in his little eyes, his flattened, slightly turned-up nose, his cold lips, and his short chin. The forehead was low and narrow. Though his temperament was apathetic, the devout Isidore was under the influence of an excessive conjugal passion that did not wear out. In spite of his resemblance to the handsome Russian emperor and the terrible Domitian, Isidore was nothing more than a bureaucrat, incapable as bureau chief, but a man of rote molded to routine, who concealed the fact that he was a fat incompetent under a skin so thick that no scalpel could cut deep enough to expose him. In the course of his intense studies, during which he showed the patience and sagacity of an ox, his square head had deceived his parents; they took him for an extraordinary man. Meticulous and pedantic, meddlesome and fault-finding, a terror to the employees under him, whom he constantly criticized, he insisted that every *i* be dotted and every *t* crossed, rigorously enforced regulations, and came to work with such punctuality that no one dared not to arrive before him. Baudoyer wore a blue coat with gilt buttons, a chamois waistcoat, gray trousers, and a colored tie. He had big feet, poorly shod. His watch chain was adorned with an enormous bunch of old trinkets, among which, in 1824, he still wore "American beads," which were much in style in the Year VII.

In the bosom of this family, held together by the force of religious ties, by the inflexibility of its mores, and by one single philosophy, that of avarice become a guiding light, Elisabeth was forced to talk to herself rather than share her ideas with those around her, for she felt that no one could understand her better than herself. Although facts forced her to judge her husband, the devoted one did her best to keep up, as well as possible, a favorable opinion of Monsieur Baudoyer: she showed him marked respect and honored him as the father of her child and her husband, the temporal power, as the vicar of Saint-Paul's told her. Also, she would have thought it a mortal sin to make a single gesture, cast a single glance, or say a single word that would betray to others her real opinion of the imbecile Baudoyer; she professed a passive obedience to all his wishes. But she kept her ears open, she took everything in, she drew her own conclusions, and so astutely weighed and compared them in the privacy of her own mind, judging men and events, that at the time our story opens, she was the secret oracle of the two functionaries, both of whom came unwittingly to do nothing without consulting her. Old Saillard would say, innocently, "Isn't she clever, that Elisabeth of mine?" But Baudoyer, too great a fool not to be puffed up by the false reputation he had in the Quartier Saint-Antoine, denied his wife's cleverness while all the time using it for his gain.

Elisabeth had figured out that her Uncle Bidault, called Gigonnet, was rich and handled vast sums. Enlightened by self-interest, she knew Monsieur des Lupeaulx far better than the minister. Finding herself married to an imbecile, she thought life could well have gone differently for her, but she only guessed at the best without really wanting to know it. All of her tender affections found their strength in her love for her daughter, whom she spared the pains she had borne in her own childhood, and thus she saw herself as quits with the world of emotions. Only for her daughter's sake had she persuaded her father to take the big step of going into partnership with Falleix. Falleix had been introduced at the Saillards' by old Bidault, who lent him money on his merchandise. Falleix thought his old countryman extortionate and complained to the Saillards that Gigonnet demanded eighteen percent from an Auvergnat. Madame Saillard complained to her uncle.

"It is precisely because he *is* an Auvergnat that I'm only taking eighteen percent," replied Gigonnet.

Falleix, twenty-eight, had made a discovery, and in telling Saillard seemed to carry his heart in his hand (to put it in Saillard's words) and to be in for a great fortune. Elisabeth then slated him for her daughter, thus molding her own son-in-law, figuring it would take her seven years. Martin Falleix felt and showed the deepest respect for Madame Baudoyer, in whom he recognized a superior spirit. If he later had millions, he would always belong to that house, where he had found a home. The little Baudoyer girl was already trained to bring him a drink and take his hat.

Monsieur Saillard, arriving home from the ministry, found a game of Boston in play. Elisabeth was advising Falleix. Madame Saillard was knitting in the chimney corner and looking over the hand of the vicar of Saint-Paul's. Monsieur Baudoyer, motionless as a millstone, was engaged in thought, calculating how the cards were placed, and sat across from Mitral, come up from L'Isle-Adam for the Christmas holidays. No one moved as the cashier entered and wandered about the salon for a few minutes, his fat face contorted with unaccustomed cogitation.

"He's always like that after he dines at the Ministry, which, thank goodness, only happens twice a year," thought Madame Saillard, "or it would kill him." Saillard was hardly made to be in the government.

"Well, now, I do hope, Saillard," she said to him out loud, "that you're not going to keep on those silk breeches and your best Elbeuf cloth suit. Go get out of all that; don't wear them at home, my man."

"Your father has something on his mind," said Baudoyer to his wife, while the cashier was in his room, undressing without any fire.

"Perhaps Monsieur de La Billardière is dead," said Elisabeth simply, "and since he wants you to replace him, it worries him."

"If I could be of any help," said the vicar of Saint-Paul's, leaning forward, "pray use my services. I have the honor of being known to Madame la Dauphine. These are days when public offices should be given only to devout men whose religious principles are not to be shaken."

"Dear me!" said Falleix. "One needs protectors in order for men of merit to get into your position? I did well to become a founder; my customers know how to tell if something is well cast. . . . "

"Monsieur," interrupted Baudoyer, "the government is the government; never attack it in this house."

"In fact," said the vicar, "you talk like *The Constitutional*."

"*The Constitutional* never says anything else," replied Baudoyer, who never read anything at all.

The cashier believed his son-in-law to be as superior in talent to Rabourdin as God was greater than Saint Crépin, so he said; but the good man coveted this appointment in a naive way. Influenced by the feeling that leads all officials to seek promotion—a violent, unreflecting, almost brutal passion—he wanted success, just as he wanted the Cross of the Legion of Honor, without doing anything against his conscience and solely based on merit. According to him, a man who had had the patience to spend twenty-five years in an office behind an iron grill had sacrificed himself to his country and certainly deserved the Cross. To help his son-in-law out, he dreamed up nothing less than to slip in a good word to His Excellency's wife when he delivered his monthly salary.

"Well, Saillard, you look as if you've lost all your friends! Do tell us about it, my boy; do say something," cried his wife when he came back into the room.

Saillard turned on his heel, after making a sign to his daughter, to keep himself from talking politics before strangers. When Monsieur Mitral and the vicar had left, Saillard pushed back the table, sat down in an armchair, and positioned himself as he always did when he had office gossip to tell, the whole routine rather resembling the three knocks given at the Comédie-Française. After swearing his wife, his son-in-law, and his daughter to the deepest secrecy—for, however petty the gossip, their posts, according to him, always depended on their discretion—he told them of this incomprehensible enigma of the resignation of a deputy, of the very legitimate desire of the secretary-general to be appointed in his place, of the secret opposition of the minister to this ambition of one of his staunchest supporters, one of his most zealous servants; and then, too, the whole issue of age and financial qualification came up. This, of course, brought down an avalanche of suppositions, flooded with the arguments of the two officials, who hurled nonsense back and forth at each other. Elisabeth quietly asked three questions.

"If Monsieur des Lupeaulx is on our side, will Monsieur Baudoyer definitely be appointed?"

"Heavens! I should think so," cried the cashier.

"In 1814 my Uncle Bidault and Monsieur Gobseck helped him out," she thought. "Is he still in their debt?"

"Yes," answered the cashier, with a prolonged hissing emphasis on the last letter. "There was a lien on his salary, but it was removed by orders from higher up, a bill at sight."

"Where is the des Lupeaulx estate?"

"Why, don't you know? In the part of the country where your grandfather, your Great-Uncle Bidault, and Falleix are from, not far from the arrondissement of the deputy who wants to resign. . . ."

When her colossus of a husband had gone to bed, Elisabeth leaned over him, and though he always treated her remarks as women's nonsense, she said, "My friend, perhaps you really will get Monsieur de La Billardière's place."

"There goes your imagination again!" said Baudoyer. "Leave Monsieur Gaudron to speak to the Dauphine and don't meddle with politics."

At eleven o'clock, when all was quiet at the Place Royale, Monsieur des Lupeaulx was leaving the Opéra for the rue Duphot. This particular Wednesday was one of Madame Rabourdin's most brilliant evenings. Many of her regular guests came back from the theaters and swelled the company already assembled in her salon, among whom were several celebrities, including Canalis the poet, Schinner the painter, Dr. Bianchon, Lucien de Rubempré, Octave de Camps, the comte de Granville, the vicomte de Fontaine, du Bruel the vaudevillist, Andoche Finot the journalist, Derville, one of the best minds in the law courts, the comte du Châtelet, deputy, du Tillet the banker, and such fine young men as Paul de Manerville and the vicomte de Portenduère. Célestine was pouring tea when the secretary-general entered. Her dress that evening was very becoming: she wore a black velvet robe without any ornament, a black gauze scarf, her hair smoothly bound about her head and raised in a heavy braided mass, with long curls à l'Anglaise falling on either side of her face. What set this woman apart was the easy grace of an Italian artist, an understanding of all things, and the graciousness with which she granted even the smallest of wishes to her friends. Nature had given her a svelte figure that turned nimbly at the slightest word, black eyes of an oriental shape, slit, like those of Chinese women, to see out of their corners. She well knew how to manage a soft, insinuating voice, which endowed every word, even those casually uttered, with a tender charm; her feet were like those you see in portraits where the painter boldly lies and flatters his model in the only way that does not really alter the appearance. Her complexion, a little yellow by day like that of most brunettes, was dazzling at night under candlelight, which brought out the brilliance of her black hair and eyes. Finally, her slender and well-defined shape recalled an artist of the Venus of the Middle Ages found by Jean Goujon, the illustrious sculptor of Diane de Poitiers.

Des Lupeaulx stopped in the doorway and leaned his shoulder against the frame. This ferret of ideas did not deny himself the pleasure of spying on an emotion, as this woman interested him more than any of the others to whom he had attached himself. Des Lupeaulx was coming to that age when men have excessive pretensions with regard to women. The first gray hairs usher in the last passions, the most violent because they are astride waning power and dawning weakness. Forty is the age of folly—an age when a man wants to be loved for himself; for now his love does not hold up all by itself, as in the early years, when one can love wastefully and with impunity, even as a cherubim. At forty, one wants it all, as one is so afraid of not getting anything; whereas at twenty-five, one has so much, one does not know how to want anything. At twenty-five, one walks with such strength that one gives out with impunity; but at forty, one mistakes abuse for virility. The thoughts that seized des Lupeaulx's mind at this moment were no doubt melancholy ones. The nerves of the old beau relaxed, the agreeable smile that he used as a face and that served as a mask controlling his look, gave way; the real man appeared, and he was horrible. Rabourdin caught sight of him and thought: "What's happened to him? Can he be disgraced?" The secretary-general was only remembering how he was recently too quickly dropped by Madame Colleville, whose intentions were exactly those of Madame Rabourdin. Rabourdin caught this fake statesman with his eyes fixed on his wife, and he recorded the look in his memory.

Rabourdin was too keen an observer not to understand des Lupeaulx to the very core of his being; he deeply despised him. But, as with most very busy men, his feelings never came to the surface. Being absorbed in a well-liked task is practically the same as the cleverest of disguises, and so the opinions of Rabourdin were a closed book to des Lupeaulx. The bureau chief was not happy to see this political upstart in his home, but he did not want to go against Célestine's wishes. At this particular moment, while he chatted confidentially with a supernumerary who was destined to play a part in an intrigue brought about by the death of La Billardière, he kept a very candid eye on Célestine and des Lupeaulx.

At this point we might explain, as much for foreigners as for our own grandchildren, what a supernumerary in Paris is.

The supernumerary is to the Administration what a choirboy is to the church, what the company's child is to the regiment, what the understudy is to the theater: someone naive, innocent, a being blinded by illusions. Without illusions where would anyone be? They give us strength to bear the *res angusta domi* of arts, to bear the initiation into any science, by inspiring us with faith. Illusion is faith without bounds! So the supernumerary has faith in the Administration! He never thinks it as cold, atrocious, and hard as it really is. There are only two kinds of supernumeraries: rich and poor. The poor supernumerary is rich in hope and needs a post; the rich supernumerary is poor in spirit and needs nothing. A wealthy family is not so foolish as to put its able men into the Administration. The rich supernumerary is given a position higher up or is put close to the general-director, who initiates him into what Bilboquet, that profound philosopher, called the high comedy of the Administration; he is spared all the horrors of probation until he is appointed to some office. The rich supernumerary never alarms the bureaus. The bureaucrats know he is hardly a threat: the rich supernumerary seeks only the highest positions in the Administration.

About this time, many families were saying to themselves, "What can we do with our children?" The army hardly offered a chance for fortune. Special careers, such as civil and military engineering, the navy, mining, the military, the professorial chair, were all blocked by regulations or entrance competitions; whereas the spinning wheel that transforms state employees into prefects, subprefects, assessors, and collectors, etc., into good old boys as if by the power of some magic lantern is not subject to a single regulation and has no entrance competitions. Through this loophole came the supernumeraries who drove in carriages, dressed well, had mustaches—all of them as rude as parvenus. Journalists were apt to persecute the rich supernumeraries who were cousins, nephews, brothers, or other relatives of some minister, deputy, or an influential peer; whereas the employees, accomplices to this type of supernumerary, sought their protection.

The poor supernumerary—the *real* one, the only supernumerary—is almost always the son of some former civil servant's widow, who lives on a meager pension and kills herself to support her son until he can get a position as copy clerk, and then dies leaving him no closer to the head of his department, but as some writer of deeds, order-clerk, or maybe even deputy chief. Always living in some area where rents are low, this supernumerary leaves home early in the morning; for him the Eastern Question relates only to the morning skies! To go on foot, not to get muddy, to save his clothes, to allow for the time he may lose standing under an overhang in case of a downpour—these are his big concerns! Sidewalks on the streets, the flagstones of the quays and boulevards, these were a godsend to him. When, for some extraordinary reason, you happen to be in the streets of Paris at seven-thirty or eight o'clock in the winter, when you see, through the piercing cold, in the rain, in whatever horrible weather, a pale young man appear without a cigar, take notice of his pockets. You will be sure to see the outline of a roll his mother has given him so that, without retaliation from his stomach, he can ford the nine hours from breakfast to dinner.

The guilelessness of the supernumerary does not last for long, however. A young man, enlightened by glimpses of Parisian life, soon measures the frightful distance that separates him from a clerkship, a distance which no mathematician—neither Archimedes, nor Newton, nor Pascal, nor Leibnitz, nor Kepler, nor Laplace—was ever able to figure, the distance that exists between zero and the number 1, or between an idea and its application! The supernumerary thus soon enough perceives the impossibilities of his career. He hears talk of favoritism; he discovers the intrigues of the different bureaus—i.e., he sees the questionable means by which his superiors have pushed their way up: one married a young woman who made a mistake; another, the natural daughter of a minister (shouldering the responsibility for another's mistake); that one, full of talent, risked his health by doing, with the perseverance of a mole, the tons of work that sometimes goes beyond one's limits. Everything is common knowledge in the bureaus. The incapable man has a wife with a clear head who has pushed him along, who got him nominated for deputy; if he has no talent for an office, he cabals in the Chamber. The wife of another has a statesman at her feet. Another is the secret informant of a powerful journalist.

So the disgusted supernumerary submits his resignation. About three-quarters of the supernumeraries leave the Administration without even obtaining an appointment, so that either the young and stubborn are left, or the real idiots who say to themselves, "I have been here for three years. I'll end up by getting some position," or those young men who feel a calling. Obviously, the position of supernumerary is, in the Administration, precisely what the novitiate is in a religious order—a trial. It is a rough trial. The state discovers how many of them can bear hunger, thirst, and poverty without cracking; how many can toil without revolting; and whose constitution will bear this horrible existence or, if you like, this disease of the bureaus. From this point of view, the supernumerary, far from being an infamous device of the government to obtain free labor, becomes a useful institution.

The young man with whom Rabourdin was speaking was a poor supernumerary named Sébastien de La Roche, who had tiptoed over from the rue du Roi-Doré in the Marais without getting in the least bit dirty. He talked of his mother, and did not dare raise his eyes to Madame Rabourdin, whose house affected him like the Louvre. He did not show his gloves, cleaned with an eraser. His poor mother had put a hundred sous in his pocket in case it became absolutely necessary that he should play cards, suggesting he take nothing, remain standing, and be very careful not to knock over a lamp or some pretty little bric-à-brac from an étagère. His dress was all of the strictest black. His fair face and his eyes, a fine shade of green with golden reflections, were in keeping with a handsome head of auburn hair. The poor lad looked furtively at Madame Rabourdin, whispering to himself, "What a beautiful woman!" When he got home, he thought of this fairy queen just as he closed his eyes to sleep.

Rabourdin had noted in Sébastien a dedication to his work, and since he took the supernumerary seriously, felt a sharp interest in the poor boy. He had, moreover, guessed the poverty reigning in the home of a poor widow with a pension of seven hundred francs, whose son, just out of school, had used up her savings. Furthermore, he was very paternally inclined toward this poor supernumerary; he often fought to get him some stipend from the Council, and sometimes paid it out of his own pocket when the fighting between the dispensers of fees and himself was too fierce. He allowed him to take du Bruel's place, the playwright known in dramatic circles and on billboards by the name Cursy, who paid him one hundred ecus out of his salary. Rabourdin, in the minds of Madame de La Roche and her son, was at once a great man, a tyrant, and an angel; on him hung all their hopes, Sébastien always with his eyes fixed on the day when he would become a state employee. Ah! The day they are commissioned is a great day for the supernumeraries! All of them can taste their first month's pay, and they will not give it all to their mothers! Venus always smiles upon these first fruits of the ministerial payroll. This hope could only be realized for Sébastien by Monsieur Rabourdin, his only protector; also, his dedication to his boss was really without limits. The supernumerary dined twice a month in the rue Duphot, but always at a family dinner, invited by Rabourdin himself; Madame never asked him to evening parties, except when she needed partners.

The heart of the poor supernumerary would pound whenever he saw the imposing des Lupeaulx, whom a car would pick up, often at four-thirty, just as he was putting on his raincoat at the door of the ministry, and take him to the Marais. The secretary-general upon whom his destiny depended, who with one word could give him a position paying twelve hundred francs (yes, twelve hundred francs was the height of his ambition—on that income, he and his mother could be happy!), well, this secretary-general did not even know him! Des Lupeaulx hardly even knew that a Sébastien de La Roche existed. But if the son of de La Billardière, the rich supernumerary in Baudoyer's bureau, happened also to be at the door, des Lupeaulx never failed to greet him with a friendly nod. Monsieur Benjamin de La Billardière was the son of a cousin of a minister.

At that moment Rabourdin was scolding this poor little Sébastien, the only person who was in the know about his immense labors. The supernumerary copied and recopied the famous memoranda, written on a hundred and fifty spread sheets, not to mention the attached tables and the summaries, which on one page had, in brackets, the captions in English script and the subtitles in round script. Full of enthusiasm for his merely mechanical participation in the great idea, the lad of twenty would rewrite whole pages because of a single blot and made it his pride and glory to touch up the writing, an element of so noble an enterprise. Sébastien had committed the great imprudence of carrying the draft of the most dangerous work into the general office in order to copy it. It was a list of all the state employees in the central offices of all the ministries in Paris, with notations concerning their fortunes, actual and prospective, along with their personal activities outside of work.

In Paris, every bureaucrat who has not, like Rabourdin, a patriotic ambition or other marked capacity, usually supplements his salary with some outside job, in order to eke out a living. He does as Monsieur Saillard did: he invests in a business as a partner and spends his evenings keeping the books of his associate. Many civil servants are married to linen maids, tobacconists, directors of the public lotteries or reading rooms. Some, like the husband of Madame Colleville, Célestine's rival, play in a theater orchestra. Others, like du Bruel, write vaudeville shows, comic operas, and melodramas, or direct productions. In this group, we may mention Messieurs Sewrin, Pixerécourt, Planard, etc. In their day, Pigault-Lebrun, Piis, Duvicquet had their posts. Monsieur Scribe's head librarian was an employee in the Treasury.

Besides such information, the list made by Rabourdin contained an inquiry into the moral capacities and physical faculties necessary to recognize those in whom were found intelligence, aptitude for work, and sound health, three indispensable preconditions for men who must bear the burden of public affairs, who must do everything in a timely and expedient manner.

But this great work, the fruit of ten years' experience, of a long working knowledge of men and things gained by interaction with the various ministries, would smell of spying and police subversion to anyone who did not understand to what it pertained. If one single page were to be read, Monsieur Rabourdin would be lost. Admiring his boss no end, yet ignorant of the evils of the bureaucracy, Sébastien had the follies of innocence as well as all its grace. Furthermore, having already been scolded once for bringing in this work, he had the courage fully to acknowledge his error; he had sealed both the draft and the copy in a box where no one could find them, but when he realized the magnitude of his mistake, a couple of tears rolled down his cheeks.

"Come, come!" said Rabourdin kindly. "Don't do it again and don't worry about it anymore. Come into the office very early tomorrow morning; here's the key to a small safe in my rolltop desk, it shuts with a combination lock. You can open it with the word *sky*; lock the copy and the draft inside."

This proof of confidence dried the tears of the good supernumerary, whom the boss advised to take a cup of tea and some cakes.

"Mother won't let me drink tea on account of my chest," said Sébastien.

"Well, then, my dear child," said the imposing Madame Rabourdin, who wished to make a point of appearing gracious, "here are some sandwiches and cream; come and sit by me."

She made Sébastien sit down beside her at the table, and the boy's heart leapt into his throat as he felt the dress of this divinity brush the sleeve of his coat. Just then the beautiful Rabourdin caught sight of Monsieur des Lupeaulx, smiled at him, and, not waiting for him to come to her, went over to him.

"Why do you stand there as if you were sulking?" she asked.

"I'm not sulking," he replied. "But coming over to bring you some good news, I couldn't help thinking that it will only add to your severity toward me. I saw myself six months from now almost a stranger to you. Yes, you are too clever, and I too experienced, too blasé if you like, for either of us to deceive the other. Your goal has been reached without it costing you more than a few smiles and gracious words. . . . "

"Deceive each other! What can you mean?" she cried in a seemingly hurt tone.

"Yes, Monsieur de La Billardière is doing even worse tonight than yesterday, and from what the minister told me, your husband will be appointed division head."

He then related what he called his "scene" at the minister's, the jealousy of the countess and what she had said about the invitation that he arranged for Madame Rabourdin.

"Monsieur des Lupeaulx," said Madame Rabourdin with dignity, "allow me to tell you that my husband is the senior bureau chief as well as the most capable, that the appointment of the old la Billardière was a breach of order which excited many rumors in the bureaus, that my husband has been in suspension for the last year expecting this promotion, and that therefore we have neither competitor nor rival."

"That is true."

"Well then," she resumed, smiling and showing the loveliest of teeth, "can the friendship I feel for you be marred by any thought of self-interest? Why should you think me capable of that?"

Des Lupeaulx made a gesture of admiring denial.

"Ah!" she continued. "The heart of a woman will always be a mystery to even the cleverest of you. Yes, I saw you coming here with the greatest of pleasure, and behind my pleasure there was a motive of self-interest."

"Ah!"

"You have," she whispered in his ear, "a future without limit: you will be deputy, then minister!"

(What joy for an ambitious man to hear such things as these softly spoken in his ear by the sweet voice of a lovely woman!)

"Oh yes! I know you better than you know yourself. Rabourdin is a man who could be of immense service to you in your career; he would do the work while you were in the Chamber. Just as you dream of the Ministry, so I want Rabourdin to be in the Council of State and to have a general-directorship. I therefore took it upon myself to bring together two men who can never injure and who can powerfully serve one another. Isn't that a woman's job? Friend, you will both rise the faster, and it is high time that each of you set sail. I have burned my boats," she added, smiling. "But you are not as frank with me as I have been with you."

"You don't want to listen to me," he replied with a melancholy air in spite of the deep inward satisfaction Madame Rabourdin had given him. "What would such future promotions avail me if you dismiss me now?"

"Before I listen to you," she replied with her Parisian liveliness, "we must be able to understand one another."

And she left the old fop to go and chat with Madame de Chessel, a countess from the provinces who seemed about to leave.

"That woman is extraordinary," said des Lupeaulx to himself. "I don't know my own self when I am with her."

And accordingly, this roué—who six years earlier had kept a ballet girl, and who now, thanks to his position, made himself a seraglio of the pretty wives of state employees, who lived in the world of journalists and actresses—was charming the whole evening for Célestine and was the last to leave.

Célestine fell asleep thinking about her debts, calculating that, in three years, by an annual withholding of six thousand francs, she could liquidate them. She was far from imagining that a woman who had never set foot in a salon, a nagging and self-seeking petite bourgeoise, devout and buried in the Marais, was thinking of seizing the position toward which she was pushing her Rabourdin. Madame Rabourdin would have hated Madame Baudoyer if she had known her to be her rival, for she had overlooked the power of smallness, that power of the worm that nibbles away under the bark of the elm.

If it were possible in literature to make use of the microscopes of the Leeuwenhoeks, Malpighis, and Raspails, as was attempted by Hoffmann from Berlin, and if we magnified and drew those teredos, those shipworms that placed Holland within inches of disaster by eating away at her dikes, then we might dis   cover   figures   in some ways resembling those of Gigonnet, Mitral, Baudoyer, Saillard, Gaudron, Falleix, Transon, Godard, and company—worms who have demonstrated their power in the thirtieth year of this century. And so, now is the time to expose the worms who were crawling around in the bureaus that are the principal scenes of our study.

PART II

The Bureaus

Three-Quarter-Length Portraits
of Certain Civil Servants

In Paris, nearly all bureaus resemble each other. In whatever ministry you go to, to ask some slight favor or to obtain redress for a trifling wrong, you will find dark corridors, poorly lighted stairways, doors with oval panes of glass like eyes, just like at the theater, through which you see fantasies worthy of Callot, and on which you find incomprehensible signs. When you discover what you are looking for, you find yourself in a first room where the office boy of the bureau sits; in the second are the lower employees; the private office of a deputy chief follows, either to the left or right; and farther on is that of the bureau chief. As to the important person called division chief under the Empire, sometimes director under the Restoration, and once again become division chief, he resides either above or below the offices of his two or three different bureaus, or sometimes beyond the office of one of his bureau chiefs. His quarters are always set apart by their size, a prized privilege among those individual cells of that honeycomb in the hive called Ministry or General Directory, if there even is such a thing as one single general direction! Today nearly all of the ministers have consolidated their administrations, which at one time were divided. As to this conglomeration, the general directors lost all their glory when they lost their government homes, their own staffs, their salons, and their minicourt. Today, who would recognize the man walking up to the

Treasury, on the second floor, as the General Director of Forestry or Indirect Revenues, who at one time was housed in a magnificent mansion in the rue Sainte-Avoye or rue Saint-Augustin, or who is an adviser, minister of state, and peer of France? (Messieurs Pasquier and Molé, among others, were content to be general directors after having been ministers, thus putting into practice the words of the duc d'Antin to Louis XIV, "Sire, when Jesus Christ died on Friday, he knew full well he would be back on Sunday.") If in his loss of luxuries the director-general were to gain administrative authority, the loss would not be so great; but today this person, with great trouble, finds himself Master of Petitions, with only a sorry twenty thousand francs. As a token of his former power, he is allowed one uniformed usher with silk stockings and a coat *à la française*, as if the usher were the last to be reformed.

In the administrative sense, a bureau consists of an office boy, several supernumeraries attending to the daily routine gratis for a certain number of years, basic copy clerks, writers of bills and deeds, order clerks, head clerks, one deputy chief, and one chief. The division, usually comprised of two or three bureaus, sometimes includes more. These titles vary according to the administrations; for instance, the order clerks are sometimes called auditors or bookkeepers, etc.

Paved like the corridor and hung with shabby paper, the room where the office boy is stationed is furnished with a stove, a large black table with inkstand, pens, and paper, and benches without mats for the general public's feet; but the boy, seated in a good armchair, has a rug to put his up on. The office of the employees is a large room, more or less well-lighted, usually without a wooden floor. Wooden floors and fireplaces are specially set apart for bureau and division chiefs, as are the armoires, tables, and desks of mahogany, red or green morocco leather armchairs, sofas, silk curtains, and other articles of administrative luxury. The office of the employees has a stove, the pipe of which feeds into a blocked-off chimney, if there even is a chimney. The wallpaper is plain and one color, green or brown. The tables are of black wood. The ingenuity of the employees is demonstrated by the ways they sit at their desks: one who is cold has a wooden footstool under his feet; the man with a hot temperament only has a little something Spartan; the sluggard who dreads the opening and closing of doors, as well as other causes of fluctuations in temperature, constructs a little windbreak out of boxes. There is a wardrobe where everyone keeps his work coat with linen sleeves, glasses, caps, skullcaps, and other tools of the trade. Nearly every day the fireplace is full of bottles of water, glasses, and leftovers from lunch. In some out-of-the-way areas there are lamps. The door of the deputy chief's office is always open so he can keep an eye on the workers, prevent them from chatting too much, or come out and talk with them if something big is up. The furnishings of the offices indicate to the observer the caliber of those who inhabit them. The drapes are white or of some colored cloth, either cotton or silk; the chairs are cherry or mahogany, trimmed with straw, leather, or cloth; the wallpaper is more or less new. Yet, to whichever administration all of these public possessions belong, as soon as it changes, there is nothing quite so uncanny as all of this furniture that has seen so many masters and so many administrations, that has weathered so many disasters. For of all moving, the most hideous moves in Paris are those of administrations. Hoffmann in his genius, that bard of the impossible, never imagined anything more fantastic. You do not realize what goes on in tumbrels, the *cartons baîllent*, leaving a trail of dust in the streets. Tables with all four legs in the air, overturned armchairs, all sorts of unimaginable tools with which France is administered—all have a horrible appearance. It all looks like a combination of theater props and acrobatic equipment. Even on the obelisks you find traces of intelligence and ghosts of writing that trouble the imagination, like anything we see without understanding its purpose! Finally, all of this stuff is so old, so worn out, so faded, that even the filthiest of kitchen utensils are infinitely more pleasant to look at than the instruments of the administrative kitchen.

Perhaps it would do to portray the division of Monsieur de La Billardière in order to give foreigners and those who live in the country a clear idea of the inner workings of the bureaus, for their principal characteristics are surely the same in any of the European administrations.

First and foremost, picture the man who is thus described in the Yearly Register:

Chef de Division

Monsieur le baron Flamet de La Billardière (Athanase-Jean-François-Michel), formerly Provost-Marshal of the Department of the Corrèze, Gentleman in Ordinary of the Bedchamber, Master of Petitions for outstanding service, President of the College of the Department of the Dordogne, Officer of the Legion of Honor, Knight of Saint Louis and of the Foreign Orders of Christ, Isabelle, Saint Wladimir, etc., member of the Academy of Gers, and other learned bodies, Vice President of the Society of Belles Lettres, member of the Association of Saint-Joseph and the Society of Prisons, one of the mayors of Paris, etc., etc.

The character who takes up so much typographic space presently took up five feet, six inches by thirty-six and one-eighth of an inch in bed, his head adorned with a cotton nightcap tied on with flame-colored ribbons and attended by the illustrious Desplein, the king's surgeon, and the young doctor Bianchon, flanked by two elderly female relatives; he was surrounded by phials of all kinds, bandages, remedies, and various mortuary instruments, and watched over by the curate of Saint-Roch, who was advising him to think of his salvation. His son, Benjamin de La Billardière, asked the two doctors every morning, "Do you think I enjoy taking care of my father?" Why that very morning the scion had a slip of the tongue, transposing the word *misfortune* for *good fortune*.

La Billardière's division was located at seventy-one degrees longitude under the latitude of an attic in the ministerial ocean of a great mansion, in the northeast corner of a courtyard, where squirrels once lived and which is now occupied by Clergeot's division. A wide landing separated its two offices, the doors of which were labeled, running the entire length of a long corridor illuminated by days of suffering. The private offices and antechambers of Monsieurs Rabourdin and Baudoyer were downstairs on the second floor, and beyond that of Monsieur Rabourdin were the antechamber, salon, and two offices of Monsieur de La Billardière.

On the first floor, divided in two by a mezzanine, were the living quarters and office of Monsieur Ernest de La Brière, a mysterious and powerful character who must be described in a few words, for he well deserves a parenthesis.

This young man was, for the whole tenure of this administration, the private secretary to the minister. His apartment was connected by a secret door to the private office of His Excellency, and behind the office was yet another room adjacent to the main rooms where His Excellency received, so that he could work secretly with his private secretary and, in turn, also confer with important persons without his secretary. A private secretary is to the minister himself what des Lupeaulx was to the ministry. Between young La Brière and des Lupeaulx was the difference between an aide-de-camp and a chief of staff. This ministerial apprentice camps and decamps with his protector. If the minister enjoys the royal favor when he falls and has parliamentary ambitions, he takes his secretary out with him only to bring him back in later; otherwise he puts him out to graze in some administrative pasture—in the Court of the Exchequer, for instance, that wayside refuge where secretaries wait for the storm to blow over. The young man is not precisely a government official, but he is a politician—sometimes a politician for one man. When you think of the infinite numbers of letters he has to open and read, besides all his other duties, is it not clear that under a monarchy his services would be well paid! A victim of this kind costs ten or twenty thousand francs a year in Paris; but he enjoys the opera boxes, the social invitations, and the carriages of the minister. The emperor of Russia would be very glad to have, for fifty thousand a year, one of these nice constitutional poodles, so gentle, so well groomed, so affectionate, so docile, always spick-and-span—careful watchdogs besides—and loyal! But the private secretary is born, propagated, developed, produced only in the hothouses of a representative government. Under a monarchy you still find only courtiers and vassals, whereas under a constitution you are served, flattered, and caressed by free men. Ministers in France are better off than women or kings: they have someone who thoroughly understands them. Perhaps, indeed, the private secretary is to be pitied as much as women and white paper: they must bear everything. Like a chaste woman, they are allowed no talent except hidden ones, and those only for their ministers: if they have talent in public, they are ruined. The private secretary is therefore a friend provided by the government. However, let us return to the bureaus.

Three office boys lived in peace in the La Billardière division: one for the two bureaus, another to service the two chiefs, and one for the division chief. All three were put up and clothed by the state, wearing that well-known state livery: blue coat with red pips for lesser occasions, and broad blue, white, and red braid for great occasions. La Billardière's man had the uniform of a gentleman-usher. To flatter the ego of some minister's cousin, the secretary-general tolerated this breach of protocol, which nevertheless added an air of dignity to the administration. Veritable pillars of the ministry, experts in all bureaucratic procedures, these boys, without want, kept warm and clothed at the state's expense, rich in their sobriety, saw right through the employees.

They had nothing better to do for fun than to observe them, studying their ways. They also knew how to get ahead with them by way of assignment draws, carrying out their various commissions with absolute discretion; going to pawn or take out of pawn at the Mont-de-Piété, buying up bills when due, and lending without interest, although no employee ever took the least sum from them without returning some small "gratuity," and so there came to be jobs in the so-called short workweek. These servants without a master received a salary of nine hundred francs a year; New Year's gifts and "gratuities" brought their remuneration up to twelve hundred francs, and they made almost as much from the employees, because the meals of those who ate work passed through their hands. The position of concierge for the Ministry of Finances was once worth almost four thousand francs to Big Father Thuillier, whose son was one of the workers in La Billardière's division. The boys sometimes found a hundred sous in their right hand, coins slipped there by hurried callers and greeted with rare impassiveness. The senior one only wore his state uniform at the ministry; he went home dressed as a bourgeois.

The one for the bureaus, the richest moreover, worked the whole lot of employees over. A man of sixty with cropped white hair, stout, pudgy, with the neck of an apoplectic, a rather vulgar pockmarked face, gray eyes, and a mouth like a furnace door—such is the portrait of Antoine, the oldest office boy in the ministry. He had brought in from Echelles in Savoie his two nephews, Laurent and Gabriel, and got the one placed with chiefs and the other with the director. Dressed in ordinary uniforms like their uncle, thirty to forty years old, with the faces of a commissioner, recipients of complimentary tickets to an evening at the Royal Theater, thanks to de La Billardière's influence, these two Savoyards were married to washerwomen of lace who also mended cashmeres. The bachelor uncle, his nephews, and their wives all lived together, and much better than most deputy chiefs. Gabriel and Laurent, having barely ten years' seniority, had not yet come to hold the government uniform in contempt; they would go out in livery, proud as a playwright with a box-office smash. Their uncle, to whom they catered fanatically and who seemed to them a shrewd man, slowly initiated them into the mysteries of the profession. All three came in to open the offices, cleaned them between seven and eight in the morning, and read the newspapers or talked division politics among themselves, comparing their respective "news." Furthermore, as all modern servants who know their masters' affairs perfectly well, at the ministry they were like spiders at the center of a web, where they felt even the slightest commotion.

On Thursday mornings, the day after the ministerial reception and Madame Rabourdin's soirée, just as the uncle was trimming his beard and his nephews were assisting him in the antechamber of the division on the second floor, they were surprised by the unexpected arrival of one of the employees.

"That's Monsieur Dutocq," said Antoine. "I know him by that pickpocket step of his. It's as if that man slid around on skates! He pops up behind you without you knowing where he came from. Yesterday, uncharacteristically, he was the last man to stay in the division bureau, something that hasn't happened three times since he's been at the ministry."

Thirty-eight years old, oblong face and bilious complexion, frizzy gray hair always close-cropped, a low forehead, heavy connected eyebrows, a crooked nose, pinched lips, bright-green eyes that shunned the look of another, the right shoulder slightly higher than the left; brown coat, black waistcoat, silk cravat, yellowish trousers, black woollen stockings, and shoes with floppy tassels—there you have Monsieur Dutocq, order clerk in Rabourdin's bureau. Incapable and a loafer, he hated his boss. Rabourdin had not a single vice to flatter, no bad or weak side Dutocq could manipulate to make himself useful. Far too noble to put down an employee, he was also too clearsighted to be deceived by any pretense. Dutocq survived solely through Rabourdin's generosity and gave up any hope of advancement so long as this chief headed the division. Although he knew himself to be without the skills for an advanced position, Dutocq knew the bureaus well enough to realize that incapacity hardly precludes advancement, and he rested his case, pointing to the search for a Rabourdin among the writing clerks, the case of La Billardière being the most striking and disastrous example of what can happen.

Wickedness coupled with self-interest made for a lot of ambition; very evil and very self-interested, this civil servant had taken it upon himself to consolidate his position by becoming the bureau spy. Since 1816, he had assumed a marked religious tone, sensing the favor toward those whom, in those days, fools indiscriminately called Jesuits. Belonging to the Congrégation without being admitted to its rites, Dutocq went from one bureau to the next, sounding out consciences by recounting immoral jests, and then went and made paraphrased "reports" to des Lupeaulx, whom he informed of every trivial event. The secretary-general would often surprise even the minister with the depth of his knowledge of the most personal matters. *Bonneau tout de bon de ce Bonneau*, Dutocq solicited the privilege of delivering the secret messages of des Lupeaulx, who tolerated this vile man, thinking that by chance he might someday be useful, if only to get him or some important friend out of a scrape through some disgraceful marriage. The two understood each other well. Dutocq was betting on that good fortune, seeing in it a good post, and so remained a bachelor.

Dutocq had succeeded Monsieur Poiret, Sr., who retired to a bourgeois boardinghouse and was pensioned off in 1814 at a time when big reforms occurred among the state employees. He lived on the fifth floor, rue Saint-Louis–Saint-Honoré, close to the Palais-Royal in a *maison à allée*. Having a passion for collections of old engravings, he wanted every Rembrandt and every Charlet, every Silvestre, Audran, Callot, Albrecht Dürer, etc. Like most people with collections who manage them themselves, he claimed that he bought works at a good price. He lived in a boardinghouse in the rue de Beaune and spent his evenings in the Palais-Royal, sometimes going to the theater, thanks to du Bruel, who gave him an author's ticket about once a week.

And now a word about du Bruel. Although backed up by Sébastien, whom he paid the small supplement you know of to do his work, du Bruel nevertheless came to the office, but only for the sake of seeing himself as, and being addressed as, deputy chief, and in order to draw a salary. He wrote short plays for a ministerial publication, for which he also wrote articles commissioned by the ministers—a very well-known, clearly defined, and quite unassailable position. Du Bruel, moreover, lacked none of those little diplomatic ruses that could win general goodwill. He offered Madame Rabourdin a loge seat for every opening performance, picked her up in a carriage and brought her home, his attention to which she took to very well. Furthermore, Rabourdin, very tolerant and loath to pester his employees, let him go off to rehearsals, make his own hours, and work on his vaudevilles. Monsieur le duc de Chaulieu knew that du Bruel was writing a novel to be dedicated to him. Dressed with the careless ease of a vaudevillian, the deputy chief each morning wore strapped-down trousers, slipper shoes, a waistcoat conspicuously altered, an olive frock, and a black cravat. In the evening he wore an elegant outfit as he played the gentleman. Du Bruel lived, and for good reason, in the house of Florine, an actress for whom he wrote parts. Florine then lived in the house of Tullia, a dancer noted more for her beauty than her talent. This living arrangement allowed the deputy chief frequently to see the duc de Rhétoré, oldest son of the duc de Chaulieu, one of the king's favorites. The duc de Chaulieu had arranged the Cross of the Legion of Honor for du Bruel after his eleventh *pièce de circonstance*. Du Bruel—or, if you prefer, Cursy—was at this time working on a play in five acts for the Française. Sébastien liked du Bruel a lot; he got tickets for the main floor from him and applauded, with the good faith of youth, the parts which du Bruel told him were of doubtful merit; Sébastien saw him as a great writer. It was to Sébastien that du Bruel said, the day after the opening performance of a vaudeville production which, like every vaudeville coauthored by three people that at times elicits whistles, "The audience picked up on the scenes written by the other two."

"Why don't you write alone?" replied Sébastien naively.

There were good reasons why du Bruel did not write alone: he was only one-third author. A dramatic writer, as few people know, is made up of: first, the Man of Ideas, responsible for coming up with the subject and constructing the framework, or scenario, of the vaudeville; then the Plodder, in charge of drawing up the play; and finally, the Man of Details, who sets the couplets to music, arranges the choruses and musical numbers, sings them, and superimposes them onto the story. The Plodder also makes the play a success— that is, oversees the publicity by never letting the director get away without featuring another of their plays the next time round. Du Bruel, a true Plodder, read the latest books at the office, extracting from them their words of wit, and memorized them to add color to his dialogues. Cursy (his name in the war) was well liked by his coauthors on account of his total precision; with him the Man of Ideas, sure of being understood, could just sit back and relax. The employees of the division liked the vaudevilles well enough that all of them attended and supported his plays, for he really deserved to be called a "good chap." With an easy hand in his pocketbook, never needing to be asked twice to buy ices or punch, he would loan fifty francs without ever asking to be repaid. Owning a country house at Aulnay and investing his money, du Bruel had, besides the four thousand, five hundred francs of his salary, a pension of twelve hundred francs from the Civil List, and eight hundred of the hundred-thousand-ecus endowment for the arts voted by the chambers. Add to these diverse resources nine thousand francs earned by his quarter-, third-, and half-shares in vaudevilles playing in three different theaters, and you will understand that physically he was big, fat, and round, with the face of a happy proprietor. As to his morals, du Bruel fancied himself as the true love of Tullia's heart and also, as always, preferred over the brilliant duc de Rhétoré, the lover in title.

Dutocq, not without dread, witnessed what he called the liaison of des Lupeaulx with Madame Rabourdin, and his silent wrath on the subject mounted. Moreover, he had much too prying an eye not to have guessed that Rabourdin was engaged in some great work outside of his official duties, and he was beside himself for not knowing anything about it, whereas little Sébastien was, wholly or in part, in on the secret. Dutocq had attempted to link up with Godard, deputy chief to Baudoyer and colleague of du Bruel; he was successful. The high esteem in which Dutocq held Baudoyer was the original cause of his acquaintance with Godard; not that Dutocq was sincere, but by praising Baudoyer and keeping quiet about Rabourdin, he satisfied his hatred after the fashion of little minds.

Joseph Godard, a cousin of Mitral on the mother's side, based upon this kinship with Baudoyer, however remote, pretensions to the hand of Mademoiselle Baudoyer; consequently, in his eyes, Baudoyer shone like a star. He claimed to esteem Elisabeth and Madame Saillard greatly, without yet having realized that Madame Baudoyer was fixing Falleix up with her daughter. He brought Mademoiselle Baudoyer little gifts—silk flowers, bonbons on New Year's Day, and pretty boxes for her special occasions. He was twenty-six years old, a worker working without purpose, well-mannered as a young lady, dull and apathetic, detested cafés, cigars, and horsemanship, went to bed regularly at ten o'clock and rose at seven, and was gifted with several social talents, such as playing quadrille music on the flageolet, which brought him into good favor with the Saillards and the Baudoyers. A fife player in the National Guard in order to avoid night-guard duty, Godard was interested above all in natural history. This boy collected minerals and shells, knew how to stuff birds, stored in his bedroom a host of odd things bought at a good price: landscaping stones, models of palaces made out of cork, petrified relics from the Saint-Allyre spring at Clermont (Auvergne), etc. He hoarded phials and perfume bottles for his barium oxide samples, his sulfates, salts, magnesia, corals, etc. He collected butterflies in shadow boxes and pinned the walls with Chinese parasols—in fact dried fish skins. He lived with his sister, a silk-flower maker, in the rue de Richelieu. Although much admired by mothers, this model of a young man was looked down upon by his sister's shopgirls, especially by the counter girl, who for a long time had tried to net him. Thin and slim, medium height, with dark circles under his eyes, a thin beard, and breath which, according to Bixiou, could kill a passing fly, Joseph Godard took little care of himself: his clothes were poorly cut, his wide trousers baggy; he wore white stockings all year round, a hat with a narrow brim, and laced shoes. Seated at his desk in a cane chair with a broken seat adorned with a round green leather cushion, he complained a lot about indigestion. His principal vice was a mania for proposing country parties at Montmorency during the summer, picnics on the grass, and visits to the creameries on the boulevard du Montparnasse. For the past six months Dutocq had taken to visiting Mademoiselle Godard from time to time, hoping to do some business in that household or to discover some female treasure.

Hence, in the bureaus, Baudoyer had in Dutocq and Godard two flatterers. Monsieur Saillard, incapable of seeing through Dutocq, once in a while paid him a visit at his desk. Young La Billardière, the director's son, placed as supernumerary with Baudoyer, was another member of this group. The smart ones in the bureaus laughed at this alliance of incompetents. Baudoyer, Godard, and Dutocq were dubbed by Bixiou the "Trinity without Spirit" and little La Billardière, the "Pascal Lamb."

"You got up this morning," said Antoine to Dutocq with a chuckle.

"And you too, Antoine," answered Dutocq. "And you can see the newspapers sometimes also get here earlier than when you give them to us."

"Today they did by chance," replied Antoine unruffled. "They have never come at the same time twice."

The two nephews looked at each other as if to say, in admiration of their uncle, "What nerve!"

"Although I get two sous to bring him his breakfast," muttered Antoine, once he heard Dutocq close the door, "I'd give them up to get that man out of our division."

"Ah, you're not the first here today, Monsieur Sébastien," said Antoine to the supernumerary a quarter of an hour later.

"Who else is in?" asked the poor lad, turning pale.

"Monsieur Dutocq," answered Laurent, the usher.

Virgin natures, more so than others, have the inexplicable gift of second sight, the reason for which lies perhaps in the purity of their nervous systems, which are, in a way, brand new. Sébastien had guessed Dutocq's hatred of his revered Rabourdin. Thus, hardly had Laurent uttered this name than, possessed by a dreadful premonition, he cried out, "I suspected that!" and flew like an arrow into the corridor.

"There's going to be a row in the bureaus!" said Antoine, shaking his head as he put on his livery. "It is very certain that Monsieur le Baron is off to account to God. . . . Yes, Madame Gruget, the nurse, told me he wouldn't make it through the day. What a stir there'll be here! Oh, won't there be! Go along, you fellows, and see if the stoves are drawing properly. Hell! our world is going to come crashing down on us."

"It's true," said Laurent, "that poor young lad looked like he'd been struck by lightning when he heard that that Jesuit of a Dutocq had got here before him."

"I for one have told him—for after all one owes a good worker the truth—and what I call a good worker is one like that little fellow who gives us without fuss his ten francs on New Year's Day—," said Antoine, "I told him, 'The more you work, the more they'll make you work, and the less they'll promote you.' Oh well, he doesn't listen to me; he kills himself staying here till five o'clock, an hour longer than everyone else." He shrugged his shoulders. "It's crazy, you don't get anywhere like that! The proof is that not a word has been said about giving him an appointment, even though he would make an excellent civil servant. After two years, too! It makes my blood boil, really."

"Monsieur Rabourdin is very fond of Monsieur Sébastien," said Laurent.

"But Monsieur Rabourdin isn't a minister," retorted Antoine. "It will be a hot day when that happens, and hens will have teeth; he is much too . . . . Never mind. When I think that I carry salaries to those clowns who stay home and do as they please, while that poor little La Roche works himself to death, I ask myself if God ever thinks of the bureaus! And what do they give you, these pets of Monsieur le Maréchal and Monsieur le Duc? They *thank* you" (Antoine gives a patronizing nod). "'Thank you, my dear Antoine!' Pack of good-for-nothings! Go to work, or you'll be the cause of another revolution. You should have seen if this would have gone on under Monsieur Robert Lindet; as for me, I came to this pit under Robert Lindet. And under him the employees really worked! You should have seen how they scratched paper here till midnight, the stoves all gone out without anyone noticing; but it was also like that because there was the guillotine! And that's a whole lot different from nowadays when they just get checked off for coming in late!"

"Uncle Antoine," said Gabriel, "since you're so talkative this morning, just what do you think a bureaucrat is?"

"He is," replied Antoine gravely, "a man who writes sitting in a bureau. And just what do I mean by that? Without the state employees, what would we be? . . . Go along and look after your stoves, and the rest of you, mind you never speak ill of the employees! Gabriel, the stove in the large office draws like the devil; you have to turn the damper."

Antoine positioned himself on the landing, a vantage point from which he could see all the workers from under the porte-cochere; he knew everyone in the ministry and observed their manner, noting the differences in their dress.

Now before diving into this drama, we must sketch the main characters in La Billardière's division, who will, moreover, provide variations within the genus "civil service workers" and will later justify not only Rabourdin's observations but even the title of this work, so fundamentally Parisian. In fact, do not be misled! Between misery and eccentricity, there are civil servants and then there are civil servants, just as there are men and men. Make sure you distinguish between a state employee in Paris and a state employee in the country. In the country, the employee is happy: he is spaciously housed; he has a garden; he is more or less comfortable in his office; he drinks good wine at a good price, doesn't end up eating horsemeat, and knows luxury in desserts. Instead of borrowing, he saves. Maybe he is not quite sure of what he will eat, but one thing is sure: *he doesn't eat his paycheck!* If he is a bachelor, mothers greet him as he passes by; if he is married, he and his wife attend the balls at the receiver-general's, the prefect's, the subprefect's, and the intendant's. People are interested in his personality; he is well-off; he is known for his wit; his loss would be grieved; the whole town knows him, takes an interest in his wife and kids. He gives dinner parties, and, if he has the means, with a father-in-law in retirement, he can become a deputy. His wife is surveyed by the intricate spy network of small towns, and if it is unhappy from within, he knows about it, whereas in Paris, state employees can be oblivious. Finally, the state employee in the country is *something*, while the state employee in Paris is hardly even *someone*.

The first to arrive after Sébastien was a writer in Rabourdin's bureau, an honorable family man named Phellion. Owing to his boss's influence, he had a fifty percent scholarship to the Collège Henri IV for both of his two boys; and a good thing too, for Phellion still had a daughter being educated gratis at a boarding school where his wife gave piano lessons and he himself taught a geography course in the evenings. A man of forty-five, sergeant-major of his company in the National Guard, openly compassionate in word but with never a penny to spare, the writer lived in the rue Faubourg-Saint-Jacques, not far from Sourds-Muets, in a house with a garden, where his rent, in true Phellion style, was only four hundred francs. Proud of his post, satisfied with his lot, he applied himself faithfully to serve the government, thought himself useful to his country, and boasted of his indifference to politics, in which he never saw anything except power. Monsieur Rabourdin pleased him whenever he asked him to stay a half-hour extra to finish some work, of which he would later say to the ladies at La Grave (for he dined at the school where his wife claimed to teach music): "Ladies, business necessitated that I stay at the bureau. When a man serves the government, he is no longer his own master." He had put together question-and-answer books on various practices of girl's boarding schools. These "little filling treatises," as he called them, were sold at the university library under the name of "Historical and Geographic Catechisms." Feeling obliged to offer a parchment copy, bound in red morocco leather, of each new "catechism" to Madame Rabourdin, he always delivered them dressed to the nines: silk breeches, silk stockings, shoes with gold buckles, etc.

Monsieur Phellion received on Thursday evenings; the boarders had gone to bed; he served beer and cakes. They played *bouillotte* for five sous a game. In spite of the small stakes, on some wild Thursdays, Laudigeois, an employee in the mayor's office, would manage to lose ten francs. Hung in American wallpaper, green with a red border, this living room was still adorned with portraits of the king, the dauphine, and Madame, two engravings of Mezeppa as seen by Horace Vernet, and yet another work, the *Convoi du Pauvre* as seen by Vigneron, "a painting of sublime inspiration, and which," according to Phellion, "should console the lowest ranks of society by demonstrating to them that they have more faithful friends than mere mortals whose concern goes beyond the tomb!" Based on this, you can well imagine the man who every year, on All Souls' Day, took his three children to the Cimetière de l'Ouest to show them the twenty-meter plot, purchased in perpetuity, in which his father and his wife's mother had been buried. "We shall all be there someday," he would tell them, to get them used to the idea of death. One of his pastimes was to explore the area around Paris; he even bought himself a map. Already completely familiar with Antony, Arcueil, Bièvre, Fautenay-aux-Roses, Aulnay—all so famous for the residence of several great writers—he hoped, in time, to grow familiar with the area west of the outskirts of Paris. He was grooming his eldest boy for the Administration, and the second for the Ecole Polytechnique. He would often tell his eldest, "Just wait until you have the privilege of being employed by the government!" But he rather suspected a leaning toward the exact sciences, which he tried to suppress, threatening to make him pay his own way if he persisted.

Phellion had never yet dared to invite Monsieur Rabourdin to dine with him, although he would have regarded such a day as one of the finest of his life. He said that if he could leave one of his sons following in the steps of Monsieur Rabourdin, he would die the happiest father in the world. He sang the praises of this distinguished and respectable chief so highly in the ears of the demoiselles at La Grave, that they longed to see the great Rabourdin, as a young man might long to see Monsieur de Chateaubriand. "How happy they would be," they said, "to be able to instruct *his* demoiselle!" When by chance the carriage of the minister went out or returned, whether empty or not, Phellion doffed his cap with the utmost respect and professed that France would be better off if everyone respected authority enough to honor even its symbols. When Rabourdin sent for him to come down and receive instructions for some task, Phellion gathered all his wits about him—listening to every word the chief said, as a dilettante listens to an air at Les Italiens. Quiet at the office, his feet up on a wooden desk and hardly moving, he conscientiously studied his task. In his official correspondence, he had a grave, almost religious tone, took everything seriously, and hung on the orders relayed by the minister in solemn sentences.

This man, ever so strict about rules and conventions, had had one disaster in his career as a writer, and what a disaster! In spite of the minute care with which he drafted his work, it had come to pass that the following phrase escaped him: "You will meet in the restroom with the necessary paper." Overjoyed to have a good laugh at the expense of this innocent creature, the copy clerks went behind his back to tell Rabourdin who, knowing the character of his writer, could not help laughing and modifying the sentence in the margin to read: "You will meet at that location with the indicated documents." Phellion, to whom they went to show the correction, studied it, weighed the difference between the two expressions, was able to admit that it would have taken him two hours to come up with the like, and exclaimed, "Monsieur Rabourdin is a genius!" He still thought, though, that his colleagues had been a little out of line in running so quickly to the boss; but he had too much respect for the hierarchy of command to deny their right to do as they had done, all the more so as he had been absent. Nevertheless, in their place he would have held back, as the letter was not urgent. This whole affair cost him several nights' sleep. When they wanted to irritate him, they had only to allude to the cursed sentence by asking him on his way out, "Do you have the necessary paper?" The fine writer would then turn back, cast a terrifying glance over the employees, and reply, "Your comments are way out of line, gentlemen." One day there was such a heated row over this topic that Monsieur Rabourdin had to intervene and forbid the employees to repeat this sentence.

Monsieur Phellion had the face of a pensive battering ram—pale, scarred by smallpox, big sagging lips, light-blue eyes—and was of above average height. Neat and clean as a master of history and geography in a young ladies' school ought to be, he wore fine linen, a pleated jabot, a black cashmere waistcoat left open to show a pair of braces embroidered by his daughter, a diamond pen, a black coat, and blue trousers. In the winter he added a nut-colored boxcoat with three capes and carried a weighted stick, necessitated by the "profound solitude of the quarter in which he lived." He had given up snuff and claimed this reform as a striking example of the self-control a man could exercise. He mounted stairs slowly, for he feared asthma, having what he called an "adipose chest." He greeted Antoine with dignity.

The next in line after Monsieur Phellion was a copy clerk who made for a strange contrast to this virtuous gentleman. Vimeux was a young man of twenty-five with a salary of fifteen hundred francs, well built and of good stature, with an elegant, romantic face and jet-black hair, beard, eyes, and brows, fine teeth, lovely hands, and sporting a mustache so thick and well kept that he seemed to have made a business and commodity of it. Vimeux had such an aptitude for work that he always finished it before anyone else. "That young man is gifted!" said Phellion when he saw him, legs crossed, with nothing to do for the rest of the day after having finished all his assignments. "And look, what a dandy!" the editor would say to du Bruel. Vimeux breakfasted on a roll and a glass of water, dined at Katcomb's for twenty sous, and lived in a furnished room for twelve francs a month. His happiness, his sole pleasure in life, was his dress. He went broke to pay for his fabulous waistcoats, fitted or partially fitted, his trousers, pleated or embroidered, his fine boots, his well-made coats that showed off his figure, his elaborate collars, crisp gloves, and hats. With his hand adorned by a signet ring worn over his glove and armed with a cane, he set out to give himself the air and manner of a wealthy man. And so he went, toothpick in mouth, to stroll in the Tuileries as though he were a millionaire who had just left the dinner table. In the hope that a woman—an Englishwoman, a foreigner of some sort, or a widow— might fall in love with him, he practiced the art of twirling his cane and casting a glance, à l'américaine, as Bixiou would say. He smiled to show off his lovely teeth. He wore no socks and had his hair done every day. Vimeux, in accordance with fixed principles, was willing to marry a hunchback with an income of six thousand livres a year, or a woman of forty-five for eight thousand, or an Englishwoman for a thousand ecus. Delighted with his handwriting and seized with compassion for the young man, Phellion preached to him on the duty of giving lessons in penmanship, an honorable profession, and one that would improve one's existence and even render it agreeable; he promised him room and board with the demoiselles at La Grave. But Vimeux had such fixed views that no human being could prevent him from believing in his star. So he continued to starve in order to keep himself on exhibition like one of Chevet's sturgeons, despite three years of having displayed his mustache in vain. Thirty francs in debt for his meals, every time Vimeux passed by Antoine he lowered his eyes to avoid contact; and yet, around noon, he never failed to ask him to buy him a roll.

After having tried to get a few reasonable ideas into this foolish head, Rabourdin finally gave up the notion. Monsieur Vimeux, the father, was a court clerk to a justice of the peace in the Département du Nord. Adolphe Vimeux had recently saved on dinners at Katcomb's and lived entirely on crusts of bread in order to buy a pair of spurs and a riding crop. They called him the Villiaume-pigeon, poking fun at his matrimonial calculations. Any jokes at the expense of this hollow Amadis could only be attributed to the malicious genius that will create a vaudeville, for in fact he really was a good chap and harmed no one but himself. The standing joke about him in the bureaus took the form of bets on whether he wore a corset. Originally posted in Baudoyer's bureau, Vimeux maneuvered to get himself transferred to Rabourdin's, on account of Baudoyer's extreme severity toward "the English," a name the employees gave their creditors. The "Day of the English" is the day on which the bureaus are open to the public. Certain of finding their debtors there, the creditors swarm and tear in to torment them, asking when they intend to pay up and threatening to garnish their wages. The implacable Baudoyer compelled the employees to remain at work. "It is up to them not to get into debt," he said. He considered his severity a duty he owed the public weal. In contrast, Rabourdin protected the employees from their creditors, whom he showed the door, saying that the government bureaus were open not for private but public business. A lot of fun was made of the two bureaus when the clank of Vimeux's spurs resounded in the corridors and on the staircases. The practical joker of the ministry, Bixiou, circulated in the Clergeot and La Billardière divisions a piece of paper on which Vimeux's head was caricatured on top of a pasteboard horse, asking for contributions to buy him a real horse. Monsieur Baudoyer was down for a quintal of hay from his own forage allowance, and each employee added his own little epigram at his neighbor's expense. Vimeux himself, good sport that he was, contributed under the name of "Miss Fairfax."

The fair employees of the genus Vimeux have their post to live off and their good looks on which to make their fortune. True to masked balls during Carnival, they attend them to seek their good fortune, which often escapes them even there. Many of them end up marrying either milliners taken out of exasperation, or old women, or even young women whose faces charm them and with whom they pursue a star-studded romance of stupid love letters, which nevertheless have their effect. These civil servants are sometimes more brazen: seeing a lady pass by in a train on the Champs-Elysées, they get hold of her address, hurl random passionate epistles at her, and unfortunately find themselves encouraged in this kind of ignoble speculation.

This Bixiou (pronounced "Bisiou") was a draftsman who ridiculed Dutocq as readily as he did Rabourdin, whom he nicknamed "La Vertueuse Rabourdin." To convey the commonness of his boss, he dubbed him "La Place Baudoyer"; he christened the vaudevillist "Flon-Flon." Without a doubt the cleverest man in the division, or even at the ministry (but clever like a monkey, without sense or object), Bixiou was so essentially useful to Baudoyer and Godard that they protected him in spite of his malicious ways; he did their work for them under the table. Bixiou wanted either Godard's or du Bruel's position, but his conduct interfered with his advancement. Sometimes he sneered at the bureaus, usually after he had made a good hit, such as the publication of portraits in the famous Fualdès case (for which he drew faces at random), or his sketches of the debate on the Castaing affair. At other times, possessed with a desire to move up, he really applied himself to work, though he would soon leave off to write a vaudeville that would hardly ever be finished. A thorough egotist, a miser and spendthrift in one—that is to say, spending his money solely on himself—sharp, aggressive, and indiscreet, he made mischief for mischief's sake. He attacked the weak, respected nothing and believed in nothing—neither in France, nor God, art, the Greeks, the Turks, the Champ d'Asile, the monarchy—and above all insulted everything he did not understand. It was he who was the first to paint a black cap on Charles X's head on the five-sous coin. He mimicked Dr. Gall when lecturing until he made the starchiest of diplomats pop their buttons. The standing trick of this terrible joker was to overheat the stoves in the office so as to make anyone who foolishly left that sauna catch cold; in addition, he also had the satisfaction of burning the government's wood. Famous for his practical jokes, he varied them with such elaborate care that he always found a victim. His big secret was the power of guessing everyone else's secret desires; he knew the way to every castle in Spain, the dream in which a man is gullible because he wants to deceive himself, and he made such men "pose" for him for hours.

And yet, this astute observer, who displayed unrivaled tact in developing a practical joke, was unable to utilize the same power to make men further his fortunes and promote him. The one he liked to annoy the most was young La Billardière—his black sheep, his nightmare—whom he was nevertheless forever buttering up so as to get at him better; he wrote him love letters signed "Comtesse de M——" or "Marquise de B——" and so led him to the Opéra on gala evenings to "wait under the clock," only to stick him with some grisette after having called everyone's attention to him. An ally of Dutocq (whom he regarded as a "real" joker) in his hatred for Rabourdin and his praise of Baudoyer, he fondly supported him. Jean-Jacques Bixiou was the grandson of a Parisian grocer. His father, who died a colonel, left him in the care of his grandmother, who remarried his first office boy, named Descoings, and who died in 1822. Finding himself without prospects upon leaving college, he tried painting; but in spite of his intimacy with Joseph Bridau, his childhood friend, he gave it up for caricature, vignettes, and drawing for books, which twenty years later is known as "illustration." The influence of the ducs de Maufrigneuse and de Rhétoré, whom he knew through stage girls, got him his position in 1819. On good terms with des Lupeaulx, with whom in society he stood on an equal footing, and on familiar terms with du Bruel, he was living proof of Rabourdin's theory about the steady deterioration of the administrative hierarchy in Paris when a man acquires personal importance outside the bureaus. Short in stature but well formed, with a delicate face remarkable for its vague likeness to Napoleon's, thin lips, a straight chin, chestnut whiskers, twenty-seven years old, fair hair, with a piercing voice and sparkling eyes—that was Bixiou. This man, all senses and wit, abandoned himself to the mad pursuit of pleasure of every description, which threw him into constant wasting. Intrepid hunter of grisettes, smoker, jester, diner-out and snacker, always in tune with the occasion, shining equally in the background or at the grisettes' ball in the Allée des Veuves, he was as entertaining at the dinner table as at a fun get-together, as on top of things at midnight on the streets as in the morning when he jumped out of bed. And yet at heart he was gloomy and melancholy, like most great comedians.

Thrust into the world of actresses and actors, of writers, artists, and certain women whose fortunes are flighty, he lived well, went to the theater without paying, gambled at Frascati and often won. In fact, this artist, truly profound—though only in flashes—balanced himself in life as on a swing, without thought for a time when the ropes would snap. The liveliness of his wit and wealth of his ideas made him sought out by persons who took pleasure in the lights of intellect; but not one of his friends liked him. Unable to hold back a good zinger, he would burn those next to him at dinner even before the first course was over. In spite of his superficial gaiety, he would allow a secret dissatisfaction with his social position to creep into his conversations; he aspired to something better, but the fatal demon remained hidden within the seriousness that so impresses fools. He lived in the rue Ponthieu on the second floor, in three rooms surrendered to all the chaos of a bachelor pad, a regular bivouac. He often talked of leaving France to go seek his fortune in America. No fortune-teller could foresee the future of a young man in whom all talents were incomplete, who was incapable of perseverance, intoxicated with pleasure, and loved as if the world would end tomorrow.

As to his dress, he was not given to the ridiculous, and for that reason was perhaps the only one in the entire ministry whose attire did not inspire the comment "There goes a bureaucrat!" He wore elegant boots, stirruped black trousers, a fancy waistcoat, a becoming blue frock coat, a collar—the perennial gift of grisettes—a Bandoni hat, and a pair of dark-colored kid gloves. His bearing, firm and simple, was not without grace. Moreover, when he was once called in by des Lupeaulx for a too impertinent remark he had made about the Baron de La Billardière and was on the verge of being dismissed, he simply reacted by saying, "You'll take me back for the way I dress." Des Lupeaulx could not help laughing. The best joke by Bixiou in the bureaus was the one he played on Godard, to whom he gave a butterfly brought back from China, which the deputy chief now has in his collection and shows off to this day, without realizing that it is colored paper. Bixiou had the patience to work up the little masterpiece for the sole purpose of getting at his superior.

The Devil always puts a victim in Bixiou's path. Baudoyer's bureau had its martyr, a poor copy clerk twenty-two years old, with a salary of fifteen hundred francs, named Auguste-Jean-François Minard. Minard had married a silk-flower maker for love, a potter's daughter who worked for Mademoiselle Godard and whom Minard had seen in her rue de Richelieu shop. Still a virgin, Zélie Lorain had many a fantasy about escaping her lot. At first a pupil at the Conservatoire, in turn a danseuse, a singer, and an actress, she had thought of doing as so many working women do, but fear of straying and falling into horrible misery kept her from the vice. She was drifting along in a haze when Minard appeared on the scene with a marriage proposal in hand. Zélie earned five hundred francs a year; Minard, fifteen hundred. Believing that they could live on two thousand francs, they married without settlements and in the most economical way possible. They went like turtledoves to live near the Barrière de Courcelles in a little apartment for one hundred ecus on the third floor: plain white-cotton curtains in the windows, plaid paper costing fifteen sous a roll on the walls, well-polished brick floors, walnut furniture, and a tidy little kitchen. First, there was a room where Zélie made her flowers; then a living room furnished with dark chairs covered in a rough fabric, a round table in the center, a mirror, a clock in the shape of a revolving crystal fountain, gilt candlesticks with a dimmer; and finally, a bedroom done in white and blue, with a bed, a mahogany chest and writing-desk, a small striped rug at the foot of the bed, six armchairs and four regular chairs, and in one corner the cherry crib in which a little boy and girl slept. Zélie nursed her children herself, did the cooking, made her flowers, and kept house.

There was something very touching in this happy and tedious mediocrity. Feeling that Minard loved her, Zélie truly loved him. Love begets love; it is the *abyssus abyssum* of the Bible. The poor man got up in the morning while his wife still slept and went to do her shopping. He delivered the finished flowers on his way to the office and on the way home picked up her raw materials. Then, while waiting for dinner, he cut out the leaves, trimmed the twigs, or mixed her colors. Small, slim, wiry, and nervous, with frizzy red hair, eyes of a light yellow, a strikingly fair complexion marked by freckles, he was a man of quiet and hidden strength. He knew the science of writing as well as Vimeux. At the office he kept to himself, did his work, and had the reflective air of a hard-working and thoughtful man. His blond eyelashes and lack of eyebrows earned him the nickname "the white rabbit" from the implacable Bixiou. Minard, the Rabourdin of a lower rank, obsessed with the desire to place his Zélie in good circumstances, combed the sea of luxury items and Parisian activity for ideas, for a find, for something perfect that would make him a quick fortune. His apparent dullness was really caused by the continual tension in his mind: he went from the *Double Pâte des Sutanes* to the *Cephalic Oils;* from phosphorescent to portable gas, from hinged clogs to hydrostatic lamps—in short, through all the little inventions of material civilization. He bore Bixiou's jests as a busy man bears the buzzing of an insect: he never let them upset him. In spite of his cleverness, Bixiou never perceived the profound contempt that Minard felt for him. Minard never dreamed of quarreling, seeing it as a waste of time. After a while, he even wore out his tormentor's patience. He came to work very simply dressed, wore his twill trousers until October, shoes and gaiters, a mohair waistcoat, a beaver-skin overcoat in the winter and a merino one in the summer, a straw hat or an eleven-franc silk hat, depending on the season—all because Zélie was his pride and joy; he would even have skipped meals to buy her a dress. He always had breakfast with his wife and ate nothing at the office. Once a month he took Zélie to the theater with tickets given him by du Bruel or Bixiou, for Bixiou was capable of anything, even doing a kindness. Zélie's mother gave up her place and came to take care of the child. Minard had replaced Vimeux in the Baudoyer bureau. Monsieur and Madame Minard paid their visits in person on New Year's Day. Seeing them, one had to wonder how the wife of a lowly civil servant paid only fifteen hundred francs managed to keep her husband in a black suit and herself in an Italian hat with flowers, embroidered muslin dresses, silk petticoats, prunelle shoes, magnificent fichus, and a Chinese parasol, and could arrive in a coach, and yet be virtuous; all the while Madame Colleville and other such *ladies* could hardly make ends meet, they who lived on two thousand, four hundred francs.

In each of these bureaus, there were two employees who were such close friends as to make their friendship ridiculous, because everything is a laughing matter in the bureaus. The one in Baudoyer's bureau was senior draft clerk and, had it not been for the Restoration, would long since have been deputy chief, or even chief. He had in Madame Colleville a wife as superior in her manner as Madame Rabourdin was in hers. Colleville, son of a first violinist at the Opéra, fell in love with the daughter of a celebrated danseuse. Flavie Minoret, one of those capable and charming Parisians who know how to make their husbands happy all the while maintaining their own liberty, made the Colleville home a rendezvous for all our best artists and orators of the Chamber. At her place one almost forgot the humble position of Colleville. Flavie's manner, a little too voluble, was such food for gossip that Madame Rabourdin had declined all her invitations. Colleville's friend, named Thuillier, held the same position in Rabourdin's bureau as Colleville and was stuck in his administrative career for the same reasons. Whoever knew Colleville knew Thuillier, and vice versa. Their friendship, born in the bureau, was the result of their both having entered the Administration at the same time. The lovely Madame Colleville had, so it was said in the bureau, taken up the care of Thuillier, whose wife had left him childless. Thuillier, called "Beau Thuillier," an ex-Lothario, led as idle a life as Colleville led a busy one. Colleville, first clarinet at the Opéra-Comique and bookkeeper in the mornings, worked hard to support his family, though he was not without influential friends. He was looked upon as a very shrewd man, all the more so as he hid his ambitions under a show of indifference. Apparently content with his lot, liking his work, he found everyone, even the chiefs, ready to assist his brave existence. Only several days before, Madame Colleville had made an evident change in the household and seemed to be taking to piety; it was also rumored in the bureaus that she was seeking out even stronger support in the Congrégation than that of the famous orator François Keller, one of her most faithful admirers, who until then had not secured a better position for Colleville. Flavie had turned—and this was one of her mistakes—to des Lupeaulx.

Colleville had a passion for reading the horoscopes of famous men in the anagrams of their names. He spent entire months decomposing and recomposing words to discover a meaning in them. "Un Corse la finira," found in the words "Révolution française"; "Vierge de son mari," in "Marie de Vigneros," niece of the Cardinal de Richelieu; "Henri-ci mei casta dea," in "Catharine de Médicis"; "Eh c'est large nez," in "Charles Genest," an abbé at the court of Louis XIV so renowned for his huge nose that he amused the duc de Bourgogne. At any rate, every known anagram was a marvel to Colleville. Elevating the anagram to a science, he declared that the destiny of every man was written in the sentence yielded by the transposition of the letters of his names, titles, and characteristics. Since the accession of Charles X, he had busied himself with the king's anagram. Thuillier, who was fond of making puns, declared that an anagram is nothing more than a pun on letters. Colleville—a man of real feeling, almost indissolubly bound to Thuillier, the model of an egoist—presented a insoluble problem that the many employees of the division explained by these words: "Thuillier's rich and the Colleville family is a burden." In fact, Thuillier lent money in order to add interest income to his salary; he was often sought out to talk with negotiators, with whom he met for several minutes in the corridor, but only on account of Mademoiselle Colleville, his sister. This friendship, consolidated by time, was based on feelings, on facts that naturally explained it, an account of which may be found elsewhere, and that to include here would be what the critics call "long-winded." We may remark in passing, though, that if Madame Colleville was well known in the bureaus, Madame Thuillier was almost unknown. Colleville, an active man burdened with children, was fat, round, and jolly; whereas Thuillier, "the Beau of the Empire," without apparent anxieties, at leisure, and having a slender figure, exhibited a pale, almost melancholy air. "We never know," said Rabourdin, speaking of these two employees, "whether our friendships are born of contrast or of likeness."

In contrast to these twins, Chazelle and Paulmier were two employees forever at war: one smoked, the other took snuff, and they were forever arguing about who practiced the better way of taking tobacco. A mutual deficiency, which made one as tiring as the other to the employees, was their arguing about the cost of consumer goods: the prices of peas, mackerel, cloth, umbrellas, clothes, hats, canes, and the gloves of their coworkers. They showed off their new finds to each other while keeping them for themselves. Chazelle collected bookstore prospectuses and printed or illustrated flyers, but he never bought a thing. Paulmier, Chazelle's fellow chatterbox, spent his time saying that if he were to have this or that fortune, he would do this or that. One day Paulmier went to the renowned Dauriat to congratulate him for having got the publisher to print books with glossy paper and printed bindings, to encourage him to continue on his track of improvement, when in fact Paulmier did not even own a single book! Chazelle's home, tyrannized by his wife, who wanted to seem independent, furnished a source of endless jibes for Paulmier; at the same time, Paulmier, a bachelor, often half-starved like Vimeux, with ragged clothes and disguised poverty, was a bountiful source of slurs for Chazelle. Both were beginning to show a potbelly: Chazelle's, small, round, protruding, so Bixiou said, was so rude as to enter a room first; Paulmier's flopped from right to left; Bixiou measured them every trimester. Both of them were between thirty and forty; both, rather inane, did nothing after hours; they were specimens of a sort of pure-blooded bureaucrat, numbed by his paperwork and by long tenure in the bureaus. Chazelle often fell asleep while working; and his pen, which he still hung onto, would mark out his breathing with little dots. Paulmier, though, blamed this sleepiness on the situation at home. To rebut this dig, Chazelle accused Paulmier of being on medication for four out of twelve months and said that a grisette would be his end. Paulmier came back by pointing out that Chazelle kept a record in an almanac of all the days on which Madame Chazelle found him appealing. The two civil servants, by dint of airing their dirty laundry and hurling back and forth the details of their private lives, had gained the disrepute they deserved. "Do you take me for a Chazelle?" was a remark that tabled any annoying discussion.

Monsieur Poiret, Jr.—to distinguish him from his brother Monsieur Poiret, Sr., now retired to the Maison Vauquer boarding-house, where Poiret, Jr., would occasionally go to have dinner and where he also intended to finish` his days—had thirty years' tenure. Even nature herself is not as entrenched in her ways as this poor man was in his daily routine: he always put his things in precisely the same place, laid his pen on the same grain mark in the wood, always took his seat at the same time, and warmed himself at the stove at the same moment of every day, for his single vanity consisted in wearing an infallible watch, set daily at the Hôtel de Ville, which he passed on his way from the rue du Martroi where he lived. From six to eight o'clock in the morning he kept the books of a large novelty shop in the rue Saint-Antoine, and from six to eight o'clock in the evening, those of the Maison Camusot in the rue des Bourdonnais. He thus earned a thousand ecus a year, including the salary from his post. As in just a few months he would reach the necessary tenure for a pension, he showed the utmost indifference to the intrigues of the bureaus. Like his older brother, for whom retirement had proven a fatal blow, he would go under when he could no longer come from the rue Martroi to the Ministry, sit in the same chair, and copy documents. In charge of keeping the newspapers to which the bureau subscribed as well as issues of the *Moniteur*, this collecting became his passion. If some employee lost an issue, that is, checked it out without returning it, Poiret, Jr., obtained a leave, went straight to the journal's publisher, got another copy, and returned all excited by the cashier's politeness. He always dealt with charming young fellows; and, according to him, reporters were definitely nice but relatively unknown people.

A man of modest height, Poiret had dim eyes, a weak gaze totally without warmth, dark and wrinkled skin, a gray complexion dotted with bluish pockmarks, a snub nose, and a sunken mouth in which a few rotted teeth still held on. Thuillier also said that it was no use for Poiret to look at himself in the mirror, since he would not see himself (i.e., his teeth) in it. His long, gray arms ended in huge hands lacking any hint of whiteness. His gray hair, flattened by the pressure of his hat, gave him the look of a cleric, a rather unflattering analogy for him, for he hated priests and the clergy, though without being able to explain his views on religion. This antipathy, however, did not prevent him from being extremely attached to whatever government happened to be in power. He never buttoned his old green coat, even in the coldest weather; he only wore shoes with ties, and black trousers. He shopped in the same stores for thirty years. When his tailor died, he requested leave to go to his funeral and shook hands with the son over the father's grave, reassuring him in his practice. On good terms with all the suppliers, he chatted with them, heard their complaints, and paid their accounts. If he had to write one of these *messieurs* to change his order, he always adhered to the politest of etiquette, writing "Monsieur" on a separate line, dating and making a draft of the letter, which he kept in a box labeled "My Correspondence."

No life was ever more organized. He had every approved memo, all of his receipts, even the smallest, and his annual account books wrapped up in old shirts according to year, starting with that of his entry into the Ministry. He even ate at the same restaurant and the same table at the Veau-qui-Tette in the Place du Châtelet; the waiters would just save "his" table. Never giving the Cocon d'Or, the famous silk shop, even five more minutes than was its due, at eight-thirty he arrived at the Café David, the best known in the quarter, and stayed there until eleven o'clock; he was a regular, as at the Veau-qui-Tette, for thirty years, and had a "bavaroise" at ten-thirty. He listened to conversations about politics, his arms crossed over his walking stick, his chin resting on his right hand, without ever participating. The lady at the counter, the only woman he enjoyed talking to, was the confidante of the little things in his life, because his table was up there by the counter. He played dominoes, the only game he ever understood. When his partners did not show up, he was sometimes found asleep with his back against the paneling, holding a newspaper, the spine of which rested on his marble table. He was interested in everything that went on in Paris and spent his Sundays walking around surveying the new construction. He questioned the old guy in charge of keeping people out of the fenced-in areas and concerned himself with holdups with the masons, lack of materials or capital, problems the architect had encountered. He was often heard to say, "I saw the Louvre emerge from its rubbish; I saw the birth of the Place du Châtelet, the Quai aux Fleurs, and the Markets!" He and his brother, both born to a farmhand at Troyes, had been sent to Paris to learn in the bureaus. Their mother earned herself the reputation of making a disastrous lapse in judgment, for the two brothers had the grief of learning of her death in the hospital at Troyes, in spite of funds they sent on numerous occasions. Not only did they thus both vow never to marry, but they came to abhor children; not only did they feel uneasy in their presence, they feared them as others fear lunatics and watched them with haggard eyes. Both of them had had the life crushed out of them by drudgery under Robert Lindet. The Administration had not been fair to them back then, yet they saw themselves as fortunate in having kept their heads and so only complained between themselves of this ingratitude, for they had "organized the Maximum." When they played the joke on Phellion by making him change his famous sentence at Rabourdin's suggestion, Poiret took Phellion aside in the corridor as he was leaving and told him, "Believe me, Monsieur, I did all I could to prevent what happened." From the day when he first came to Paris, he had never left the city. Since that time, he began to keep a journal of his life in which he recorded the big events of the day; du Bruel told him that Lord Byron did the same thing. This similarity filled Poiret with delight and led him to buy the works of Lord Byron, translated by Chastopalli, of which he did not understand a thing. At the office, you could often catch him in a melancholy attitude, looking as though he were in deep contemplation; in fact, he was thinking of nothing at all. He did not know a single person in the house where he lived and always kept the key to his apartment himself. On New Year's Day, he went around delivering his own cards to all the employees in the division, but never paid visits.

Bixiou took it into his head, one scorching hot day, to put a layer of lard under the lining of a certain old hat that Poiret, Jr. (he was fifty-two years old), had worn for the last nine years. Bixiou, who had never seen any other hat on Poiret's head, dreamed about it and had visions of it when he ate; he therefore resolved, for the sake of his digestion, to relieve the bureaus of the sight of that foul hat. Poiret, Jr., left around four o'clock. As he walked along the streets of Paris, where the sun's rays, reflected up from the pavements and off walls, produced a tropical heat, he felt his head being inundated— he, who never perspired! Believing that he was ill, or on the verge of being so, instead of going to the Veau-qui-Tette, he went home, took from his desk the journal of his life, and recorded the fact in the following manner: "Today, 3 July 1823, taken by extraordinary perspiration, a sign, perhaps, of the sweating-sickness, a malady that prevails in Champagne; I am about to consult Doctor Haudry. The disease first appeared as I reached the top of the Quai des Ecoles."

All of a sudden, without a hat on, he realized that the mysterious sweat had some cause independent of his own person. He wiped his face, examined the hat, and could find nothing, for he did not venture to take out the lining. So he noted the following in his journal: "Carried my hat to the 'Sieur Tournan, hatmaker in the rue Saint-Martin, for I suspect some other cause for this perspiration, but nevertheless the result of some recent or former alteration to the hat."

Monsieur Tournan recognized on the spot, as was his custom, the presence of a greasy substance obtained by the processing of a hog or sow. The next day Poiret appeared with a hat lent him by Monsieur Tournan while he awaited the new one; but he did not go to bed that night without adding the following sentence to his journal: "It is asserted that my hat contained lard or pig fat." This inexplicable fact occupied Poiret's thoughts for better than fifteen days, and he never figured out how this could have come to pass. There was talk in the office of showers of frogs and other canicular wonders, of an outline of Napoleon's head seen in the root of an elm tree, as well as hundreds of other quirks of nature. Vimeux informed him that one day his hat, Vimeux's, had stained his face black, and that the hatmakers were selling drugs. Poiret paid many visits to 'Sieur Tournan to reassure himself about his means of production.

In the Rabourdin bureau, there was yet another employee, a man

of seeming courage who professed Left-Center opinions and rebelled against the tyrannies of Baudoyer for the sake of the miserable slaves of that bureau. This lad, named Fleury, boldly subscribed to an Opposition newspaper, wore a gray hat with a broad
brim, red stripes on his blue trousers, a blue waistcoat with gilt buttons, and a double-breasted overcoat like that of a quartermaster of
the gendarmerie. Though unyielding in his opinions, he continued
on as an employee in the bureau, but he foretold a disastrous future
for the government if it persisted in mixing with religion. He openly expressed his support for Napoleon, now that the death of that great
man had put an end to the laws against "the partisans of the usurper." Fleury, ex-captain of a regiment of the line under the emper-
or, a tall, dark, handsome fellow, was controller at the Cirque-
Olympique. Bixiou never ventured a stab at Fleury, for this rough
trooper, who was a good shot and proficient at fencing, seemed
quite capable of extreme brutality if provoked. An ardent subscriber to "Victoires and Conquêtes," Fleury refused to pay, all the
while keeping the issues, alleging that they exceeded the number proposed in the brochure. He adored Monsieur Rabourdin, who had
saved him from dismissal. He was once caught saying that if any harm
should come to Monsieur Rabourdin through anyone's doing, he
would kill that person. Dutocq stroked Fleury, so much did he fear
him.

Fleury, crippled by debt, played countless tricks on his creditors.
Expert in legal matters, he never signed a promissory note and had
his own wages garnished under the names of fictitious creditors, so
that he was actually able to draw nearly the whole of it himself.
Very close friends with a supernumerary in the Porte-Saint-Mar-
tin, at whose place he kept his furniture, he happily played *écarté*,
was the life of the party with his talents, downed a glass of champagne
in one shot without wetting his lips, and knew all the songs of
Béranger by heart. He was proud of his full and sonorous voice. The

three great men he admired were Napoleon, Bolívar, and Béranger. Foy, Laffitte, and Casimir Delavigne he merely esteemed. Fleury, as you might have guessed, coming from the Midi, would end up as editor of some Liberal paper.

Desroys, the mystery man of the division, interacted with no one, talked little, and hid his private life so carefully that no one knew where he lived, who were his protectors, or what he lived on. Searching for the causes of this reserve, some of his colleagues thought him a *Carbonaro*, others an Orleanist; some thought him a spy, others a "deep" man. Desroys was simply the son of a "Conventionnel," who did not vote for the king's death. Cold and reserved by temperament, he had judged the world and relied on no one but himself. A closet Republican, secret admirer of Paul-Louis Courier, friend of Michel Chrestien, he looked to time and common sense to bring about the triumph of his opinions in Europe. He also dreamed of Young Germany and Young Italy. His heart swelled with that stupid collective love which we must call humanitarianism, the eldest son of defunct philanthropy, which is to the divine Catholic charity what system is to art: reason substituted for works. This conscientious puritan of freedom, this apostle of an impossible equality, regretted being forced by poverty to serve the government and took steps toward finding work in some shipping office. Tall, lean, lanky, and solemn as a man who expects someday to be called to lay down his life for a cause, he lived off a page of Volney, studied Saint-Just, and set about rehabilitating Robespierre, whom he regarded as the successor of Jesus Christ.

The last of the individuals who merits a couple of strokes of the pen is the little La Billardière. Having, to his great misfortune, lost his mother, under the protection of the minister and therefore safe from the snubs of the "Place Baudoyer," received in all the ministerial salons, he was hated by everyone because of his impertinence and conceit. The chiefs were polite to him, but the workers excluded him from their circles by way of a grotesque politeness invented solely for him. A pretty youth of twenty-two, tall and slender, with the manners of an Englishman, he was an affront to the bureaus with his gaudy ways, his curled hair, perfumes, collars, yellow gloves, and always newly lined hat; he carried fancy glasses, went to the Palais-Royal for breakfast, was a joke under the veneer of fake manners: Benjamin de La Billardière thought himself a charming fellow and possessed all the vices of high society without any of its graces. Certain of having been created a "somebody," he thought of writing a book to obtain the Cross as a writer and ascribing it to his administrative talent. He cajoled Bixiou with an eye to exploiting him, but had not yet gone ahead with this plan. This noble heart impatiently awaited the death of his father in order to succeed to the title of "Baron" recently bestowed upon him, had his cards printed "le Chevalier de La Billardière" and his framed coat of arms hung in his office (a blue field with three stars and two swords in saltire on a sable background, with the motto: A Toujours Fidele)! Possessed by a mania for discussing the art of heraldry, he had asked the young vicomte de Portenduère why his arms were configured in a certain way and drew down upon himself the nice little answer, "I did not make them." He talked of his devotion to the monarchy and the favors the dauphine paid him. He stood well with des Lupeaulx, often ate with him, and thought him a friend. Bixiou posed as his mentor, hoping to rid the division and France of the young "prima donna" by leading him to debauchery, and openly avowed that intention.

Such were the principal figures in La Billardière's division, which also housed also some other employees whose mores and appearance were more or less the same as these. In Baudoyer's bureau one came across some workers who were balding, icy, bundled up in flannel, perched on the fifth floor and growing flowers there, had pine walking sticks, old threadbare clothes, and never without an umbrella.

These people, who hold the ground between happy caretakers and disgruntled workers, too far removed from the administrative centers to hope for any kind of advancement, represent the pawns in the bureaucratic chess game. Glad to be drafted to avoid going to the bureau, capable of doing anything for a price, their very existence is a problem even for those who employ them and an indictment against the state that fosters and accepts this misery. As for the various aspects of these strange faces, it is difficult to decide if these quill-bearing mammals become morons as the result of their jobs, or if they do these jobs because they are a little moronic from birth. Perhaps the blame falls equally between nature and government. "The villagers," according to someone unknown, "are submitted, without realizing it, to the influence of atmospheric conditions and external circumstances.   Linked in some way with the nature of the surroundings in which they live, they unconsciously absorb the ideas and feelings their environment projects and express them in their actions and their appearance in accordance with their organization and individual personality. Thus molded and shaped over time by the objects that continually surround them, they are books most interesting and true to life for whoever feels himself drawn to this aspect of physiology—so little understood and yet so rich—which explains the relationship of the moral being to the outside forces of nature." Moreover, nature to a bureaucrat is the bureau: his horizon is bordered on all sides by green boxes; for him, atmospheric conditions are the air of the corridors, the masculine fumes trapped in rooms without ventilators, the smell of paper and quill; his soil is tile or parquet, strewn with a curious litter moistened by the office boy's watering can; his sky is the ceiling toward which he yawns; and his element is dust. The observation about the villagers applies to the state employees identified in terms of the nature of the milieu in which they live. If several distinguished doctors doubt the influence of this "nature," at once savage and civilized, on the moral being trapped in those dreadful compartments called bureaus, where the sun seldom penetrates, where thought is tied down to tasks similar to that of the horses who turn a merry-go-round, who yawn distressingly and die quickly. . . .

Rabourdin thus had very good reason to weed out the employees, seeking very good salaries for them and a lot of hard work. Men are never weary when they are doing great things. Moreover, as they are set up, the bureaus, during the nine hours the employees owe the state, spend four in conversation, as we shall see—in gossip, arguments, and most of all, in intrigues.

The Machine in Motion

You would have had to haunt the bureaus to recognize the degree to which their little world resembled that of the colleges; and yet whenever men live collectively, this similarity is striking: in regiments, in tribunals, you will find a more or less enlarged college. All of these state employees, brought together for their eight-hour sessions in the bureaus, saw in this a sort of class session where there were lessons to write, where the chiefs acted as schoolmasters, and where the payoffs were like awards for good conduct handed out to favorites, where you made fun of others, disliked others, but there nevertheless existed a sort of camaraderie more relaxed than that in a college. To the degree to which a man moves ahead in life, egoism develops and loosens secondary bonds of affection. In sum, is not the bureau a microcosm of society, with its oddities, its loves and hatreds, its envy and greed, its relentless march onward despite everything, its frivolous gossip that inflicts so many wounds, and its perpetual spying?

At this time, the division of Monsieur le Baron de La Billardière was prey to an extraordinary state of excitement, well justified by the event that was about to take place, for division chiefs do not die every day, and there is no "tontine" insurance brokerage where the chances of life and death are calculated with more sagacity than in the bureaus. Self-interest stifles all compassion, just as in children;

but bureaucrats add hypocrisy to boot.

Around eight o'clock, the employees of Baudoyer's office arrived, whereas at nine those of Rabourdin's had seldom scarcely begun to wander in, which in no way kept work from getting done much faster in Rabourdin's office than in Baudoyer's. Dutocq had serious reasons for coming in so early. Having sneaked into Sébastien's work area the previous evening, he had caught him copying something for Rabourdin; he hid himself and saw Sébastien leave without taking any papers with him. Sure of finding this rather lengthy document and its copy hidden somewhere, after rummaging through one box after another, he finally found the fatal list. He hurried off to the director of an autographic printing house to have two copies of the document made, and thus even had it in Rabourdin's own writing. So as not to arouse suspicion, he hastened to put the document back in its box by being the first one in the office. Kept out until midnight in the rue Duphot, Sébastien was, in spite of his diligence, superseded by hatred. Hatred lived in the rue Saint-Louis–Saint-Honoré, whereas devotion lived far off in the rue du Roi-Doré in the Marais. This slight delay would weigh on the rest of Rabourdin's life.

Sébastien, in a hurry to look in his box, found therein the memorandum along with his unfinished copy, all in order, and locked them in his boss's desk. By the end of December it was not very light in the offices in the mornings, and there were several in which the lamps were kept on until ten o'clock; therefore Sébastien did not happen to notice the imprint of the copying machine upon the paper. But at nine-thirty, when Rabourdin looked at his memorandum, he recognized much more clearly the effects of the copying process—all the more so as he dealt with them a lot to see whether these autographic presses could replace copy clerks. The bureau chief sat down in his armchair, took his fire tongs, and proceeded methodically to rearrange his fire, so absorbed in thought was he; then, curious to know in whose hand his secret was, he called in Sébastien.

"Did anyone get to the office before you?" he asked.

"Yes," replied Sébastien, "Monsieur Dutocq."

"Good, he's on time. Send Antoine to me."

Too big a man to upset Sébastien unnecessarily by blaming him for a misfortune now beyond remedy, Rabourdin said no more. Antoine came in, and Rabourdin asked him if on the previous evening any employees had stayed after four o'clock. The boy replied that Monsieur Dutocq had worked later than Monsieur de La Roche. Rabourdin dismissed the lad with a nod and picked up the thread of his thoughts.

"Twice I have prevented his dismissal," he said to himself, "and this is my reward."

This morning was for the bureau chief like the solemn hour in which great commanders weigh all the odds before deciding a battle. Knowing better than anyone the spirit of the bureaus, he knew that here one pardons no more than in a college, prison, or army, anything that hints of demotion or espionage. A man capable of informing on his comrades is disgraced, lost, despised: ministers in such cases will disavow their own people. An employee must then give his resignation and leave Paris, his honor is forever stained: explanations are no use, no one asks for them or wants to hear them. In this game, a minister is a great man, he is supposed to choose his people; but a mere employee will pass as a spy, no matter what his motives.

As he weighed the hollowness of such folly, Rabourdin knew that it was powerful and saw himself crushed. More surprised than overwhelmed, he now sought the best course to follow under the circumstances, and so stayed in the dark as to the excitement in the offices, all stirred up by the death of Monsieur de La Billardière; he only learned of it thanks to the young La Brière, who knew how to appreciate the sterling value of the bureau chief.

Meanwhile, in the Baudoyer bureau (the bureaus were simply referred to as Rabourdin's and Baudoyer's), at around ten o'clock, Bixiou was describing the director of the division's last moments to Minard, Desroys, Monsieur Godard, whom he had called from his cubbyhole, and Dutocq, who had rushed over to Baudoyer's with an ulterior motive. Colleville and Chazelle were absent.

Bixiou (standing with his back to the stove, to which he held up the sole of each boot alternately to dry): "This morning, at seventhirty, I went to inquire after our most worthy and respected director, Knight of the Order of Christ, et cetera, et cetera. And, my God, yes, gentlemen, the baron was yesterday still twenty et ceteras, but today he is nothing, not even a bureaucrat. I asked how his night was. His nurse, who gives in but does not die, said that, as of five in the morning, he was concerned about the Royal Family. He had read off to him those among us who had come by for news of him. Finally he said, 'Fill my snuffbox, give me the newspaper, bring my spectacles, and change my ribbon of the Legion of Honor, it is very dirty.' You know him, he wears his orders to bed. He was fully conscious, had all his wits about him, all his usual thoughts. But, presto! Ten minutes later the water rose, rose, rose, and reached his heart and lungs; he knew he was dying, for he felt the cysts break. At that fatal moment he proved what a strong character he had, what a great intellect he was! Ah, we never really appreciated him, the rest of us! We made fun of him, we thought him a fool, the most foolish of fools, isn't that right, Monsieur Godard?"

Godard: "I? I always rated Monsieur de La Billardière's talents higher than anybody."

Bixiou: "I'm sure you're including yourself, too!"

Godard: "Nevertheless, he wasn't a bad man; he never harmed anyone."

Bixiou: "To do harm you must do something, and he never did anything. If it wasn't you who said he was hopelessly inept, it must have been Minard."

Minard (shrugging his shoulders): "I!"

Bixiou: "Well then, it was you, Dutocq!" (Dutocq made a vehement gesture of denial.) "Great! Nobody then! He was seen by everyone here as an intellectual Hercules. Well then, you were right: he finished as a man of wit, talent, character—in fact, as the great man that he was."

Desroys (impatiently): "Pray what did he do that was so great? Did he go to confession?"

Bixiou: "Yes, Monsieur, he received the Holy Sacraments. But in order to receive them, do you know what he did? He put on his uniform as gentleman-in-ordinary, all his orders, and even had himself powdered; they tied his queue (that poor queue!) with a fresh ribbon. Now I say that only a man of great character would have his queue tied on his deathbed; here we are, eight of us, and not one of us would have had that done. But that's not all," he said, "for you know that on their deathbeds all famous men make a *speech*" (an English word for a long-winded parliamentary speech). "'I must attire myself to meet the King of Heaven, I, who have so often dressed in my best for an audience with the king on earth.' Thus Monsieur de La Billardière departed, taking it upon himself to justify the saying of Pythagoras, 'No man is known until he dies.'"

Colleville (rushing in): "At last, gentlemen, I bring you great news. . . . "

All: "We know."

Colleville: "I bet you don't! I have been working on it ever since the accession of His Majesty to the thrones of France and Navarre. Last night I figured it out, albeit with such trouble that Madame Colleville asked me what in the world was worrying me."

Dutocq: "Do you think we have time to worry about anagrams when the great Monsieur de La Billardière has just left us?"

Colleville: "I do know you, my Bixiou! I just came from Monsieur de La Billardière's; he was still alive, although they expect him to die soon. . . . " (Godard, seeing through the hoax, goes back to his cubicle.) "Gentlemen! You would never guess what events are revealed in the anagram of this sacramental sentence." (He pulls out piece of paper and reads.) "'*Charles dix, par la grâce de Dieu, roi de France et de Navarre.*'"

Godard (reentering): "Spit it out this instant, and don't tease these people."

Colleville (triumphantly unfolding the hidden part of his piece of paper): "'*A H. V il cedera; De S. C. l. d. partira; En nauf errera. De-cede á Gorix.*' Every letter is there!" (He repeats it.) "'*A Henri cinq cedera* (his crown), *de Saint-Cloud partira; en nauf* (that's an old French word for skiff, vessel, felucca, corvette—anything you like) *errera.* . . . '"

Dutocq: "What a bunch of absurdities! How can the king cede his crown to an Henri V who, according to your nonsense, must be his grandson, with Monseigneur le Dauphin around? You're already prophesying the dauphin's death."

Bixiou: "What's Gorix? The name of a cat?"

Colleville (provoked): "It's the lapidary abbreviation of the name of a town, my friend; I looked it up in Malte-Brun: Goritz, in Latin Gorixia, situated in Bohemia or Hungary, at any rate, in Austria. . . . "

Bixiou: ". . . Tyrol, the Basque provinces, or South America. You should have thought up a melody so you could play it on the clarinet too."

Godard (shrugging his shoulders and leaving): "What nonsense!"

Colleville: "Nonsense! Nonsense! I wish you all would take the trouble to study fatalism, the religion of the Emperor Napoleon."

Godard (irritated at Colleville's tone): "Monsieur Colleville, Bonaparte may well be called emperor by historians, but this should not be recognized in the bureaus."

Bixiou (smiling): "Get an anagram out of that, my dear fellow. Actually, as for anagrams, I like your wife better; she's easier to convince." (In a low tone.) "Flavie would do well, if only to subject you to Godard's nonsense."

Dutocq (supporting Godard): "If that wasn't nonsense, you would lose your job for prophesying events disagreeable to the king; every good Royalist must understand that two stays in exile are enough."

Colleville: "If my job is taken from me, François Keller would gladly shake up your minister." (Dead silence.) "I'd have you know, Master Dutocq, that all known anagrams have actually come to pass. Look here—you'd better not marry; there's *coqu* in your name."

Bixiou: "And *d* and *t* are left for *detestable*."

Dutocq (without seeming to be angry): "I don't care, as long as it is only in my name."

Paulmier (quietly to Desroys): "Got ya, my little Colleville!"

Dutocq (to Colleville): "Have you done *Xavier Rabourdin, Chef de Bureau*?"

Colleville: "I have!"

Bixiou (fixing his pen): "And what did you find?"

Colleville: "It comes out as follows: '*D'abord rêva bureaux, E-u.* . . . Get it? . . . And he had! '*E-u fin riche*,' which means that after having begun in the Administration, he left it to go make his fortune elsewhere." (He repeats.) "*D'abord rêva bureaux, E-u fin riche*."

Dutocq: "At least it's original!"

Bixiou: "And Isidore Baudoyer?"

Colleville (mysteriously): "I don't want to tell that to anyone but

Thuillier."

Bixiou: "Bet you breakfast I can tell you what it is."

Colleville: "I'll pay if you figure it out."

Bixiou: "Then I'll be your guest. But you won't be sore, will you? Two artists like us will laugh ourselves to pieces! . . . *Isidore Baudoyer* gives *Ris d'aboyeur d'oie!*"

Colleville (struck with amazement): "You stole it from me!"

Bixiou (with dignity): "Monsieur Colleville, do me the honor to believe me rich enough in absurdity not to have to steal my neighbor's nonsense."

Baudoyer (entering with a dossier in hand): "Gentlemen, I ask you to shout a little louder; you bring the office into such high repute with the administrators. The Honorable Monsieur Clergeot, who did me the honor just now to come and ask me a question, overheard your subject matter." (Goes into Monsieur Godard's office.)

Bixiou (in a low voice): "The watchdog is very quiet this morning, we're in for a change in the weather."

Dutocq (whispering to Bixiou): "I have something I want to say to you."

Bixiou (fingering Dutocq's waistcoat): "You've got a pretty waistcoat that surely cost you next to nothing. Is that what you want to say?"

Dutocq: "What! Not at all! I've never paid so much for anything. This costs six francs a yard in the best shop in the rue de la Paix—a wonderful matte fabric that's great for deep mourning."

Bixiou: "You understand fabrics but you are ignorant of the laws of etiquette. You can't know everything! Silk is not acceptable in deep mourning. Therefore I only wear wool. Monsieur Rabourdin, Monsieur Clergeot, and the minister all wear wool; the Faubourg Saint-Germain is all in wool. There's no one but Minard who doesn't wear wool; he's afraid of being called *laniger* in bucolic Latin; that's why he exempted himself from putting on mourning for Louis XVIII, great legislator, author of the Charter, and a man of wit, a king who will hold his place in history as he held it on the throne and as he held it everywhere. Do you know the best part about his life? No? Well, at his second ascension, when he received all of the allied sovereigns, he went in first on the way to the table."

Paulmier (looking at Dutocq): "I don't understand . . ."

Dutocq (looking at Paulmier): "Neither do I."

Bixiou: "Don't you see? Well, he did not see himself as being in his own house. It was inspired, great, epigrammatic. The sovereigns didn't understand any more than you, even offering each other money to understand; it is true, though, that they were almost all strangers. . . . "

Baudoyer (during this conversation he is sitting by the fire in his deputy chief's office, and the two are speaking in low voices): "Yes, the fine man is dying. The two ministers are there for his last breath; my father-in-law has just been notified of the event. If you want to do me a big favor, you will take a cab and go let Madame Baudoyer know what is happening, for Monsieur Saillard cannot leave his desk and I don't dare leave the office unattended. Put yourself at her disposal: she had, I believe, her ideas and may want to have several concurrent steps taken on her own." (The two functionaries leave together.)

Godard: "Monsieur Bixiou, I am leaving the office for the rest of the day; so take over for me."

Baudoyer (to Bixiou, benignly): "Let me know if anything comes up."

Bixiou: "This time, La Billardière is really dead."

Dutocq (in Bixiou's ear): "Come outside with me a minute." (Bixiou and Dutocq, in the corridor, gaze at each other like birds of ill-omen.)

Dutocq (whispering in Bixiou's ear): "Listen. Now is the time for us to work together to get ahead. What would you say to being made chief and I deputy chief?"

Bixiou (shrugging his shoulders): "Come, come, don't talk nonsense!"

Dutocq: "If Baudoyer is appointed, Rabourdin won't stay on and will hand in his resignation. Between you and me, Baudoyer is so incompetent that if du Bruel and you don't help him, in two months he'll be dismissed. If I figure right, we'll have before us three empty positions."

Bixiou: "Three positions that will pass right under our noses, that will be given to some pot-bellied flunkies, spies, men of the Congrégation—to Colleville perhaps, whose wife has ended up where all pretty women end up, in 'piety.'"

Dutocq: "It's up to you, my friend, whether you want for once in your life to use your mind logically." (He stopped as if to study the effect of his adverb on Bixiou's face.) "Come, let's put our cards on the table."

Bixiou (impassive): "Let's see your hand then."

Dutocq: "I don't want to be anything more than deputy chief. I know I don't have, as you do, the skill to be chief. Du Bruel can become director, and you his bureau chief; he will leave you his place once he has made a bundle, and I, I'll bob along, under your protection, until I'm pensioned."

Bixiou: "You sly dog! But how do you expect to carry out a plan that entails forcing the minister's hand and getting rid of a man of real talent? Between us, Rabourdin is the only capable man in the division, maybe even in the whole Ministry. Then again, it's a question of putting in his place that square lump of stupidity, that cube of idiocy, Baudoyer!"

Dutocq (strutting about): "My dear fellow, I am in a position to rouse the whole division against Rabourdin. You know how devoted Fleury is to him. Well, Fleury will despise him."

Bixiou: "Despised by Fleury!"

Dutocq: "Not a soul will stand by Rabourdin. The employees will go en masse to complain about him to the minister; and it won't just be our division, but Clergeot's division, Bois-Levant's division, and the other ministries. . . ."

Bixiou: "That's it! Infantry, cavalry, artillery, and marines of the guard, forward march! You're dreaming, my friend! And I, what part am I to play in all this?"

Dutocq: "You are to make a scathing caricature: a picture that can kill."

Bixiou: "Will you pay for it?"

Dutocq: "A hundred francs."

Bixiou (to himself): "There's something behind this."

Dutocq (continuing): "You'd have to make Rabourdin out to be a butcher, but a good likeness. Find analogies between an office and a kitchen, put a skewer in his hand, draw in the important employees of the various ministries looking like some sort of poultry caged up in a huge coop labeled 'Administrative Executions,' and make him the one who has to cut their throats one by one. He can have geese and ducks with heads kind of like ours, you see! He'll be holding his winged creatures in one hand. Like Baudoyer, for example—he'll make a perfect turkey."

Bixiou: "*Ris d'aboyeur d'oie!*" (He has been watching Dutocq carefully for some time.) "Did you come up with that yourself?"

Dutocq: "Yes, all by myself."

Bixiou (to himself): "Do evil feelings, then, really bring men to the same end as talents?" (To Dutocq): "My friend, sure I'll do it . . . " (Dutocq lets out a sigh of delight.) "when" (a dramatic pause) "I am sure of what I can count on; because if you don't succeed, I will lose my position, and I have to make a living. You are still a curious kind of innocent, my dear colleague!"

Dutocq: "All right, then, don't draw the picture until success is evident."

Bixiou: "Why don't you just spill the beans right now?"

Dutocq: "First we have to go feel out the mood in the bureau; we'll talk about that later." (Goes off.)

Bixiou (alone in the corridor): "That fish—for he's more of a fish than a bird—that Dutocq has a good idea there; I can't figure out where he got it. If Baudoyer should succeed La Billardière, it would be a joke, even more than a joke; we would profit!" (Goes back into the office.) "Gentlemen, there are going to be great changes: La Billardière really is dead. No joke, word of honor! There goes Godard running errands for our most respected Chief Baudoyer, successor, heir apparent to the deceased." (Minard, Desroys, and Colleville raise their heads in amazement; they put down their pens, and Colleville blows his nose.) "We're all going to move up! Colleville will be deputy chief at the very least; Minard may become head drafter, and why shouldn't he, he's as dumb as I am. Hey, Minard, if you got twenty-five hundred francs, your little wife would be very happy and you could buy yourself a pair of boots."

Colleville: "But you don't have them yet, those twenty-five hundred francs."

Bixiou: "Monsieur Dutocq gets that in Rabourdin's bureau, so why shouldn't I get that this year? Monsieur Baudoyer got that."

Colleville: "Through Monsieur Saillard's influence. No other draft clerk in Clergeot's division gets that."

Paulmier: "As a matter of fact, Monsieur Cochin, doesn't he get three thousand? He succeeded Monsieur Vavasseur, who served for ten years under the Empire at four thousand, dropped to three when the king first returned, and died getting two thousand five hundred. But, through his brother's influence, Monsieur Cochin got himself a raise; he gets three thousand."

Colleville: "Monsieur Cochin signs himself E. L. L. E. Cochin—he calls himself Emile-Louis-Lucien-Emmanuel, which anagrammed gives *Cochenille*. And so, he has ties to a hardware business in the rue des Lombards, the Maison Matifat, which made its fortune by speculating on that very colonial commodity."

Bixiou: "Poor fellow, he did a year in Florine."

Colleville: "Cochin sometimes comes to our soirées, as he is a great violinist." (To Bixiou, who has not yet gone to work.) "You should come to our place for a concert next Tuesday. They're playing a quintet by Reicha."

Bixiou: "Thanks, I'd rather look at the score."

Colleville: "Are you saying that to be funny? An artist of your caliber must enjoy music."

Bixiou: "I would go, but it would be for Madame."

Baudoyer (returning): "Monsieur Chazelle isn't around yet. If you will be so kind as to convey my compliments, gentlemen."

Bixiou (who had put a hat on Chazelle's chair when he heard Baudoyer's steps): "Excuse me, Monsieur, he has gone to the Rabourdins' to make an inquiry on your behalf."

Chazelle (entering with his hat on and not seeing Baudoyer): "Father La Billardière is done for, gentlemen! Rabourdin is division chief and Master of Petitions; he didn't steal *his* promotion, he...."

Baudoyer (to Chazelle): "You found that appointment in your second hat, didn't you?" (He points to the hat on the chair.) "This is the third time this month you have come in after nine o'clock; if you persist in this, you will take a hike to you-know-where!" (To Bixiou, who is reading the newspaper.) "My dear Monsieur Bixiou, do, pray, leave the newspapers to these gentlemen who are about to have breakfast and come with me for the day's orders. I don't know what Monsieur Rabourdin wants with Gabriel; he keeps him to do his private errands, I believe; I've rung three times." (Baudoyer and Bixiou go into the private office.)

Chazelle: "Damn fate!"

Paulmier (delighted to annoy Chazelle): "Why didn't they tell you downstairs that he had already come up? Well, you could have looked when you came in to see the hat in your chair and the elephant . . . "

Colleville (laughing): ". . . in the menagerie."

Paulmier: "He's big enough not to miss."

Chazelle (dismally): "Good God! For the seventy-five centimes the government gives us a day, I don't see why we have to work like slaves."

Fleury (entering): "Down with Baudoyer! Long live Rabourdin! That's the cry of the division."

Chazelle (exasperating himself): "Baudoyer can ruin me if he likes, I won't be any the worse for it. In Paris there are a thousand ways of earning five francs a day. You can do that at the Palais, copying for lawyers."

Paulmier (still goading Chazelle): "So you say, but a post is a post, and that strong guy Colleville, who works like a slave outside the office, who could earn, if he were to lose his post, more than his salary, even by only staging musical performances, chooses to keep his post. You, devil of a fool, you can't just give up your hopes."

Chazelle (continuing his philippic): "Him! But not me! Do we have another chance? My God! There was a time when nothing was more alluring than an administrative career. There were so many men in the army that they were short in the Administration. Those without teeth, the maimed, the sick, like Paulmier, the nearsighted, all got rapid promotions. Families whose children swarmed the lycées let themselves become enchanted with the brilliant life of a young man with glasses, dressed in blue with a red ribbon blazing from his buttonhole, who earned around a thousand francs a month; responsible for going to whatever ministry for several hours, going in to check up on something there, getting there late and leaving early; having, just like Lord Byron, two hours of leisure time, romancing, strolling in the Tuileries, endowed with a slightly arrogant air; being seen everywhere, at big events, at balls; admitted to societies' best circles; spending his salary; and in all this giving back to France all that France had given unto him, even doing something in return. In fact, the state employees were at one time, like Thuillier, fussed over by pretty ladies; they seemed to be bright and did not spend too much time in the bureaus. Empresses, queens, princesses, the high society of this 'belle époque' had its whims. All of these fine ladies had the passions a noble should: they loved to play the protector. Furthermore, one could in twenty-five years reach a high position, be auditor to the Conseil d'Etat or Master of Petitions, and have ties to the emperor as you amused yourself with his august family. You had fun and everyone worked together. Everything got done efficiently. But nowadays, ever since the Chamber invented specialization for expenditures and divisions entitled personnel, we are even lower than the soldiers. The most menial posts are at the mercy of a thousand variables, because there are a thousand sovereigns. . . . "

Bixiou (returning): "Chazelle is crazy. Where does he see a thousand sovereigns? . . . In his own pocket by any chance?"

Chazelle: "Shall we add them up? Four hundred over there at the end of the Pont de la Concorde (so called because it leads to the scene of perpetual discord between the Right and Left of the Chamber); three hundred more at the end of the rue de Tournon. The Court, which ought to count for three hundred, has to have seven hundred times the power of the emperor to get *one* of its protégés any post whatsoever. . . . "

Fleury: "All of which means that, in a country where there are three powers, you can bet a thousand to one that a single bureaucrat who is protégé to none but himself will never get ahead."

Bixiou (looking alternately at Chazelle and Fleury): "Ah, my children, you have yet to learn that in these days the worst state of life is the state of belonging to the state."

Fleury: "Because of the constitutional government."

Colleville: "Gentlemen, let us not talk politics."

Bixiou: "Fleury is right. Nowadays, gentlemen, serving the state is no longer serving the prince who knew how to punish and reward. Today, the state is anybody and everybody. Furthermore, everybody cares for nobody. To serve everybody is to serve nobody. Nobody cares about anybody. The state employee lives between these two negations! The world has neither pity nor respect, neither heart nor head; everybody is selfish and forgets tomorrow the service of yesterday. Now you may be lucky, like Monsieur Baudoyer, from the tenderest of years an administrative genius, the Chateaubriand of reports, the Bossuet of circulars, the Canalis of memos, the gifted child of dispatches, but there is a dark law counter to administrative genius: that is the law of promotion by averages. This inevitable average is based on the statistics of promotion and the statistics of mortality combined. It is certain that upon entering whichever administrative branch even at the age of eighteen, you will only get eighteen hundred francs a year when you're thirty; to get sixty-five hundred, Colleville's case is living proof that the genius of a wife, the influence of several Peers of France, of influential deputies, are to no avail. Now there is no free and independent career in which, in twelve years, a young man who has studied the humanities, been vaccinated, exempted from military service, of sound mind yet without transcendent intelligence, has not accrued a capital of forty-five thousand francs and a couple of centimes, which represents permanent interest income equal to our rather volatile salaries, since they are not even for life. In this time a grocer could have earned enough to give him ten thousand francs in interest a year, gone bankrupt, or gained a seat on a Commercial Tribunal. A painter can paint a mile of canvas and be decorated with the Legion of Honor or pose as a great unknown. A man of letters becomes professor of something or other, or a journalist at a hundred francs for a thousand lines; he writes feuilletons or finds himself at Sainte-Pélagie for a brilliant pamphlet that offends the Jesuits, which is, after all, a feather in his cap and makes him into a politician. Finally, even an idler who hasn't done a thing—for there are idlers who *do* do something—has debts and a widow who pays them. A priest finds time to become a bishop *in partibus*. A vaudevillist becomes a proprietor even if, like du Bruel, he never wrote a whole vaudeville. An intelligent and sober young fellow who begins investing with very little capital, like Mademoiselle Thuillier, soon buys a share in a broker's business. So let's go right down the ladder! A petty clerk becomes a notary; a rag picker gets a thousand francs; the poorest workmen often become manufacturers; whereas, in the vertigo of this present civilization, which mistakes perpetual division and subdivision for progress, someone like Chazelle has lived on twenty-two sous per person, argues with his tailor and bootmaker, gets into debt, is absolutely nothing! He becomes a moron! Come, gentlemen, let's take a stand! How about it, let's all hand in our resignations! Fleury, Chazelle, plunge yourselves into something else and become two great men at it! . . . ”

Chazelle (calmed down by Bixiou's speech): "Thanks." (General laughter.)

Bixiou: "You are wrong; in your position I would go to the secretary-general."

Chazelle (uneasily): "And what would he have to say to me?"

Bixiou: "Odry would say to you, 'Chazelle,' with more charm than des Lupeaulx will ever put on for you, 'the one open post for you is the Place de la Concorde.'”

Paulmier (clasping the stove-pipe): "My God! Baudoyer will have no mercy on you! Let's go."

Fleury: "Another one of Baudoyer's stabs! Ah! what a weird fellow you have in him! Now, Monsieur Rabourdin, there's a man for you! He put work on my table that would take three days to get done in here; well, *he'll* have it by four o'clock this afternoon. Yet he is not always on my heels to keep me from coming to talk with my friends."

Baudoyer (appearing): "Gentlemen, you must admit that if you have the right to find fault with the Chamber's system or the Administration's protocol, you must at least do it somewhere other than in the office." (To Fleury): "What are you doing here, Monsieur?"

Fleury (insolently): "I came to alert these gentlemen to a shake-up. Du Bruel has been sent for by the secretary-general, and Dutocq has gone too. Everybody is asking who will be appointed."

Baudoyer (retiring): "That, monsieur, is not your affair. Go back to your office, and don't come to disturb mine."

Fleury (in the doorway): "It would be a terrible injustice if Rabourdin lost it! I swear, I'd quit the Ministry. Did you find your anagram, Papa Colleville?"

Colleville: "Yes, here it is."

Fleury (leaning over Colleville's desk): "Great! Wonderful! This is just what will happen if the Administration continues to play the hypocrite." (He signals the employees that Baudoyer is listening.) "If the government would frankly state its intentions without any second thoughts, the Liberals would know what they have to deal with. A government that sets its best friends against itself, and the men of the 'Débats,' like Chateaubriand and Royer-Collard, is a sorry one indeed!"

Colleville (after consulting his colleagues): "Come, Fleury, you're a good fellow, but don't talk politics here—you don't know what harm you're doing us."

Fleury (dryly): "Well, adieu, gentlemen. I have my work to do."

(He returns and speaks softly to Bixiou.): "They say Madame Colleville has ties with the Congrégation."

Bixiou: "How?"

Fleury (bursting out laughing): "You're never caught off guard!"

Colleville (worried): "What do you mean?"

Fleury: "Our theater took in a thousand ecus yesterday with our new play, even though it's the fortieth showing! You really should come see it, the sets are superb."

Meanwhile, des Lupeaulx was receiving du Bruel at the Secretariat, after whom Dutocq followed. Des Lupeaulx had learned of Monsieur de La Billardière's death from his valet and wanted to please the two ministers by issuing an obituary that very evening.

"Good morning, my dear du Bruel," said the semiminister to the deputy chief as he entered and not inviting him to sit down. "You have heard the news? La Billardière is dead; both ministers were present when he received the last sacraments. The worthy man strongly recommended Rabourdin, saying that he would die unhappy unless he knew he had as his successor the man who had filled his shoes all along. It seems deathbed is a situation in which one tells all. . . . The minister more readily agreed that it was his intention, as well as that of the Council, to reward Monsieur Rabourdin's many services." (He shakes his head.) "The Conseil d'Etat lays claim to his expertise. They say that Monsieur de La Billardière, Jr., is to leave the division of his late father and go to the Commission of Seals; that's as though the king made him a present of a hundred thousand francs: the post is like a notary's and can be sold. The news will delight your division, for it was conceivable that Benjamin might have been placed there. Du Bruel, we must knock off ten or twelve lines about the worthy late director; His Excellency will look them over—he reads the papers. Do you know the particulars of old La Billardière's life?"

Du Bruel made a sign indicating ignorance.

"No?" continued des Lupeaulx. "Well, then: he was mixed up in the affairs of La Vendée, and he was one of the confidants of the late king. Like Monsieur le Comte de Fontaine, he always refused to compromise with the first consul. He was a bit of a *chouan*. Born in Brittany of a parliamentary family, so young that he was ennobled by Louis XVIII. How old was he? It doesn't matter! Let's just say his loyalty was untarnished, his religion enlightened (the poor old fellow had a habit of never setting foot in a church), make him out to be a 'pious vassal.' Bring in, gracefully, the fact that he sang the Song of Simeon at the accession of Charles X. The comte d'Artois thought very highly of La Billardière, for, unfortunately, he cooperated in the Quiberon affair and took the whole responsibility upon himself. You know about that don't you? La Billardière defended the king in a printed pamphlet in reply to an impudent history of the Revolution written by a journalist; you can stress his devotion. Finally, weigh your words well so that the other newspapers cannot laugh at us, and bring me the article when you've written it. Were you at Rabourdin's yesterday?"

"Yes, monsigneur," said du Bruel. "Oh! I beg your pardon."

"No harm done," answered des Lupeaulx, laughing.

"His wife was delightfully lovely," added du Bruel. "There are no two women like her in Paris: some are as clever as she, but there's no one so gracefully witty, perhaps a woman as lovely as Célestine, yet it is doubtful that she would be so multifaceted in her beauty. Madame Rabourdin is far superior to Madame Colleville," went on the vaudevillist, recalling des Lupeaulx's past adventure. "Flavie owes what she is to the men about her, whereas Madame Rabourdin is all things in herself. She knows everything; you can't tell a secret in Latin with her around. If I had a wife like that, I believe I could succeed at everything."

"You have more mind than an author is allowed," retorted des Lupeaulx with a conceited air. Then he turned around to look at Dutocq. "Ah, good morning, Dutocq. I sent for you to lend me your Charlet, if you have finished it. Madame la Comtesse knows nothing of Charlet."

Du Bruel withdrew.

"Why do you come in without being summoned?" said des Lupeaulx harshly, when he and Dutocq were alone. "Is the state in danger that you come here to find me at ten o'clock in the morning, just as I am going to breakfast with His Excellency?"

"Perhaps it is, monsieur," said Dutocq. "If I had had the honor of seeing you earlier, you would probably not have been so willing to support Monsieur Rabourdin after reading his opinion of you."

Dutocq opened his coat, took a folder of papers stamped on their backs and laid it on des Lupeaulx's desk, opened to a specifically marked passage. Then he went to bolt the door, fearing an explosion. This is what the secretary-general read while Dutocq bolted the door. "MONSIEUR DES LUPEAULX. A government degrades itself by openly employing such a man, whose real vocation is diplomatic police work. He is fit to deal with the political filibusters of other cabinets, and it would be a pity, therefore, to employ him in our internal police: he is above a common spy, he understands a plan; he could skillfully carry out a necessary bit of dirty work and skillfully cover his retreat."

Des Lupeaulx was succinctly analyzed in five or six sentences, the essence of the biographical portrait given at the beginning of this story. As he read the first words, the secretary-general felt himself to be judged by a man stronger than himself; but he wanted to hold himself back so as to examine this work, which reached far and wide, without conferring his secrets on a man like Dutocq. The secretary-general—like lawyers and magistrates, like diplomats and anyone who must pry into the human heart—was past being surprised by anything. Versed in treachery, in all the tricks of hatred, and in traps, he could take a stab in the back without letting it show in his face.

"How did you get hold of this paper?"

Dutocq explained his good luck. As he listened to him des Lupeaulx's face showed no sign of approval. So the spy ended in terror the account which he had begun in triumph.

"Dutocq, you have put your finger between the bark and the tree," replied the secretary-general dryly. "If you do not wish to make powerful enemies, I advise you to keep this a deep secret, as it is a work of the utmost importance and already well known to me."

So saying, des Lupeaulx dismissed Dutocq with one of those glances that are more expressive than words.

"Ha! That scoundrel of a Rabourdin is in this too!" thought Dutocq, terrified at finding a rival in his boss. "He is in the big leagues while I am left out in the cold. I never would have believed it!"

To all his other reasons for aversion to Rabourdin he now added a worker's jealousy of a colleague, one of the most volatile ingredients of hatred.

When des Lupeaulx was alone, he fell into a strange meditation. Of what power was Rabourdin the instrument? Should he use this singular document to destroy him, or should he keep it as a weapon to succeed with his wife? This mystery was unfathomable for des Lupeaulx, who in terror tore through those pages on which men he knew were judged with unheard-of profundity. He admired Rabourdin yet felt torn to the heart by him. The breakfast hour caught des Lupeaulx by surprise in his reading.

"You will keep His Excellency waiting if you do not go down at once," the minister's bailiff came to tell him.

The minister always breakfasted with his wife and children and des Lupeaulx, without servants present. The morning meal affords the only private moment statesmen can snatch from the current of overwhelming business matters. Yet in spite of the precautions they take to keep this hour for open conversation and interaction with their family and close friends, a good many great and small people contrive to infringe upon it. Business matters often manage, at times like this, to throw themselves in the way of their pleasures.

"I thought that Rabourdin was a man above ordinary employees, and here he is, not ten minutes after La Billardière's death, sending through La Brière this ticket to what sounds like a real show. Look," said His Excellency, handing des Lupeaulx a piece of paper he was twirling in his fingers.

Too noble of mind to think of the embarrassing meaning La Billardière's death lent to his letter, Rabourdin had not withdrawn it from La Brière's hands after hearing the news from him. Des Lupeaulx read as follows:

Monseigneur,

If twenty-three years of irreproachable service may claim a favor, I entreat your Excellency to grant me an audience this very day. It is a matter in which my honor is involved.

Followed by respectful cordialities.

"Poor man!" said des Lupeaulx, in a tone of compassion that confirmed the minister in his error. "We are among ourselves; have him come over. You have a meeting after the Chamber session, and Your Excellency must respond to the Opposition today; there is no other time you could receive him."

Des Lupeaulx rose, called the servant, said a few words, and returned to his seat at the breakfast table. "I have called for him during dessert," he said.

Like all other ministers under the Restoration, this minister was a man without youth. The charter granted by Louis XVIII had the defect of tying the hands of the kings by forcing them to hand over the destinies of the nation to the quadrigenarian of the Chamber and the septuagenarians of the Peerage, of robbing them of the right to lay hands on a man of statesmanlike talent wherever he might be found, no matter how young or how poor his condition might be. Napoleon alone was able to employ young men as he chose, without being constrained by any consideration. Furthermore, after the overthrow of that mighty will, vigor deserted power. Moreover, to instate slothfulness for strength is a polarity more dangerous in France than in any other country. In general, ministers who were old when they entered office were mediocre, whereas ministers recruited when young were an honor to the European monarchies and to the republics whose affairs they directed. The world still rings with the struggle between Pitt and Napoleon, two men who conducted politics at the age when the Henri de Navarres, the Richelieus, the Mazarins, the Colberts, the Louvois, the princes of Orange, the Guises, the La Rovères, the Machiavellis—in short, all of the renowned great men, coming from the ranks or born close to the throne—began to rule the state. The Convention, that model of energy, was composed in great measure of young minds; no sovereign can ever forget that it was able to raise fourteen armies against all of Europe. Its policy, fatal in the eyes of those who cling to so-called absolute power, was nevertheless dictated by strictly monarchical principles, for it acted essentially like one great king.

After ten or twelve years of parliamentary struggle, having pondered politics to the point of wearing himself out, this minister was actually enthroned by his party, which saw him as their man for business. Happily for him, he was closer to sixty than fifty; if he had retained even a vestige of youth's vigor he would have quickly been broken. But, used to being broken, to retreating and returning to take charge, he could let himself be struck again and again—

by his party, by the Opposition, by the Court, by the clergy—by running up against inertia with a substance at once soft and consistent; and so he reaped the fruits of his misfortune. Living hell on earth in the thousand questions of government, like the thoughts of an old lawyer after pleading every angle, his mind no longer had the keen edge of solitary minds or the power to make quick decisions, like men used to action from early on and who distinguish themselves among the young military ranks. Could he be anything else? He had always juggled rather than exercised judgment; he had criticized effects without seeing to the causes; his head was full of the reforms a party throws at its leader, programs that private interests take to an up-and-coming speaker, smothering him in plans and advice impossible to implement. Far from coming in fresh, he came in weary from his advances and counteradvances. Then, when he took his position at the long-desired top, he got tangled up in a thousand thorny bushes with a thousand conflicting wills to conciliate. If the statesmen of the Restoration had been able to follow through on their own ideas, their ability would doubtless have been less subject to criticism; but though their wills were influenced, their age saved them by not allowing them to exert the resistance that youth can deploy to oppose those intrigues, both high and low, which at times vanquished even Richelieu, and to which, in a lower sphere, Rabourdin was to succumb. After the throes of their first struggles, these men, less old than aged, have to face the wrangling of ministries. And so their eyes have already begun to weaken just as they need to have the clear-sightedness of eagles; their minds are weary when they need to redouble in verve.

The minister in whom Rabourdin wanted to confide routinely heard men of undeniable superiority expound upon the most ingenious of theories applicable to the affairs of France. Such men, from whom the difficulties of national politics were hidden, assailed this minister on his return from a parliamentary battle with the infighting of the secret follies of the Court; or it might be on the eve of a struggle with the popular will; or on the day after a diplomatic debate that split the Council into three opinions. In these circumstances, a statesman naturally keeps a yawn ready for any first sentence designed to show how to better organize public affairs. He did not dine where the most audacious speculators, the financial and political lobbyists, sum up the opinions of the Bourse and the Bank, the secrets of diplomacy, and the policy necessitated by the state of affairs in Europe. In any case, the minister had in des Lupeaulx his private secretary, a minicounselor to pre-chew all of this, to control and analyze the interests that spoke in many clever voices. In fact, his problem, that of all sextagenarian ministers, was to dodge every difficulty: with journalism, which at this time one wanted to tone down rather than flat out repress; with financial as well as industrial questions; with the clergy, as with questions of the public lands; with liberalism, as with the Chamber. After having maneuvered into power in seven years, the minister believed that he could manage every issue in the same way. It is so natural to seek to maintain a position by the means that got us there, that no one dared to condemn a system invented by mediocrity to please mediocre minds. The Restoration, like the Polish revolution, proved to nations, as to princes, the true value of a man and what happens if he is not to be found. The last and greatest weakness of the statesmen of the Restoration was their honesty in a struggle in which their adversaries employed the resources of political roguery, lies, and slander, loosing upon them, by all subversive means, the clamor of the unintelligent masses only able to understand one thing—chaos.

Rabourdin told himself all this; yet he had just made up his mind to go for it all, like a man weary of gambling who gives himself one last chance. But fate dealt him a cheater as adversary in the person of des Lupeaulx. Nevertheless, for all his shrewdness, the bureau chief, better versed in matters of administration than in parliamentary perspectives, did not imagine the whole truth: he did not know that the great work which had taken over his whole life was to be reduced to theory by the minister, and that it was impossible for the statesman not to confuse him with after-dinner innovators and fireside chatterers.

As the minister rose from the table, instead of thinking of Rabourdin, he thought of François Keller, and was detained by none other than his wife, who offered him a bunch of grapes; the bureau chief was announced by the bailiff. Des Lupeaulx had counted on the minister's mood, which should be preoccupied with his improvisations; also, seeing the statesman busy with his wife, he went up to Rabourdin and struck him a blow with his first sentence.

"His Excellency and I are informed about what you are occupying yourself with and you have nothing to fear," said des Lupeaulx, lowering his voice, "either from Dutocq or from anyone else."

"Don't worry at all, Rabourdin," said His Excellency kindly, but moving to leave.

Rabourdin came forward respectfully, and the minister could not evade him.

"Would His Excellency permit me to have a word with him in private?" said Rabourdin, as he cast a mysterious glance toward His Excellency.

The minister looked at the clock and went toward the window, followed by the poor chief.

"When may I have the honor of submitting the matter to Your Excellency and explaining to him the new administrative plan to which the paper pertains, and which is sure to sully . . ."

"An administrative plan!" exclaimed the minister, knitting his brows and interrupting him. "If you have anything of that kind to tell me about, wait for the day we do business together. I have to be at the Council today; I have an answer to make to the Chamber on the point the Opposition raised before the session ended yesterday. Your day is next Wednesday; I could not work yesterday, for I was not able to attend to ministerial affairs. Political matters are apt to interfere with purely administrative ones."

"I place my honor with all confidence in Your Excellency's hands," said Rabourdin gravely, "and I entreat him to remember that he did not allow me time for immediate explanation of the stolen paper. . . ."

"Do not be uneasy," said des Lupeaulx, coming between the minister and Rabourdin, whom he interrupted, "within eight days you will surely be appointed. . . ."

The minister chuckled as he thought of des Lupeaulx's enthusiasm for Madame Rabourdin, and he glanced at his wife, who was also smiling. Rabourdin, taken aback by this silent game, tried to fathom its meaning; his attention was diverted from the minister for a moment, and His Excellency took advantage of it to make his escape.

"We shall talk of all this," said des Lupeaulx, in front of whom the bureau chief, much to his surprise, found himself alone. "Do not be angry with Dutocq; I shall answer for him."

"Madame Rabourdin is a charming woman," said the minister's wife to the bureau chief, just to say something.

The children gazed at Rabourdin with curiosity. Rabourdin had come there expecting something official, and he was like a great fish caught in the threads of a flimsy net; he struggled with himself.

"Madame la Comtesse is very good," he said.

"Shall I not have the pleasure of seeing her some Wednesday? said the Countess. "Pray, bring her; you will do me the pleasure . . . "

"Madame Rabourdin herself receives on Wednesdays," interrupted des Lupeaulx, who knew the banality of the official "Wednesdays"; "but if you are so inclined to her, you have, I believe, an intimate soirée coming up."

The minister's wife rose in some irritation.

"You are my master of ceremonies," she said to des Lupeaulx, ambiguous words in which she expressed the annoyance she felt with des Lupeaulx for meddling in her private soirées, to which she admitted only a select few. She left, saying good-day to Rabourdin. Des Lupeaulx and the bureau chief were alone in the small salon where the minister breakfasted with his family. Des Lupeaulx fingered the confidential letter that La Brière had delivered to the minister; Rabourdin recognized it.

"You do not know me very well," he said to the bureau chief, smiling. "Friday evening we shall come to a full understanding. Just now I must go and receive callers; the minister leaves that on my shoulders today, for he must ready himself for the Chamber. But I will say it again, Rabourdin, do not worry about a thing."

Rabourdin slowly made his way downstairs, confounded by this singular turn of events. He had thought himself denounced by Dutocq and found that he had not been mistaken: des Lupeaulx had in his hands the document that judged him so severely, and des Lupeaulx was fawning over his judge. It was not to be believed! Upright men are at a loss to understand complicated intrigues, and Rabourdin was lost in this labyrinth without being able to figure out the game the secretary-general was playing.

"Either he has not read the part about himself or he is in love with my wife."

Such were the two thoughts over which the chief stopped dead in his tracks as he crossed the courtyard, for the glance he had intercepted between des Lupeaulx and Célestine the night before came back to him like a flash of lightning.

During Rabourdin's absence, his bureau was of course prey to great excitement, for in the ministries, the relationship between the workers and their superiors is so well regulated that, when the minister's messenger comes on behalf of His Excellency to a bureau chief, and, above all, at an hour when the minister is not out in public, there is no end to the comments that are made. The coincidence of this message and the death of Monsieur de La Billardière lent a strange importance to the circumstance that Monsieur Saillard learned from Monsieur Clergeot, and he went at once to confer with his son-in-law. Bixiou, who was working with his chief, left him to talk with his father-in-law and himself went to the Rabourdin bureau, where work had stopped.

Bixiou (entering): "Things haven't heated up too much in here, gentlemen? Don't you know what's going on downstairs? 'La Vertueuse Rabourdin' is done for! Yes, done for, crushed! Terrible scene at the minister's."

Dutocq (looking fixedly at him): "Is that true?"

Bixiou: "Who would be the worse for it? Not you. You'll be made deputy chief and du Bruel, chief. Monsieur Baudoyer gets the division."

Fleury: "I'll bet a hundred francs that Baudoyer will never be division chief."

Vimeux: "I'm in, too. How about you, Monsieur Poiret?"

Poiret: "I retire the first of January."

Bixiou: "What! We'll never see your laced boots again? And what will the Ministry be without you? Who'll bet with me?"

Dutocq: "I can't, I'd be betting knowing the facts. Monsieur Rabourdin is appointed. Monsieur de La Billardière requested it of the two ministers on his deathbed, blaming himself for having drawn the pay of an office for which Rabourdin did all the work; he had a guilty conscience, and so, subject to orders from above, they promised him, to keep him quiet, to appoint Rabourdin."

Bixiou: "Gentlemen, are you all against me, seven of you? For I know which side you'll take, Monsieur Phellion. I'll bet a dinner for five hundred francs at the Rocher de Cancale that Rabourdin does not get La Billardière's place. It won't cost you a hundred francs each, and I'm risking five hundred; I'll take you all on myself. Any takers? Du Bruel, what do you say?"

Phellion (putting down his pen): "*Môsieur*, on what do you base that aleatory proposal, for *aleatory* is the only word for it? Nevertheless, I am wrong to call it a proposal; it is 'contract' that I wanted. The wager constitutes a contract."

Fleury: "No, no. You can only apply the 'contract' to agreements recognized in the Code, and the Code accords no action for the recovery of a wager."

Dutocq: "Proscribe a thing and you recognize it."

Bixiou: "Good for you, my little Dutocq."

Poiret: "For example!"

Fleury "True! It's just like refusing to pay one's debts; that's recognizing them."

Thuillier: "You would make fabulous lawyers."

Poiret: "I am as curious as Monsieur Phellion to find out what grounds Monsieur Bixiou has for . . ."

Bixiou (shouting across the office): "Are you in, du Bruel?"

Du Bruel (appearing at the door): "Damn it, gentlemen, I'm working on something very tricky, the obituary of Monsieur de La Billardière. Please! A little quiet. You can joke and make bets later."

Thuillier: "Joke and make bets! You're stepping on my puns!"

Bixiou (going into du Bruel's office): "That's true, du Bruel, the eulogy of a chump, I mean champ, is a very difficult thing to write. I'd much rather draw a caricature of him!"

Du Bruel: "Help me, Bixiou."

Bixiou: "Sure I will, although these kinds of articles are so much easier to write while eating."

Du Bruel: "We'll have dinner together." (Reading) "'*The Church and the Monarchy are daily losing some of those who fought for them in Revolutionary times . . .*'"

Bixiou: "Bad. Why don't you say, '*Death carries on its ravages among the oldest defenders of the monarchy and most faithful servants of the king, whose heart bleeds for every blow.*' (Du Bruel writes quickly.) '*Monsieur le Baron Flamet de La Billardière died this morning of dropsy in the chest, caused by a heart condition.*' You see, it's not a matter of indifference that we have a heart in the bureaus. Should we slip in a little dig about the emotions of the Royalists during the Terror? Hey! That wouldn't hurt. But wait, the petty reporters would say the emotions came more from the intestines than the heart. Better leave that out. What have you got?"

Du Bruel (reading): " '*Descended from old parliamentary stock . . .*'"

Bixiou: "That's great! It's poetic, and 'stock' is true all right."

Du Bruel (continuing): "'*Where devotion to the throne was hereditary, as was also attachment to the faith of our fathers, Monsieur de La Billardière . . .*'"

Bixiou: "I'd say 'Monsieur le Baron.'"

Du Bruel: "But he wasn't in 1793."

Bixiou: "Doesn't matter. You know that, under the Empire, Fouché was telling an anecdote about the Convention in which he was talking to Robespierre, and he said, 'Robespierre called out to me, "duc d'Otrante, go to the Hôtel de Ville."' So there's a precedent."

Du Bruel: "Let me just jot that down! But let's not put *le Baron*, because I've saved the honors bestowed on him for the end."

Bixiou: "Oh! Very good! Dramatic effect, the credits at the end of the article."

Du Bruel: "You get it? '*In appointing Monsieur de La Billardière Baron, Gentleman-in-Ordinary . . .*'"

Bixiou (aside): "Very ordinary."

Du Bruel (continuing): "'. . . *of the Bedchamber, etc., the King rewarded not only the services rendered by the Provost, who knew how to reconcile the rigor of his duties with the customary urbanity of the Bourbons, but the bravery of the Vendean hero who never bent the knee to the Imperial idol. He leaves a son, who inherits his loyalty and his talents, etc.'"*

Bixiou: "Don't you think all that's too high-tone; too colorful? I'd tone down the poetry. *'Imperial idol!'*, *'bent the knee!'* Forget it! Writing vaudevilles has ruined your style; you can't come down to pedestrian prose. I would say, *'He belonged to the small number of those who, etc. . . .'* Simplify! You're talking about a simpleton."

Du Bruel: "That's another vaudeville line. You would make your fortune in the theater, Bixiou!"

Bixiou: "What have you said about Quiberon?" (He reads.) "That's all wrong! Here's how I would say it: *'He took upon himself, in a recently published work, all the responsibility for the Quiberon expedition, thus demonstrating the nature of his loyalty, which did not shrink from any sacrifice.'* That's clever and witty, and saves La Billardière."

Du Bruel: "At whose expense?"

Bixiou (solemn as a priest in a pulpit): "Why, Hoche and Tallien. Don't you know the story?"

Du Bruel: "No. I subscribed to the Baudouin series, but I've never had time to open it; there's nothing about vaudevilles in there."

Phellion (at the door): "We all want to know everything, Monsieur Bixiou, about what makes you think that the worthy and honorable Monsieur Rabourdin, who has been the interim chief of the division for nine months, who is the senior bureau chief in the Ministry, and whom the minister, upon the departure of Monsieur de La Billardière, summoned, will not be appointed division chief?"

Bixiou: "Papa Phellion, do you know your geography?"

Phellion (bridling): "I should say so!"

Bixiou: "And your history?"

Phellion (modestly): "Maybe."

Bixiou (looking at him): "Your diamond pin is loose; it's going to fall out. Well, you don't know human nature; you have gone no further in that study than in that of the Paris suburbs."

Poiret (quietly to Vimeux): "Paris suburbs? I thought they were talking about Monsieur Rabourdin."

Bixiou: "Does the entire Rabourdin bureau bet against me?"

All: "Yes."

Bixiou: "Du Bruel, are you in?"

Du Bruel: "For sure. It's in our interests that our chief move on, for everyone in the bureau moves ahead."

Thuillier: "A-head." (Softly to Phellion): "He's good, that one."

Bixiou: "I'm going to win. And here's why. You'll find it hard to understand, but I'll tell you all the same. It would be right to appoint Monsieur Rabourdin" (looking straight at Dutocq), "for in him, seniority, talent, and honor are recognized, appreciated, and rewarded. Such an appointment is even in the best interests of the Administration." (Phellion, Poiret, and Thuillier listen without understanding a thing, like someone trying to see clearly in twilight.) "Well, precisely because of all his qualifications and merits, and recognizing that moderation is just and wise, I still bet that this will not come to pass. Yes, it will fall through just like the campaigns in Boulogne and Russia, when genius had gathered every chance for success! It will fall through, just as everything that seems just and good down here fails. I am only backing the Devil's game."

Du Bruel: "Who *will* be appointed then?"

Bixiou: "The more I think about Baudoyer, the more I feel that he embodies all the opposite qualities; therefore, he will be appointed division chief."

Dutocq (pushed to the brink): "But Monsieur des Lupeaulx, who sent for me to borrow my Charlet, told me that Monsieur

Rabourdin would be appointed and that La Billardière, Jr., would be made Clerk of the Seals."

Bixiou: "Appointed! Appointed! The appointment won't even be signed in under ten days. The appointment will be on New Year's Day. Hey, look at your chief there in the courtyard, and tell me if 'La Vertueuse Rabourdin' looks like a man in favor; you would think he'd been fired!" (Fleury rushes to the window.) "Gentlemen, adieu. I'll go and tell Monsieur Baudoyer of your appointment of Monsieur Rabourdin; that always makes him furious, the pious creature! Then I'll tell him of our wager, to cheer him up. That's what we in the theater call a peripateia, right, du Bruel? What will it get me? If I win, he'll take me as deputy chief." (He leaves.)

Poiret: "Everybody says that man is clever, but as for me, I can never understand a word he says." (He goes on copying.) "I listen and listen; I hear words, but I never get at any meaning: he talks about the Paris suburbs when he discusses human nature and" (lays down his pen and goes to the stove) "declares he is backing the Devil's game when talking about Russia and Boulogne! First of all, you have to suppose that the Devil plays games, and then find out which games. Dominoes comes to mind . . ." (He blows his nose.)

Fleury (interrupting): "It's eleven o'clock. Papa Poiret is blowing his nose."

Du Bruel: "So it is. Goodness! I'm off to the Secretariat."

Poiret: "What was I saying?"

Thuillier: "*Domino*, which means 'to the Lord'; we're talking about the Devil, and the Devil is suzerain without a charter. But this is more to the point than a pun. This is a play on words. Anyhow, I don't see the difference between this play on words and . . ." (Sébastien enters to gather up the different papers for signing and collating.)

Vimeux: "Ah! There you are, my fine young man. Your days of

hardship are nearly over; you'll get a commission. Monsieur Rabourdin will be appointed. Weren't you at Madame Rabourdin's last night? Aren't you the lucky one to go there! They say that really splendid women go there."

Sébastien: "I wouldn't know."

Fleury: "Are you blind?"

Sébastien: "I don't like to look at what I can't have."

Phellion (delighted): "Well said, young man!"

Vimeux: "You paid close attention to Madame Rabourdin, you devil! A charming woman."

Fleury: "Pooh! Thin as a rail. I saw her in the Tuileries, and I much prefer Percilliée, the mistress of Ballet, the victim of Castaing."

Phellion: "What does an actress have in common with the wife of a bureau chief?"

Dutocq: "They both play a comedy."

Fleury (looking at Dutocq with a scowl): "The physical has nothing to do with the moral, and if you mean . . ."

Dutocq: "I don't mean anything."

Fleury: "Of all the employees, who will be bureau chief? Do you want to know?"

All: "Tell us!"

Fleury: "Colleville."

Thuillier: "Why?"

Fleury: "Because Madame Colleville has taken the shortest path—the way of the sacristy."

Thuillier (dryly): "I am too good a friend of Colleville's not to ask you, Monsieur Fleury, not to speak lightly of his wife."

Phellion: "Women should never, without any means of defense, be the subject of our conversations. . . ."

Vimeux: "All the more so because the charming Madame Colleville didn't invite Fleury to her house, so he backbites her in revenge. . . ."

Fleury: "She did not see fit to receive me on the same footing as Thuillier, but I went. . . ."

Thuillier: "When? Where? Under the windows?"

Although Fleury was dreaded in the bureaus for his boisterousness, he quietly accepted Thuillier's last word. This resignation, which surprised the employees, was owing to a two-hundred-franc note, with a rather dubious signature, that Thuillier was to present to Mademoiselle Thuillier, his sister. After this skirmish, a dead silence prevailed. Everyone worked from one to three o'clock. Du Bruel did not return.

Around three-thirty, the preparations for departure—the brushing of hats, the changing of coats—went on simultaneously in all the offices of the Ministry. That precious half-hour spent on little personal cares cut the workday by just that much more. At that time, the overheated rooms cool down, the odor particular to the offices evaporates, silence is restored. By four o'clock, only the real employees are left, those who take their positions seriously. A minister can tell who the real workers are in his ministry by walking around at four on the dot, a sort of spying in which none of these grave figures indulges. At this hour, in the courtyards, various chiefs run into each other and exchange opinions on the day's events. In general, going off in twos and threes, they decided in Rabourdin's favor; but the old veterans like Monsieur Clergeot shook their heads, saying, *Habent sua sidera lites*. Saillard and Baudoyer were politely avoided, for nobody knew what to say to them about La Billardière's death, and everybody knew that Baudoyer desired the post, though it was certainly not his due.

When the son and the father-in-law were at a given distance from the Ministry, Saillard broke the silence, saying, "Things don't look good for you, my poor Baudoyer."

"I don't understand," replied the chief, "what Elisabeth has in mind by using Godard to have a passport made up for Falleix in such a hurry. Godard tells me she hired a post chaise on the advice of my Uncle Mitral, and that by now Falleix has already started off for his home county."

"Surely a matter connected with our business," said Saillard.

"Our most pressing business just now is to see to Monsieur de La Billardière's position."

They were just then near the entrance of the Palais-Royal in the rue Saint-Honoré. Dutocq greeted and joined them.

"Monsieur," he said to Baudoyer, "if I can be of any help to you under the circumstances, pray command me, for I am no less devoted to your interests than Monsieur Godard."

"Such an assurance is at least comforting," replied Baudoyer. "One has the good favor of honest men."

"If you were to exercise your influence to get me placed with you as deputy chief and take on Bixiou as your chief, you would secure the future of two men able to do anything for your advancement."

"Are you making fun of us, monsieur?" asked Saillard, staring at him with a stupid look.

"Far be it from me to do that," said Dutocq. "I have just come from delivering the obituary notice of Monsieur de La Billardière to the newspaper printer's office on behalf of Monsieur the Secretary-General. The article I read about you over there has given me the highest opinion of your talents. When the time comes to crush Rabourdin, I'm in a position to deal him the final blow; keep that in mind."

Dutocq disappeared.

"I'll be hanged if I understand a single word of that," said the cashier, looking at Baudoyer, whose little eyes expressed utter bewilderment. "I'll have to get the newspaper tonight."

When Saillard and his son-in-law entered the salon on the ground floor, they found a large fire going, and Madame Saillard, Elisabeth, Monsieur Gaudron, and the curate of Saint-Paul's. The curate turned to Monsieur Baudoyer, to whom his wife made a sign that was poorly understood.

"Monsieur," said the curate, "I have lost no time in coming to thank you for the magnificent gift with which you have adorned my poor church. I dared not run into debt to buy that beautiful monstrance, worthy of a cathedral. You, one of our most pious and assiduous parishioners, must have been struck more than others by the bareness of the high altar. I will be on my way in just a few minutes to see Monseigneur the Coadjutor, and he will shortly convey his personal thanks to you."

"I haven't done anything yet . . . ," began Baudoyer.

"Monsieur le Curé," interposed his wife, cutting him short, "may I betray his whole secret? Monsieur Baudoyer hopes to complete the gift by sending you a dais for the upcoming Fête-Dieu. But this acquisition depends to some extent upon the state of our finances, and our finances depend upon our promotion."

"God rewards those who honor Him," said Monsieur Gaudron, withdrawing with the curate.

"But," said Saillard to Monsieur Gaudron and the curate, "won't you do us the honor of taking potluck with us?"

"Do stay, my dear vicar," said the curate to Gaudron. "You know I have been invited by Monsieur le Curé of Saint-Roch, who is to inter Monsieur de La Billardière tomorrow."

"Monsieur le Curé de Saint-Roch might put in a word for us?" asked Baudoyer, as his wife violently tugged at his coattails.

"Do be quiet, Baudoyer," she said to him, drawing him aside to whisper in his ear: "You have given the parish a monstrance worth five thousand francs. I'll explain everything later."

The avaricious Baudoyer made a horrible grimace and remained pensive throughout dinner.

"Why did you go to so much trouble about Falleix's passport? What are you mixed up in?" he finally asked her.

"It seems to me that Falleix's affairs are a little our own, too," returned Elisabeth dryly, glaring at her husband to make him notice Monsieur Gaudron, in front of whom he ought to keep still.

"Certainly," said old Saillard, thinking of his investment.

"You got to the newspaper office in time, I hope?" asked Elisabeth of Monsieur Gaudron as she served him the soup.

"Yes, my dear lady," answered the vicar. "As soon as the editor read the little article written by the secretary of the Grand Almoner, he was no longer the least bit of trouble. The little blurb was, thanks to him, put in the most appropriate place, which I never would have thought of, but this young man at the paper was very much on top of things. The defenders of religion can enter the lists against impiety without disadvantage, for there is a great deal of talent in the royalist newspapers. I have every reason to believe that success will crown your hopes. But remember, my dear Baudoyer, to foster Monsieur Colleville; he is the object of His Eminence's attention; I was told to mention him to you."

"If I am division chief, I will make him one of my bureau chiefs if he likes!" said Baudoyer.

The clue to the puzzle arrived after dinner. The ministerial newsletter, picked up by the porter, contained among its Paris news, the following two articles or paragraphs.

Monsieur le Baron de La Billardière died this morning, after a prolonged and painful illness. In him, the king loses a devoted servant, the church, one of its most pious sons. Monsieur de La Billardière's end was a worthy crown to his noble life, entirely consecrated in troubled times to perilous missions, and then later devoted to the most arduous of tasks. Monsieur de La Billardière was provost of a department, where his strength of character triumphed over all the obstacles multiplied by the rebellion. He subsequently accepted a very trying directorship, where his light was no less useful than the graciousness of French manners in conciliating the weighty matters thereto pertaining. No rewards have ever been more truly deserved than those with which King Louis XVIII and His Majesty took pleasure in crowning a loyalty that never faltered under the usurper. This old family lives on in a son as heir to the talents and devotion of the outstanding man whose death now afflicts so many warm friends. Already, His Majesty has let it be known in a gracious word that Monsieur Benjamin de La Billardière is counted among the Gentlemen-in-Ordinary of the Bedchamber.

The numerous friends who have not already received notification of this sad event, or will not receive it in time, are hereby informed that the funeral will take place tomorrow at four o'clock, at the church of Saint-Roch. The eulogy will be delivered by Monsieur l'Abbé Fontanon.

Monsieur Isidore Baudoyer, representing one of the oldest bourgeois families of Paris and bureau chief in Monsieur de La Billardière's division, has lately revived memories of the old traditions of piety that distinguished these great families, so jealous of the splendor of Religion, and so in love with her monuments. The church of Saint-Paul has lacked a monstrance in keeping with the magnificence of that basilica, owing to the Society of Jesus. Neither the vestry nor the curate was endowed to decorate the altar. Monsieur Baudoyer has bestowed upon the parish the monstrance that many persons have admired at Monsieur Gohier's, the king's goldsmith. Thanks to this pious gentleman, who did not shrink from the immensity of the price, the church of Saint-Paul today possesses this masterpiece of the goldsmith's art, executed from Monsieur de Sommervieux's designs. It gives us pleasure to publish a fact that proves how empty the declamations of liberalism have been in the spirit of the Parisian bourgeoisie. For all time, the upper bourgeoisie has been Royalist, and will always prove to be Royalist when called upon.

"The price was five thousand francs," said the Abbé Gaudron. "But since the payment was in cash, the court goldsmith lowered his price."

"'Representing one of the oldest bourgeois families of Paris'!" repeated Saillard to himself. "There it is in print, and even in the official newspaper!"

"Dear Monsieur Gaudron, do help my father come up with a little word or two he could slip into Madame la Comtesse's ear when he takes her the monthly allowance, a single sentence that would say it all! I must leave you. I must go out with my Uncle Mitral. Would you believe it, I could not find my Uncle Bidault this afternoon. Oh, what a kennel he lives in! Then, Monsieur Mitral, who knows his ways, said he finishes his work between eight o'clock and noon, and that after that he can only be found at a so-called Café Thémis, a rather odd name. . . . "

"Is justice meted out there?" said the Abbé Gaudron, laughing.

"How does he get to a café at the corner of the rue Dauphine and the Quai des Augustins? Yet they say he plays dominoes there every night with his friend Monsieur Gobseck. I don't want to go there all alone, my uncle is taking me and bringing me home."

At this moment Mitral showed his yellow face below a wig that seemed to be made of straw bristles and made a sign to his niece to come at once so as not to waste time at two francs an hour. Madame Baudoyer rose and left without explaining anything to her father or husband.

"Heaven," said Monsieur Gaudron to Baudoyer when Elisabeth had disappeared, "has granted you this woman, a perfect treasure of prudence and virtue, a model of wisdom, a Christian in whom is found divine understanding. Religion alone is able to form a character so complete. Tomorrow I shall say a mass for the success of the good cause. You must, in the interests of the monarchy and religion, be appointed. Monsieur Rabourdin is a Liberal, a subscriber to the 'Journal des Débats,' a dangerous newspaper that attacked Monsieur le Comte de Villèle to serve the frustrated interests of Monsieur de Chateaubriand. His Eminence will read the newspaper tonight, if only on account of his poor friend Monsieur de La Billardière, and Monseigneur the Coadjutor will talk about you and Rabourdin. I know him, Monsieur le Curé. When you think of his precious church, he won't forget you in his sermon. More than that, he has the honor at this very moment of dining with the coadjutor at the Curate of Saint-Roch's."

These words made Saillard and Baudoyer begin to see that Elisabeth had not been idle ever since the moment Godard had informed her.

"Isn't she sharp, that 'Lisabeth of mine!" cried Saillard, appreciating more clearly than Monsieur l'Abbé the rapid, molelike progress his daughter had made.

"She sent Godard to Monsieur Rabourdin's to find out which newspaper he takes," said Gaudron, "and I mentioned it to the secretary of His Eminence, for we live at a time when the church and the throne must recognize who are their friends and who are their enemies."

"It's been five days that I have been trying to find the right thing to say to His Excellency's wife," said Saillard.

"All Paris reads this," cried Baudoyer, whose eyes were riveted on the paper.

"Your eulogy cost us four thousand eight hundred francs, my sonny boy!" exclaimed Madame Saillard.

"You have adorned the house of God," replied the Abbé Gaudron.

"We could have gotten salvation without that," she retorted. "But if Baudoyer gets the post, it's worth another eight thousand, so the sacrifice isn't that great. And if he doesn't get it? Hey, mama!" she added, looking at her husband. "What a drain! . . ."

"Oh well," said Saillard, enthusiastically, "we'll make it up through Falleix, who is going to expand his business and tap his brother, whom he has made a stockbroker on purpose. Elisabeth could have told us why Falleix took off. But let's think of a line. This is what I've come up with: 'Madame, if you would say a word to His Excellency . . .'"

"Not, 'would say,'" said Gaudron; "'would deign,' to sound more respectful. Besides, you must know, above all, whether Madame la Dauphine will grant you her protection, for then you could suggest to her the idea of cooperating with the wishes of Her Royal Highness."

"You ought to mention the vacant post," said Baudoyer.

"'Madame la Comtesse,'" began Saillard, getting up and glancing over toward his wife with an agreeable smile.

"Christ! Saillard, you look ridiculous like that! Look out, my boy, you're going to make that woman laugh."

"'Madame la Comtesse.' Is that better?" he said, looking at his wife.

"Yes, my darling."

"'The post of the worthy late Monsieur La Billardière is vacant. My son-in-law, Monsieur Baudoyer . . . '"

"'Man of talent and extreme piety,'" prompted Gaudron.

"Write, Baudoyer," cried father Saillard, "write the sentence down."

Baudoyer simply took up a pen and wrote, without a blush, his own praises, precisely as Nathan or Canalis might have reviewed one of their own books.

"'Madame la Comtesse . . .' Don't you see, mother," said Saillard to his wife, "I am pretending you are the minister's wife."

"Do you think I'm stupid? I figured *that* out," she retorted.

"'The place of the worthy late Monsieur de La Billardière is vacant; my son-in-law, Monsieur Baudoyer, a man of consummate talent and extreme piety . . . '" After looking at Monsieur Gaudron, who was reflecting, he added, "'. . . would be very happy to have it.' Ha! That's not bad; it's short and says it all."

"But just wait, Saillard. Don't you see that Monsieur l'Abbé has something on his mind? Don't disturb him."

"'. . . would be very happy if you would deign to interest yourself on his behalf,'" resumed Gaudron, "'and in saying a few words to His Excellency you will particularly please Madame la Dauphine, by whom he has the honor of being protected.'"

"Ah! Monsieur Gaudron, that sentence itself is worth the monstrance. I'm not so sorry about the four thousand eight hundred. . . . Besides, Baudoyer my lad, you'll repay them! Have you got it all down?"

"I'll have you repeat that, my mother," said Madame Saillard, "and you'll recite it for me morning and night. Yes, it certainly is well polished, it is, that line! How lucky you are, Monsieur Gaudron, to be so smart. That's what it is to have studied in seminaries; you learn how to speak to God and his saints."

"He is as good as he is smart," said Baudoyer, pressing the priest's hands. "Did you write that article?" he asked, pointing to the newspaper.

"No," answered Gaudron," that article was written by the secretary to His Eminence, a young abbé who is greatly indebted to me and who takes an interest in Monsieur Colleville. I paid his tuition at seminary."

"A good deed is always rewarded," said Baudoyer.

While these four were sitting down to their game of Boston, Elisabeth and her Uncle Mitral reached the Café Thémis, after having discussed on the way the issue of what Elisabeth's tact had come up with as the strongest lever by which to force the minister's hand. Uncle Mitral, a former bailiff well versed in chicanery and full of expedients and legal precautions, saw the honor of his family involved in the appointment of his nephew. His avarice had led him to sound out the contents of old Gigonnet's strongbox, and so he knew his nephew Baudoyer would be the successor; he therefore wanted a position in keeping with the fortunes of the Saillards and old Gigonnet, all of which would go to the little Baudoyer girl. And what couldn't she be with an income of a hundred thousand francs! He adopted the ideas of his niece Elisabeth and thoroughly understood them. Also, he had helped Falleix hurry off, explaining to him how much faster it was to travel by post. Then, over dinner, he had thought about the twist he wanted to work in the sting dreamed up by Elisabeth.

When they reached the Café Thémis he told his niece that he alone could manage the deal with Gigonnet, and he made her wait in the coach so she could come in at the right moment and in the right place. Through the windows Elisabeth saw the faces of Gobseck and her Uncle Bidault, which stood out against the bright-yellow background of the old café's paneling like two cameo heads, cold and impassive in the rigid mien their engraver had impressed upon them. These two avaricious Parisians were surrounded by old faces on which "thirty-percent discount" seemed to be written in circular wrinkles that started at the nose and came up around the glacial cheekbones. These remarkable physiognomies brightened up on seeing Mitral, and their eyes gleamed with tigerish curiosity.

"Hey, hey! It's Papa Mitral!" cried Chaboisseau, this little old man who discounted for a bookstore.

"Yes, my word!" answered a paper merchant named Métivier. "Ah, it's an old dog who knows every trick."

"And you, you're an old crow you recognize from among corpses," retorted Mitral.

"True," said the stern Gobseck.

"What are you here for, my boy? Come to seize our friend Métivier?" asked Gigonnet, pointing to the paper merchant, who had the whiskey-worn face of a retired porter.

"Your great-niece Elisabeth is here, Papa Gigonnet," whispered Mitral in his ear.

"What! Bad news?" asked Bidault.

The old man scowled and assumed the tender air of an executioner about to go to work. In spite of his Roman look, he must have been touched, for his very red nose lost some of its color.

"Well, suppose it is misfortune, wouldn't you help out Saillard's daughter, a girl who's been knitting your socks for the last thirty years!" cried Mitral.

"If it's safe, I won't say no!" replied Gigonnet. "Falleix is in with them. Your Falleix has just set up his brother as a broker; he's doing as much business as the Brézacs, and with what! . . . his brains? Right! Well, Saillard's no new kid on the block."

"He knows the value of money," said Chaboisseau.

That remark, uttered among these old men, would have made an artist shudder, as they all nodded their heads.

"But the problems of those around me are none of my business," went on Bidault-Gigonnet. "My principle is never to be off my guard with friends or relatives, because you only die as a result of your weakest spot. Go talk to Gobseck, he's soft."

The discounters all applauded these doctrines with a shake of their metallic heads, and anyone watching them would have thought he was hearing the squeaks of poorly greased machinery.

"Come, Gigonnet, show a little tenderness," said Chaboisseau. "They've knit your stockings for thirty years."

"That counts for something," added Gobseck.

"Are you all alone? . . . can we talk?" said Mitral after carefully examining the heads around him. "I come with a good piece of business."

"Why are you coming to us if it's so good?" said Gigonnet bitterly, interrupting Mitral.

"A fellow who was Gentleman of the Bedchamber, an old *chouan*, his name? . . . La Billardière is dead."

"Right," said Gobseck.

"And the nephew is giving monstrances to churches!" said Gigonnet.

"He is not such a fool as to give them; he sells them, old man," said Mitral proudly. "It's a question of Monsieur de La Billardière's post, and in order to get it, you must seize . . ."

"*Seize*! you're ever a bailiff," said Métivier, striking Mitral kindly on the shoulder. "I like that, I do!"

" . . . seize one Monsieur Chardin des Lupeaulx in our clutches," continued Mitral. "Elisabeth has discovered how, and he is . . ."

"Elisabeth!" cried Gigonnet, interrupting again. "Dear little creature, she takes after her grandfather, my poor brother! Bidault never had his equal! Ah, if you'd seen him at old furniture sales—what tact! what shrewdness! What does she want?"

"Hey, hey!" cried Mitral. "How quickly you regain your bowels of compassion, Papa Gigonnet! This phenomenon must have its reasons."

"You kid," said Gobseck to Gigonnet. "You always jump the gun."

"Come, Gobseck and Gigonnet, my masters, you need des Lupeaulx; don't you remember having plucked him? Are you afraid he'll ask for some of his feathers back?" said Mitral.

"Can we tell him the whole thing?" Gobseck asked Gigonnet.

"Mitral is one of us; he wouldn't play a nasty trick on his old customers," replied Gigonnet. "Okay, Mitral, we had, just between the three of us," he said in the bailiff's ear, "bought some debts, the payment of which depends on the decision of the Liquidation Committee."

"How much can you lose?" asked Mitral.

"Nothing," said Gobseck.

"Nobody knows we are in it," added Gigonnet. "Samanon is our front man."

"Listen to me, Gigonnet," said Mitral. "It's cold and your niece is waiting. You'll get it in three words. You must, between the two of you, without interest, send two hundred and fifty thousand francs to Falleix, who at this moment is tearing up the road thirty leagues from Paris with a courier out in front."

"Is that possible?" said Gobseck.

"Why, he's on his way to the magnificent lands of des Lupeaulx," replied Mitral. "He knows the country; he is going to buy around the secretary-general's shack, for the said two hundred and fifty thousand francs, prime land, always worth its price. We have nine days to record the notarized deeds (don't forget that!). With this little addition, des Lupeaulx's property will pay one thousand francs in taxes. Ergo, des Lupeaulx becomes an elector of the Grand Collège—eligible, count, and whatever he pleases! Do you know which deputy has stepped down?"

The two misers nodded in agreement.

"Des Lupeaulx would cut off a leg to be a deputy," continued Mitral, "but he wants to have in his name the title deeds that we'll show him, mortgaged, of course, for our loans with the right to foreclose and sell. . . . (Ha! Ha! Are you with me?) First of all, we must get Baudoyer's appointment. Then we'll hand des Lupeaulx back over to you! Falleix will stay in the country and get the electoral matters set up; and so you have a loaded gun at des Lupeaulx's head through Falleix for the duration of the election, since this is a regional one in which Falleix's friends make up the majority. Now do you see Falleix's hand in all this, Papa Gigonnet?"

"I see Mitral's in it too," said Métivier. "It's well done."

"We'll go for it," said Gigonnet, "right Gobseck? Falleix can sign the counterdeeds and will put the mortgages in his name; we'll go and see des Lupeaulx when the time is right."

"And us," said Gobseck, "we're robbed!"

"Ha, papa?" said Mitral. "I'd love to meet the thief."

"Hey! Nobody can be robbed except by himself," answered Gigonnet. "I told you we were doing good business in buying up the debts from all des Lupeaulx's creditors at sixty-percent discount."

"You'll mortgage his estate and you'll hold him still tighter through the interest," answered Mitral.

"Maybe," said Gobseck.

After exchanging a sharp look with Gobseck, Bidault, alias Gigonnet, went to the door of the café.

"Elisabeth, run along, my girl," he said to his niece. "We have your man, but don't forget the details. The wheels are rolling, how clever! Succeed, you have your uncle's best wishes!" and he grasped her hand playfully.

"But," said Mitral, "Métivier and Chaboisseau may pull a fast one on us by going to an Opposition paper tonight, playing the ball on the rebound and striking back for the ministerial article. You go on alone, my dear, I don't want to let those two cormorants get away." And he proceeded to go back into the café.

"Tomorrow the funds will go out to their destinations at the word of the Receiver-General; we shall raise, among 'friends,' a hundred thousand ecus of his own paper," said Gigonnet to Mitral as the bailiff came over to talk to the lender.

The next day the many subscribers to a certain Liberal journal read in the Paris news a short article, inserted on the authority of Chaboisseau and Métivier, shareholders in the two newspapers, brokers for publishers, printers, and paper manufacturers, whose wishes no editor dared refuse:

Yesterday a ministerial paper evidently named the successor of Monsieur le Baron de La Billardière as Monsieur Baudoyer, one of the worthiest citizens of a populous district where his benevolence is scarcely less known than the piety on which the ministerial paper placed so much emphasis. It could have mentioned his abilities! Or did it feel that in praising the long bourgeois tradition of Monsieur Baudoyer, which certainly is a nobility as good as any other, it would point out a reason for the probable exclusion of the candidate? Gratuitous treachery! The good lady pets the one she is about to kill; what else is new! To appoint Monsieur Baudoyer would be to do honor to the virtues, the talents of the middle classes, of whom we shall ever be the supporters even though we may often feel our cause is lost. This appointment would be an act of justice and good policy; the minister will not stand for it. The religious paper has, this time, more sense than its patrons; we will have to set it straight.

The next morning, Friday, the usual day for Madame Rabourdin's dinner, which des Lupeaulx had left at midnight dazzled by beauty, on Bouffon's staircase, as he lent his arm to Madame de Camps (Madame Firmiani had recently married), the old roué awoke, his thoughts of vengeance calmed, or rather refreshed: his mind was filled with the last glance exchanged with Célestine.

"I'll make sure of Rabourdin's support by forgiving him now; I'll get even with him later. For the time being, if he didn't have his post I would have to give up a woman who is capable of becoming a most precious instrument of high political fortune. She understands everything, shrinks from nothing; and besides, I can't know before the minister does what new administrative scheme Rabourdin has dreamed up! No, my dear des Lupeaulx, the task at hand is to conquer all for your Célestine. You may have made a face, Madame la Comtesse, but you will invite Madame Rabourdin to your next intimate soirée."

Des Lupeaulx was one of those men who, to satisfy a passion, are quite able to store away revenge in some remote corner of their hearts. His mind was made up; he resolved to get Rabourdin appointed.

"I will prove to you, my dear chief, that I deserve a good place in your diplomatic ranks," he thought to himself as he sat down in his study and began to unfold the newspapers.

He already knew all too well, at five o'clock, what the ministerial paper would say to bother reading it, but opened it to look at the article on La Billardière, thinking of the predicament in which du Bruel had placed him by bringing him that satire by Bixiou. He could not keep from laughing as he reread the biography of the late comte de Fontaine, who had died a few months earlier, and which he had reprinted for La Billardière, when all of a sudden his eyes were struck by the name of Baudoyer. He read with fury the specious article that undermined the minister. He rang furiously and called for Dutocq, to send him at once to the newspaper office. But imagine his surprise on reading the reply of the Opposition paper, for it happened to be the Liberal paper he had first got his hands on. The situation was serious. He knew the game, and the man who was shuffling his cards for him was a Greek of the first order. So adroitly to engage two opposing newspapers at the same time, and in the same evening, and to start the fight by guessing the intentions of the minister! He recognized the hand of a Liberal editor he knew and resolved to question him that night at the opera. Dutocq appeared.

"Read that," said des Lupeaulx, handing him the two papers and continuing to scan the other papers to see if Baudoyer had struck any other chords. "Go find out who dared to compromise the minister like this."

"It was not Monsieur Baudoyer, though," answered Dutocq, "for he never left his office yesterday. I don't need to go to the newspaper. When I took your article over there yesterday, I saw the abbé, who came with a letter from the Grand Almoner, before which you yourself would have had to give in."

"Dutocq, you have a grudge against Monsieur Rabourdin, and it isn't right, for he has twice kept you from being dismissed. However, we are not masters of our own feelings; one sometimes hates one's benefactor. Only, remember this, if you indulge in the slightest treachery against Rabourdin before I give you the word, it will be your loss; count me as your enemy. As to my friend's newspaper, let the Grand Almonry subscribe as heavily as we do if it wants its exclusive services. We're at the end of the year, the matter of subscriptions will come up for discussion, and will we agree? As for La Billardière's post, there is only one way to settle the matter, and that is to make the appointment this very day."

"Gentlemen," said Dutocq, returning to the bureau and addressing his colleagues, "I don't know if Bixiou has the gift of seeing into the future, but if you haven't read the ministerial paper, I advise you to study the article about Baudoyer; then, since Monsieur Fleury has the Opposition paper, you can see the reply. Certainly, Monsieur Rabourdin has talent, but these days a man who gives a six-thousand-franc monstrance to the church has a devilish sort of talent, too."

Bixiou (entering): "What do you say to the First Letter to the Corinthians in our religious newspaper today, and of the Epistle to the Ministers in the Liberal paper? How's Monsieur Rabourdin, du Bruel?"

Du Bruel (coming in): "I don't know. (He takes Bixiou into his office and says in a low voice): My good friend, your way of helping people is more like that of an executioner who pulls your feet over your shoulders to break your neck all the faster. You got me a licking from des Lupeaulx that was stupidity deserved. It was nice, that article on La Billardière! I won't forget *that* one. The first sentence seemed to say to the king, 'You should die.' The one about Quiberon left no doubt that the king is a. . . . At any rate, everything was ironic."

Bixiou (laughing): "Oh come! Can't a fellow make a joke?"

Du Bruel: "Joke! Joke! When you want to be deputy chief somebody will hand you a joke, my friend."

Bixiou (in a bullying tone): "Are we angry?"

Du Bruel: "Yes!"

Bixiou (dryly): "Well then, too bad for you."

Du Bruel (uneasy): "Would *you* ever forgive this sort of thing?"

Bixiou (coaxing): "Of a friend? Indeed I would. (They hear

Fleury's voice.) There goes Fleury cursing Baudoyer. Hey, did things work out well? Baudoyer will get the post. (Confidentially): After all, so much the better. Du Bruel, just keep your eye on the consequences. Rabourdin would be a weakling to stay under Baudoyer; he'll hand in his resignation and that'll give us two positions. You'll be chief and you'll take me as deputy chief. We'll do vaudevilles together, and I'll slave away at the work in the office."

Du Bruel (smiling): "Well, I never thought of that. Poor Rabourdin! I'll feel sorry for him, though."

Bixiou: "So! That's how you love him! (Changing his tone.) Oh well, I don't pity him either. After all, he's rich; his wife gives parties and doesn't invite me—me, who goes everywhere! Come now, my dear du Bruel, good-bye, and don't hold a grudge! (He leaves by way of the office.) Adieu, gentlemen. Didn't I tell you yesterday that a man who has nothing but virtues and talents will always be poor, even with a pretty wife?"

Fleury: "You're so rich yourself!"

Bixiou: "Not bad, dear Cincinnatus! But you owe me a dinner at the Rocher de Cancale."

Poiret: "I simply cannot understand Monsieur Bixiou."

Phellion (with an elegiac air): "Monsieur Rabourdin so seldom reads the newspapers that it might perhaps be useful to bring them to him by momentarily depriving ourselves of them." (Fleury hands over his paper, Vimeux the office one. He takes the papers and leaves.)

At that moment, des Lupeaulx, on his way down to breakfast with the minister, asked himself whether, before using the sweet flower of his cunning on the husband, prudence might not dictate the sounding out of the wife's heart so as to make sure of a reward for his dedication. He was feeling the beat of what little heart he had when, on the staircase, he ran into his lawyer, who said to him, smiling, "Just a couple of words, Monseigneur," in that tone of familiarity assumed by men who know they are indispensable.

"What is it, my dear Desroches?" exclaimed the politician. "What has happened? These gentlemen get upset and cannot do as I do—wait!"

"I've come to warn you that all your debts are in the hands of the two Monsieurs Gobseck and Gigonnet, under the name of Samanon."

"Men whom I helped to make fortunes!"

"Listen," said the lawyer in his ear, "Gigonnet is named Bidault; he is the uncle of Saillard, your cashier, and Saillard is father-in-law to a certain Baudoyer, who thinks he has a right to the vacant post in your ministry. Wasn't I right to warn you?"

"Thank you," said des Lupeaulx, nodding to the lawyer with a shrewd look.

"One stroke of your pen and you're off the hook," said Desroches, leaving him.

"What a huge sacrifice!" muttered des Lupeaulx to himself. "It's impossible to explain it to a woman," he thought. "Is Célestine worth the clearing up of all my debts? I'll go and see her this morning."

And so the lovely Madame Rabourdin was to be, within a few hours, the arbiter of her husband's fate, and no power on earth could warn her of the importance of her replies or give her the least hint that she should guard her conduct and control her voice. And, unfortunately, she was sure of success, never dreaming that Rabourdin was being undermined in all directions by the silent work of the teredos.

"Well, Monseigneur," said des Lupeaulx, entering the little salon where they breakfasted, "have you read the articles on Baudoyer?"

"For God's sake, my dear friend," replied the minister, "let's forget those appointments just now! They cracked my ears last night with that monstrance. To save Rabourdin, I would have to make his promotion a matter for the Council if I don't want my hand forced. It's enough to disgust a man with public service. To keep Rabourdin, we have to promote a certain Colleville. . . . "

"Would you leave the management of this vaudeville to me and rid yourself of the worry? I could amuse you every morning with an account of the chess moves I make against the Grand Almonry," said des Lupeaulx.

"Very well," said the minister, "settle it with the chief of staff. You know nothing is more likely to strike the king's mind than those reasons in the Opposition paper. You try and run a ministry with Baudoyers!"

"A pious imbecile," said des Lupeaulx, "and as incapable as . . ."

". . . as La Billardière," finished the minister.

"But La Billardière at least had the manners of a Gentleman-in-Ordinary-of-the-Bedchamber," replied des Lupeaulx. "Madame," he continued, addressing the Countess, "it is now an absolute necessity that you invite Madame Rabourdin to your next intimate soirée. May I point out that she is a friend of Madame de Camps? They were together last night at Les Italiens. I first met her at the Hôtel Firmiani; besides, you will see whether she is of a nature to compromise a salon."

"Invite Madame Rabourdin, my dear," said the minister, "and let's talk about something else."

"So Célestine is in my clutches," said des Lupeaulx on his way back up to his room to dress for the day.

PART III

To Whom the Place?

Scenes from the Home Front

Parisian households are literally consumed with the desire to be in keeping with the luxury that surrounds them on all sides; furthermore, there are few who have the wisdom to let their external situation conform to their internal budget. But this vice is perhaps linked to a truly French patriotism, whose aim is to preserve France's supremacy in matters of fashion. France reigns through clothes over the whole of Europe, where everyone feels the need to hold a commercial scepter that makes fashion in France what the navy is in England. This patriotic ardor that leads a nation to sacrifice everything to appearances—to the *paroistre*, as d'Aubigné said in the days of Henri IV—is the cause of those great and secret labors which take up the entire morning for Parisian women, when they choose, as Madame Rabourdin did, to maintain on twelve thousand francs a year the style that many a wealthy woman does not indulge in with thirty thousand. And so, on the day of her dinner parties, Madame Rabourdin helped the chambermaid do up the rooms, for the cook went early to Les Halles and the manservant was cleaning the silver, folding the napkins, and polishing the glasses. The ill-advised individual who might happen, through the porter's oversight, to come up to Madame Rabourdin's around eleven or twelve in the morning, would find her in the midst of a very unsightly disorder—in a housecoat, her feet in old slippers, her hair a mess, trimming the lamps herself, arranging her own flowers, or quickly cooking up an extremely unglamorous breakfast. The visitor to whom the mysteries of Parisian life were unknown would certainly have learned not to step backstage at the theater, and would soon be labeled as a man capable of the darkest of deeds; a woman caught at the mysteries of her mornings would point out his stupidity and indiscretion in a manner to ruin him. Indulgent as the Parisienne is toward that which profits her, she has nothing left over for those who embarrass her. Furthermore, is not domestic invasion, not only in police terms, an invasion of privacy, the theft of that most precious of all things, *credibility*? A woman will allow herself to be surprised half-dressed, with her hair down; if her hair is her own, she scores. But she does not want to be caught doing her own housework, or she loses her *paroistre*!

Madame Rabourdin was in the full swing of preparations for her Friday, surrounded by groceries the cook had just fished from the vast ocean of Les Halles, when Monsieur des Lupeaulx slyly made his way in. The secretary-general was certainly the last person the lovely Rabourdin expected, and what's more, when she heard boots creaking on the landing, she exclaimed, "The hairdresser already!" an exclamation as little agreeable to des Lupeaulx as the sight of des Lupeaulx was agreeable to her. She immediately took refuge in her bedroom, where a huge mess of unsightly furniture prevailed, a mix of stuff of more, or rather less, elegance, a real in-house flea market. The brazen des Lupeaulx followed the lovely fugitive, so piquant did he find her in her dishabille. Who knows what enticement caught his eye: the body seen through a veil of camisole seemed a thousand times more alluring than when it gracefully rose from the curve of her back up to the vanishing line of the prettiest swan's neck that ever a lover had kissed before a ball. When the eye wanders over a woman fully dressed, showing a magnificent chest, does one not imagine dessert after a wonderful dinner? But the eye that glides across fabric wrinkled by sleep discovers secret delicacies and feasts upon it as one would devour a forbidden fruit dangling between two leaves on a trellis.

"Wait! Wait!" cried the pretty Parisienne, locking away her mess.

She rang for Thérèse, called for her daughter, the cook, and the manservant, asking for a shawl and hoping for the crew's whistle blow, as at the Opéra. And the whistle passed. With a sleight of hand, another phenomenon! The room assumed that distinctive morning air quite in keeping with an impromptu toilette put together for the glory of this woman, evidently superior in these matters.

"You!" she said, coming forward. "At this hour? What is going on?"

"Some of the most important things ever," answered des Lupeaulx. "You and I must come to an understanding today."

Célestine saw straight through this man hiding behind his glasses, and understood.

"My principal vice," she said, "is being extremely whimsical, and so I do not mix my feelings with politics. Let us talk politics, business, and then we shall see. Besides, it is not a whim, but rather a result of my artistic taste that forbids me to mix colors and put together disparate things, which compels me to avoid clashes. We women also have our policies!"

Already the tones of her voice and the charm of her manners were producing their effect and transformed the coarseness of the secretary-general into sentimental courtesy; she had reminded him of his obligations as a lover. A fine and clever woman creates about her an atmosphere in which nerves relax and feelings soften.

"You are ignorant of what is going on," said des Lupeaulx, harshly, thinking it best to maintain a show of severity. "Read that."

He gave the gracious Rabourdin the two newspapers in which he had circled each article in red ink. As she read, her shawl slipped aside without Célestine noticing, or seeming to notice. At the age when the power of fantasies increases with their frequency, des Lupeaulx could not keep up his cold front any more than Célestine could.

"What!" she exclaimed. "But this is dreadful! Who is this Baudoyer?"

"An ass," answered des Lupeaulx. "But you see, he bears relics, and thanks to the clever hand that pulls his bridle, he will get there."

The thought of her debts crossed Madame Rabourdin's mind and dazed her, as if two lightning flashes had blinded both eyes at once; her ears buzzed under the heightened pressure of the blood that pounded in her arteries; she remained quite bewildered for a moment, staring at a curtain hook without actually seeing it.

"But how faithful you are!" she said to des Lupeaulx, stroking him with a glance to hook him.

"That depends," he replied, answering her glance with a questioning look that made the poor woman blush.

"If you need a deposit, you will lose the prize," she said, laughing. "I thought you more magnanimous. And you, you think me quite small, a mere schoolgirl."

"You have misunderstood me," he said in a polished way. "I meant to say that I could not serve a man who plays against me, like l'Etourdi against Mascarille."

"What does this mean?"

"This will prove to you whether I am magnanimous or not."

He handed Madame Rabourdin the memorandum stolen by Dutocq, pointing out to her the passage in which her husband had so shrewdly analyzed him.

"Read that."

Célestine recognized the handwriting, read, and paled under this blow.

"All the ministries are listed," said des Lupeaulx.

"But fortunately," she said, "you alone possess this document, which I myself do not understand."

"The man who stole it is not such a fool as not to have kept a copy; he is too great a liar to admit it, and too clever at his work to give it up. I did not even dare ask him for it."

"Who is he?"

"Your head drafting-clerk."

"Dutocq. You're never punished except for your good deeds! But," she continued," he is only a dog who wants a bone."

"Do you know what I was offered, poor devil of a secretary-general?"

"What?"

"I owe thirty thousand and some odd miserable francs; you will despise me knowing I do not owe more, but in this, I grant you, I am small! Oh well, Baudoyer's uncle has just bought up my debts and is doubtless ready to give me a clear receipt."

"But all that is monstrous."

"Not at all. It is monarchical and religious, for the Grand Almonry is involved. . . ."

"What will you do?"

"What do you bid me do?" he said, holding out his hand with charming grace.

Célestine no longer thought him ugly, or old, or as powdered as a hoarfrost, or as secretary-general, or anything that was filthy and vile, but she did not give him her hand. The other night in her salon she would have let him take it a hundred times, but this morning, alone, the gesture constituted a commitment that was a little too strong and could go too far.

"And they say that statesmen have no heart!" she cried enthusiastically, trying to compensate for the harshness of her refusal by the grace of her words. "That frightened me," she added, assuming the most innocent air in the world.

"What slander!" replied des Lupeaulx. "One of the most impassive diplomats, one who has been in power since he was born, has just married the daughter of an actress, and has had her received in the most rigorous court in the ranks of the nobility."

"You will continue to support us?"

"I draw up the nominations. But no tricks!"

She gave him her hand to kiss and a tap on the cheek as she did so. "You are mine!" she said.

Des Lupeaulx liked that expression. (That night at the Opéra, the conceited old boy related the incident like this: "A woman not wanting to tell a man she was his, an admission a well-bred woman would never make, told him 'You are mine.' Don't you find the evasion charming?")

"But you must be my ally," he answered. "Your husband has spoken to the minister of an administrative plan in connection with the document in which I am so kindly regarded. Find out about it and let me know tonight."

"It will be done," she answered, without attaching great importance to that which had brought des Lupeaulx to her house so early in the morning.

"Madame, the hairdresser," announced the chambermaid.

"He certainly took his time. I don't know how I would have made it if he had been later," she thought.

"You do not know the extent of my devotion," said des Lupeaulx, rising. "You are to be invited to the next select soirée given by His Excellency's wife. . . ."

"Oh, you are an angel!" she cried. "And now I see how much you love me; you love me intelligently."

"This evening, dear child," he said, "at the Opéra I shall find out which journalists are conspiring for Baudoyer, and we will measure swords together."

"Yes, but you will dine here, will you not? I have sought and found the things you like."

"All of this is so much like love that it would be most pleasant to be so deceived for a long time!" des Lupeaulx said to himself as he went downstairs. "But, if she *is* tricking me, I shall find out: I'll set the cleverest of all traps for her before the signing so as to read her heart. Ah! my little cats, don't we know you! For, after all, women are all that we are. Twenty-eight years old, virtuous, and here in the rue Duphot!—a rare piece of luck worth the trouble of cultivating."

The eligible butterfly fluttered down the staircase.

"My God, that man without his glasses, powdered, must look very funny in a dressing gown," thought Célestine. "He has the harpoon in his back and will tow me where I want to go: to the minister's. He has played his part in my comedy."

When at five o'clock Rabourdin arrived home to change, his wife came in to help him dress, bringing him the list which, like the slipper in *One Thousand and One Arabian Nights*, the poor man was fated to meet at every turn.

"Who gave you that?" he asked thunderstruck.

"Monsieur des Lupeaulx!"

"So he has been here!" said Rabourdin, casting a look at his wife that would certainly have made a guilty woman turn pale but that met a marble brow and a laughing eye.

"And he is coming back to dine," she said. "Why such a startled air?"

"My dear," said Rabourdin, "I have mortally offended des Lupeaulx; such men never forgive, and yet he strokes me! Don't you think I see why?"

"The man," she said, "seems to me to have a very fine palate; I can't fault him for that. After all, I cannot think of anything more flattering to a woman than to revive a worn-out palate. After . . ."

"A truce to nonsense, Célestine. Spare an exhausted man. I cannot speak with the minister, and my honor is at stake."

"Good God, no! Dutocq will have the promise of a good post, and you will be named division chief."

"I see what you mean, dear child," said Rabourdin, "but the game you are playing is just as dishonorable as reality. A lie is a lie, and an honest woman . . ."

"So let me use the same weapons that are being used against us."

"Célestine, the more that man feels he is foolishly caught in a trap, the more he will work against me."

"And if I turn him around?"

Rabourdin looked at his wife in amazement.

"I am only thinking of your advancement, and it was about time, my poor love!" continued Célestine. "But you are mistaking the hunting dog for the quarry," she said after a pause. "In a few days des Lupeaulx will have accomplished his mission. While you are trying to speak to the minister, and before you can even see him on business, I will have spoken with him. You have sweat blood and water bearing a plan you have hidden from me, and in three months your wife will have accomplished more than you have in six years. Tell me about your nice little system."

Rabourdin, continuing to shave and after having made his wife promise not to say a word about his work, warning her that to confide a single idea to des Lupeaulx would be to put the cat near the milk jug, began an explanation of his work.

"Rabourdin, why didn't you tell me this before?" said Célestine, cutting off her husband in his fifth sentence. "You could have saved yourself all that useless effort. To be blinded by an idea for a moment, that I can understand, but for six or seven years, that I can't imagine! You want to cut the budget; that's a vulgar and bourgeois idea! Rather, we ought to arrive at a budget of two billion; France would be twice as great. A new system should be one spurred on by borrowing, as put forth by Monsieur de Nucingen. The poorest of all treasuries is the one full of ecus lying idle; the mission of a minister of finance is to fling money out the windows, it will come back to him through the cellars; and you, you want to hoard it! The thing to do is to increase jobs instead of cutting them. Instead of redeeming bonds, you should multiply the number of bondholders. If the Bourbons want to reign in peace, let them create creditors in every last town and village, and above all keep foreigners from touching French interests, for someday they will ask us for the capital. Whereas if all the bonds are in France, neither France nor credit will perish. That's what saved England. Your plan is that of a petit bourgeois. An ambitious man should only approach his minister picking up where Law left off, except for his bad luck, explaining the power of credit, demonstrating that we simply mustn't reduce the principal but interest, as the English do . . ."

"Come, Célestine," said Rabourdin. "Jumble all the ideas together, contradict them, play with them like little games! I'm used to that. But don't criticize a work you know nothing about yet."

"Do I need," she said, "to know a scheme the essence of which is to administer France with six thousand bureaucrats instead of twenty thousand? But, my dear friend, if it were the plan of a man of genius, a king of France would dethrone himself trying to execute it. You can put down a feudal aristocracy by leveling a few heads, but you can't subdue a Hydra with a thousand legs. No, you cannot crush the little folks, they are too flat underfoot. And is it with the present ministers (just between us, sorry lords) that you so want to shake men up? You can shake up interests, but you cannot shake up men: they cry out, whereas ecus are dumb."

"But, Célestine, if you keep talking and putting off the issue because of feelings, we shall never come to an understanding. . . . "

"Ah! I understand what that paper in which you classified administrative abilities, leads to," she answered, not having listened to her husband. "My God! You yourself have ground the axe to cut off your own head. Blessed Virgin! why didn't you consult me? At least I would have kept you from writing down a single word, or, at the very least, I would have copied it myself, and it never would have left this house. Why, my God, didn't you tell me? That's a man for you! Able to sleep next to a wife and keep a secret for seven years! Keeping himself from a poor woman for seven years!—doubting her devotion!"

"But," said Rabourdin, provoked, "it's been eleven years since I have been able to talk with you without your cutting me off, substituting your ideas for mine. . . . You know nothing of my work."

"Nothing! I know everything!"

"Then tell me about it!" cried Rabourdin, provoked for the first time in his married life.

"Look, it's six-thirty. Shave and get dressed," she replied, as all women do when pressed on a point where they have nothing to say. "I must go finish dressing, and we'll postpone the discussion, for I don't want to be all upset on a day when we receive. My God! The poor man!" she said, as she left the room, "to work for seven years to give birth to his own death! And not trust his wife!"

She went back into the room.

"If you had listened to me in time, you would never have interceded to keep your head copy clerk, and he no doubt has an autographed copy of this cursed document! Adieu, clever man!"

Seeing her husband's tragic expression of grief, she knew she had gone too far. She ran to him, grabbed him, all lathered with soap, and kissed him tenderly.

"Dear Xavier, don't be angry," she said to him. "Tonight we shall study your plan; I will listen as long as you wish! . . . Isn't that okay? Go on, I want nothing more than to be the wife of Mohammed."

She began to laugh. Rabourdin couldn't keep from laughing as well, for Célestine had white suds on her lips and her voice revealed the treasures of the purest and most steadfast affection.

"Go and dress, dear child. And above all, don't say anything to des Lupeaulx, swear to me? That is the only penance I impose."

"*Impose?*" she said. "Then I won't swear to anything!"

"Come, Célestine, I said in jest something very serious."

"Tonight," she replied, "your secretary-general will know whom we have to fight—and me, I can attack."

"Whom?" said Rabourdin.

"The minister," she answered, gaining two feet in stature.

In spite of the loving charm of his dear Célestine, Rabourdin, while dressing, could not prevent certain painful thoughts from clouding his brow.

"When will she be able to appreciate me?" he said to himself. "She did not even understand that she is the sole reason for this project! How wanton, and yet how intelligent! If I had not married, I would already be high up and pretty rich! it would have saved five thousand a year of my salary. Well invested, I would today yield ten thousand francs a year in interest outside of my office; I would be a bachelor and would have the chance to become somebody through a marriage. . . . Yes," he resumed, having interrupted himself, "but I have Célestine and my two children." He fell back upon his happiness. Even in the happiest of homes, there are always moments of regret. He entered the salon and looked around at his apartment. "There are not two women in Paris who understand living as well as she does. With twelve thousand livres to manage all this!" he said, looking at the planters full of flowers and thinking of the pleasure of flattered vanity with which society was about to gratify him. "She was made to be the wife of a minister. When I consider that my minister's wife is no good for him;

she is like a great, hefty bourgeoise, and when she finds herself in the château, or in the salons. . . ." He pursed his lips. Very busy men have such misguided notions about household matters that you can just as easily make them believe that with a hundred thousand francs you have nothing as that with twelve thousand you have it all.

Although impatiently awaited, and despite the flattering dishes prepared for his gourmet-emeritus tastes, des Lupeaulx did not come to dine; he came very late in the evening, at midnight, the time at which the conversation becomes, in every salon, more intimate and confidential. Andoche Finot, the journalist, had stayed on.

"I know everything," said des Lupeaulx when he was comfortably seated on a sofa by the fireplace, a cup of tea in hand and Madame Rabourdin standing before him holding a plate of sandwiches and some slices of cake, very appropriately called *pound* cake. "Finot, my dear and witty friend, you can render service to our gracious queen by letting loose a few dogs on the men of whom we are speaking. You have against you," he said to Monsieur Rabourdin, lowering his voice so as to be heard only by the three persons to whom he was speaking, "usurers and the clergy, money and the church. The article in the Liberal paper was instigated by an old moneylender to whom there were some obligations, but the little fellow who did it isn't worrying. The head editorial staff is going to change in three days, and we'll get back to that. The Royalist Opposition—for we have, thanks to Monsieur de Chateaubriand, a Royalist Opposition, that is to say, Royalists who have gone over to the Liberals, but let's not discuss high politics now—these assassins of Charles X, have promised me their support for your appointment in return for our approval for one of their amendments. All my batteries are manned. If they foist Baudoyer on us, we shall say to the Grand Almonry: 'Such and such a paper and such and such men will attack the measures you seek and the whole press will be against you' (for the ministerial papers' control will be deaf and dumb; they won't have any problem being that: they're like that often enough, isn't that so, Finot?). 'Appoint Rabourdin, and public opinion is with you.' The poor 'Bonifaces' in the country, who settle into their armchairs by the fire, so delighted with their independence from the organs of 'Opinion,' ha, ha!"

"Hee, hee, hee!" laughed Andoche Finot.

"Settle down," said des Lupeaulx. "I have arranged everything this evening. The Grand Almoner will give way."

"I would rather have lost all hope and had you to dinner," Célestine whispered in his ear, looking at him with a vexed air that could pass for an expression of mad love.

"Here is something to win my pardon," he returned, handing her an invitation for the Tuesday soirée.

Célestine opened the letter, and the reddest flush of delight lit up her features. No pleasure can be compared to that of triumphant vanity.

"You know what the Tuesday soirée is," said des Lupeaulx, assuming a mysterious air. "In our ministry it's like the Petit Château at the Court. You will be at the heart of power! The Comtesse Féraud will be there, who is still in favor in spite of Louis XVIII's death, as will Delphine de Nucingen, Madame de Listomère, the Marquise d'Espard, and your dear de Camps, whom I have invited as a support for you in case the women try to blackball you. I cannot wait to see you in the midst of such company."

Célestine tossed her head like a thoroughbred before the race, and reread the invitation just as Baudoyer and Saillard had reread their articles in the newspapers, without being able to quaff enough of it.

"*There* first, and some day at the Tuileries," she said to des Lupeaulx.

Des Lupeaulx was startled by her words and attitude, so expressive were they of ambition and security. "Will I only be a stepping-stone?" he said to himself. He got up, went into Madame Rabourdin's bedroom and was followed by her, for she understood from one of the secretary-general's gestures that he wished to speak to her in private.

"Well now, the plan," he said.

"Bah! the nonsense of an honest man!" she replied. "He wants to get rid of fifteen thousand state employees and keep only five or six thousand. You've never heard of such a monstrosity. I shall let you read the document when the copy is ready. He is in earnest. His analytic catalog of the employees was prompted by the most upright of considerations. Poor dear man!"

Des Lupeaulx was all the more reassured by the genuine laugh that accompanied these bantering and scornful words, because he was a judge of lies and knew that, for now, Célestine spoke in good faith.

"But still, what is at the bottom of it all?" he asked.

"Well, he wants to do away with the land-tax and replace it with taxes on consumption."

"Why, it is over a year since François Keller and Nucingen proposed some such plan, and the minister is considering reducing the burden of the land-tax."

"There! I told him there was nothing in it," exclaimed Célestine, laughing.

"No, but if he is on the same ground as the best financier of our times, a man who, between us, is the Napoleon of finance, he must have some ideas in his method of implementation."

"The whole thing is very ordinary," she said, pursing her lips in a disdainful pout. "Just think of him governing and administering France with five or six thousand bureaucrats, when, on the contrary, what is really needed is that there be not one soul in France who is not interested in supporting the government."

Des Lupeaulx seemed satisfied to find a mediocre man in the man to whom he had accorded superior talents.

"Are you quite sure of the appointment? Do you want a woman's advice?" she said.

"You are more adept than we at refined treachery," said des Lupeaulx, nodding his head.

"Well then, say *Baudoyer* to the Court and Grand Almoner to divert suspicion and put them to sleep, but at the last minute write *Rabourdin*."

"There are some women who say yes as long as they need a man, and no when he has played his part," replied des Lupeaulx.

"I know some," she answered, laughing. "But they are very foolish, for in politics you always run into each other again; that may do with fools, but you are a clever man. In my opinion, the biggest mistake anyone can make is to quarrel with a superior man."

"No," said des Lupeaulx, "for he forgives. There is only danger with the petty, spiteful minds who have nothing else to do but avenge themselves, and I spend my life at that."

When everyone had left, Rabourdin stayed in his wife's room, and, after insisting for once on her attention, he was able to explain his plan, making her see that it did not in any way cut back but on the contrary increased the budget, showing her in what ways the public funds were employed, explaining how the state could increase the circulation of money by putting its own, in the proportion of a third or a quarter, into the expenditures that would be supported by private or local interests; and, finally, he proved to her that his plan was less a theoretical work than a system teeming with means of implementation. Célestine, enthusiastic, sprang into her husband's arms and sat on his knee by the fire.

"At last I have in you the husband of my dreams!" she said. "My ignorance of your real merit has saved you from des Lupeaulx's claws. I slandered you to him gloriously and in good faith!"

The man wept for joy. His day of triumph had come at last. After having done everything to please his wife, he was great in the eyes of his only audience!

"And to someone who knows you are so good, so tender, so just and loving, you are ten times as great. But," she added, "a man of genius is always more or less a child; and you are a child, a dearly beloved child." She drew her invitation from that particular spot where women put what they want to hide and showed it to him.

"Here is what I wanted," she said. "Des Lupeaulx has brought me together with the minister, and were he made of bronze, His Excellency shall be my servant for a while."

»»» VIII «««

Enter Madame Rabourdin

The very next day Célestine busied herself for her introduction into the inner circle of the Ministry. It was her big day, all hers! Never did a courtesan take such pains with herself as this honest woman. Never was a dressmaker so tormented as hers, and never was a dressmaker more aware of the importance of her art. In short, Madame Rabourdin overlooked nothing. She herself went to the livery rental to choose a carriage that was neither old, bourgeois, or haughty. Her manservant, like the servants of great houses, was dressed like a lord. Then, around ten in the evening on that great Tuesday, she left home in a charming full-mourning outfit. Her hair was dressed with jet grapes of fine workmanship, an ornament commissioned at Fossin's by an Englishwoman who left without it. The leaves were of stamped iron leaf, light as real vine leaves, and the artist had not forgotten the tendrils, so graceful, which coiled among her curls as if to cling to veritable branches. The bracelets, necklace, and earrings were all made of what is called "Berlin iron"; but these delicate arabesques came from Vienna and seemed to have been fashioned by those fairies who, in fairy tales, are condemned by some jealous Carabosse to gather the eyes of ants or weave fabrics found in nutshells. Her figure, already slimmed by the black, was accented by a very well-cut dress that rose up to a strapless, curved shoulder seam. With every move, it was as if this lady, like a butterfly, was about to leave her cocoon, and yet the gown held together through one of the dressmaker's magical inventions. The gown was of *mousseline de laine*, a fabric the manufacturer had not yet introduced in Paris, a divine fabric that later became a wild success. This success surpassed fashion in France. The practical advantages of *mousseline de laine*, which spares laundering, later hurt the cotton fabric industry, as it revolutionized Rouen production. Célestine's feet, covered by finely stitched silk stockings and turk-satin shoes (for silk-satin is inadmissible in deep mourning), were of elegant proportions. And so Célestine was very beautiful.

Her complexion, revived by a bran bath, was softly radiant. Her eyes—bathed in the tide of expectation, sparkling with spirit—bore testimony to that superiority of which the happy and proud des Lupeaulx had spoken earlier.

She made a good entrance (women can well appreciate the meaning of this expression). She bowed gracefully to the minister's wife, with a balanced blend of the deference due and her own self-respect; and she did not stun her, yet all the while bore an air of majesty, for every beautiful woman is a queen. And with the minister she assumed that pretty air of sauciness that women may allow themselves with men even when they are grand dukes. She surveyed the terrain as she took her seat and found herself in the midst of one of those few select soirées where the women can eye and size one another up, where the slightest word echoes in every ear, where every glance has weight, where conversation is a duel with witnesses, where that which is second-rate becomes nothing but everything of worth is silently taken in, as though it were on the level of everyone present. Rabourdin went and confined himself to an adjoining salon where people were playing cards and stayed there, planted on his feet to watch, thus proving he was not without sense.

"My dear," said the Marquise d'Espard to the Comtesse Féraud, Louis XVIII's last mistress, "Paris certainly is unique. It puts forth, without your knowing and from who knows where, women like that one over there, who seem able to do and will everything."

"But she can and does will everything," said des Lupeaulx, puffed up with satisfaction.

At this moment, the wily Madame Rabourdin was courting the minister's wife. Carefully coached the evening before by des Lupeaulx, who knew the Countess's weak spots, she flattered her without seeming to touch them. Then she was quiet as appropriate, for des Lupeaulx, in love though he was, had noticed her faults and had told her the night before, "Above all, do not talk too much," an enormous testimony of attachment. If Bertrand Barrère left behind this sublime axiom, "Never interrupt a woman when dancing to give her advice," we may add, "Never reproach a woman for scattering her pearls," so as to make this chapter on the Female Code complete.

The conversation became general. From time to time Madame Rabourdin put in a word, just as a well-trained cat puts its paws on her mistress's lace with the claws carefully drawn in. Emotionally, the minister had few illusions; the Restoration had no statesman more accomplished in matters of gallantry, and the Opposition of *Le Miroir*, *La Pandora*, and *Le Figaro* could not come up with the slightest irregularity with which to reproach him. His mistress was *L'Etoile*, and, strangely enough, it stuck by him in bad times; it surely got something out of it! Madame Rabourdin knew this, but she also knew that ghosts return to old castles, so she had taken it into her head to make the minister jealous of the happiness that des Lupeaulx, though conditionally, was appearing to enjoy. At that moment, des Lupeaulx's throat literally gurgled with the name Célestine. To launch his supposed mistress, he was hard at work to persuade the Marquise d'Espard, Madame de Nucingen, and the Countess, in a conversation for eight ears, that they should admit Madame Rabourdin into their league, and Madame de Camps was supporting him. After an hour, the minister had been thoroughly stroked; Madame Rabourdin's wit pleased him, and she had won over his wife who, delighted with this siren, had just invited her to come whenever she pleased.

"For, my dear," the minister's wife had said to Célestine, "your husband shall soon be director; the minister's intention is to bring together the two divisions and place them under one director; and so you will then be one of us."

His Excellency took Madame Rabourdin to show her a certain room that had become famous for the alleged extravagances of which the Opposition paper had accused him, which only went to show the nonsense of journalism. He offered her his arm.

"In truth, Madame, you really must give us the pleasure, the Countess and myself, of coming often. . . ."

And he went on with a round of ministerial compliment.

"But, Monseigneur," she said, casting one of those glances that women hold in reserve, "it seems to me that that depends on you."

"How so?"

"You alone can give me the right to come here."

"Pray explain."

"No. I said to myself before I came that I would certainly not have the bad taste to play the solicitor."

"Speak! *Places* asked in this way are never out of *place*," said the minister, laughing.

There is nothing like this type of nonsense to amuse these serious men.

"Well, then, it is ridiculous for the wife of a bureau chief to come here too often, whereas a director's wife would never be out of place."

"Never mind that," said the minister. "Your husband is an indispensable man; he is appointed."

"Is that really true?"

"Would you like to see his nomination in my study? It's all drawn up."

"Well then," she said, pausing in a corner alone with the minister, the openness of which lent it a suspect urgency, "let me tell you that I can do something for you in return. . . ."

She was about to reveal her husband's plan when des Lupeaulx came up on tiptoe and emitted an angry little cough that announced he did not wish to appear to have overheard what he had been listening to. The minister, caught in the act, threw an angry look at the old dandy. Impatient for his reward, des Lupeaulx had rushed the paperwork for the appointment beyond all reason, had gotten it back to the minister that evening, and the following day wanted to deliver the nomination to the woman who passed as his mistress. Just then the minister's valet de chambre came up in a mysterious manner and told des Lupeaulx that *his* valet de chambre had bid him deliver this letter at once, indicating that it was of the utmost importance.

The secretary went over to a lamp and read the following note:

Contrary to my custom, I am waiting in your antechamber and you have not a moment to lose if you wish to come to terms with

Your servant,
Gobseck

The secretary-general shuddered as he recognized the signature, which it would be a shame not to give as an autograph; it is uncommon in the market and would be a treasure for those who seek to guess people's characters from the physiognomy of their signatures. If ever a hieroglyph represented an animal, it was certainly this name, in which the first and final letters came together like the voracious jaws of a shark—insatiable, always open, catching and devouring all, the strong as well as the weak. It is impossible to reproduce the message—it's much too fine, close and small, although neat—but you can imagine; it was only one line. Only the spirit of the usurer could have inspired a sentence so insolently imperative and cruelly irreproachable, so clear and curt, saying all and betraying nothing. "Gobseck" would mean nothing to you, except for the way that sentence made you come without being ordered, and you would have guessed it was the implacable moneylender of the rue des Grès. And so, like a dog called to heel, des Lupeaulx abandoned his present quest and went immediately to his own quarters, thinking over his compromised position. Imagine a general-in-chief whose aide-de-camp comes up to him and says: "The enemy is attacking on our right flank with thirty thousand fresh troops."

A very brief word will explain the arrival of Monsieur Gigonnet and Monsieur Gobseck on the field of battle, for they were both in des Lupeaulx's room. At eight in the evening, Martin Falleix, returning on the wings of the wind, thanks to three-francs'-worth of riders and an advance courier, had brought back the property deeds signed the day before. Taken at once to the Café Thémis by Mitral, these contracts passed into the hands of the two usurers, who hastened to the Ministry, albeit on foot. Eleven o'clock sounded. Des Lupeaulx trembled when he saw those sinister hawklike faces discharging a look as direct as a pistol shot and as brilliant as the flash itself.

"Well, what's going on, my masters?"

The usurers remained cold and motionless. Gigonnet pointed to the dossier and at the valet in turn.

"Come into my study," said des Lupeaulx, dismissing his valet with a gesture.

"You understand French wonderfully," said Gigonnet.

"Have you come here to torment a man who enabled each of you to make a couple of hundred thousand francs?" he said, letting a haughty gesture escape him.

"And who will help us to make more, I hope," said Gigonnet.

"Some business . . . ?" asked des Lupeaulx. "If you need me, I have a memory."

"So do we," answered Gigonnet.

"My debts will be paid," said des Lupeaulx disdainfully, so as not to get taken.

"True," said Gobseck.

"Let's get to the point, my son," said Gigonnet. "Don't draw into your cravat like that, with us it's no use. Take these deeds and read."

The two usurers took a mental inventory of des Lupeaulx's study while he read, amazed and stupefied, these contracts, which hit him out of the blue as if from angels.

"In us don't you have a couple of smart businessmen?" said Gigonnet.

"But to what do I owe such able cooperation?" said des Lupeaulx uneasily.

"We knew eight days ago what, without us, you would only have found out tomorrow: the president of the Commercial Court, a deputy, finds himself obliged to resign."

Des Lupeaulx's eyes dilated and grew as big as daisies.

"Your minister has been playing a trick on you," said the terse Gobseck.

"You are my masters," said the secretary-general, bowing with an air of profound respect tinged with sarcasm.

"Precisely," said Gobseck.

"But are you going to strangle me?"

"Possibly."

"Well, then, get to it, executioners!" added the secretary-general, smiling.

"You will see," resumed Gigonnet, "your debts are registered with the loan for the acquisition."

"Here are the deeds," said Gobseck, pulling the legal papers from the pocket of his greenish overcoat.

"You have three years to pay off the whole lot," said Gigonnet.

"But," said des Lupeaulx, alarmed at so much readiness to oblige and such a wonderful arrangement. "What do you want from me?"

"La Billardière's post for Baudoyer," said Gigonnet sharply.

"That's a small matter, though. I would have to do the impossible," replied des Lupeaulx. "My hands are tied."

"Then you'll gnaw the cords with your teeth," said Gigonnet.

"They're sharp enough!" added Gobseck.

"Is that all?" said des Lupeaulx.

"We'll keep the papers until the recognition of these debts comes through," said Gigonnet, putting a document before the secretary-general. "If they are not acted upon by the Commission within six days, your name on this contract will be replaced by mine."

"You're very clever," cried the secretary-general.

"Precisely," said Gobseck.

"And that's all?" exclaimed des Lupeaulx.

"Honest," said Gobseck.

"Is it a deal?" asked Gigonnet.

Des Lupeaulx nodded.

"Well, then, sign this power of attorney," said Gigonnet. "Within two days, Baudoyer's nomination; in six days, the recognition of the debts, and . . ."

"And what?" said des Lupeaulx.

"We guarantee you . . ."

"Your nomination," said Gigonnet, rising up on his heels. "We have a majority with fifty-two farm and industrial voters who will do as your lender says."

Des Lupeaulx shook Gigonnet's hand.

"Only between us are misunderstandings impossible," he said. "This is what I call doing business. So return the goodwill."

"Good," said Gobseck.

"What will it be?" asked Gigonnet.

"The Cross for your imbecile of a nephew."

"Good," said Gigonnet. "I see you know him well."

The usurers then took their leave as des Lupeaulx saw them to the staircase.

"They must be secret envoys from foreign powers," whispered the two valets between themselves.

Once in the street, the two usurers looked at each other and laughed under the glow of a street lamp.

"He will owe us nine thousand francs in interest a year; that property hardly brings in five," cried Gigonnet.

"He's in our hands for a long time," said Gobseck.

"He'll build; he'll make mistakes," replied Gigonnet. "Falleix will buy up the land."

"He wants to be a deputy; the old fox doesn't care about anything else," said Gobseck.

"Ho! Ho!"

"Hee! Hee!"

These dry little exclamations served as laughs to the two usurers, who made their way back to the Café Thémis on foot.

Des Lupeaulx returned to the salon and found Madame Rabourdin in all her glory. She was charming, and the minister, usually so gloomy, had a relaxed and gracious look on his face.

"She works miracles," said des Lupeaulx to himself. "What an exquisite woman! I must get to the bottom of her heart."

"She is definitely very nice, your little lady," said the marquise to the secretary-general. "The only thing she lacks is your name."

"Yes, her only fault is that she is an auctioneer's daughter; her want of birth will be her ruin," replied des Lupeaulx in a cold manner that contrasted with the warmth with which he had spoken of Madame Rabourdin just a moment before.

The marquise stared straight at des Lupeaulx.

"The glance you gave them did not escape me," she said, looking toward the minister and Madame Rabourdin. "It pierced through the fog on your glasses. How amusing you both are, to fight over that bone."

As the marquise turned to leave the room, the minister rushed over to her and escorted her to the door.

"Well," said des Lupeaulx to Madame Rabourdin, "what do you think of our minister?"

"He is charming. Indeed," she added, raising her voice slightly so as to be heard by His Excellency's wife, "we must know these poor ministers to appreciate them. The petty newspapers and the calumnies of the Opposition are so misleading about men in politics that we end up letting ourselves be influenced by them; but such prejudices turn to their advantage when we actually see them in person."

"He is very fine," said des Lupeaulx.

"Well, I can assure you he is quite easy to like," she said good-naturedly.

"Dear child," said des Lupeaulx, adopting in turn a good-natured and ingratiating manner, "you have achieved the impossible."

"What?" she asked.

"You have resuscitated the dead. I did not think that man had a heart; ask his wife. He has just enough for a passing fancy, but take advantage of it. Come this way, and don't be surprised." He led Madame Rabourdin into the boudoir and sat down with her on the divan. "You are very crafty, and I like you the better for it. Between ourselves, you are a superior woman. Des Lupeaulx brought you here, and that's it for him, isn't it? Besides, when one decides to love for what one can get out of someone, it is better to take a sex-agenarian minister than a quadrigenarian secretary-general; there's more profit and less nuisance. I'm a man with glasses, powdered hair, worn out by pleasure—what a wonderful love it would make! Oh! Haven't I told myself that. If you absolutely must give in to the practical, I will never be to your liking, right? One would have to be crazy not to be able to rationalize one's position. You can confess the truth to me, show me the depths of your heart: we are two partners, not two lovers. If I have some caprice, you are too superior to pay any attention to such trifles and will pass over them, otherwise you would be a little boarding-school miss or a bourgeoise of the rue Saint-Denis. Bah! We are above all of that, you and I. There's the Marquise d'Espard, who is leaving; don't you believe she also thinks so? We understood each other two years ago (the coxcomb!), and now she has only to write me one line—and it's not a long one—'My dear des Lupeaulx, you will oblige me by doing such or such a thing,' and it is done at once; at the moment we are getting a commission of lunacy on her husband. You other women, it costs you only pleasure to get what you want. So be it; beguile the minister, my dear child. I will help you; it is in my interest to do so. Yes, I wish him a woman who will influence him; he would never escape me. He does get away from me sometimes, and that stands to reason: I only have a hold through his rational faculties; but by allying myself with a lovely woman, I would have hold of him through his weak side, and that's the stronger. Therefore, let us remain good friends and share the influence you will have."

Madame Rabourdin listened most amazedly to this singular profession of roguerie. The simplicity of this political businessman precluded any thought of surprise.

"Do you believe he paid any attention to me?" she asked him, caught in the snare.

"I know him. I am certain of it."

"Is it true that Rabourdin's appointment is signed?"

"I gave him the papers this morning. But it's nothing to be director; one must be Master of Petitions. . . ."

"Yes," she said.

"Well, then, go back in and play the coquette with His Excellency."

"It is true," she said, "that until tonight I never fully understood you. There is nothing ordinary about you."

"Well, then," said des Lupeaulx, "we shall be two old friends and do away with all tender airs, tormenting love, in order to understand things as they did under the Regency, when they had real sense."

"You really are something, and you have my admiration," she said, smiling and holding out her hand to him. "You will understand that one does more for one's friends than for one's . . ."

She broke off and left.

"Dear little thing," said des Lupeaulx to himself as he watched her take on the minister, "des Lupeaulx no longer has the slightest remorse in turning against you! Tomorrow evening, when you offer me a cup of tea, you will be offering me a thing I no longer care for. . . . All is said and done. Ah! When you are forty, women always take you in; it is too late to be loved."

He entered the salon after looking himself over in a mirror, saw himself as a rather handsome politician but a perfect casualty of Cytherea.

At the same moment, Madame Rabourdin was pulling herself together. She thought of departing and did her utmost to leave in the minds of all one last graceful impression, and she succeeded. Contrary to the custom in the salons, when she had gone, everyone cried out, "What a charming woman!" and the minister himself escorted her to the door.

"I am quite sure you will think of me tomorrow," he told the family, thus alluding to the appointment.

"There are so few high functionaries whose wives are agreeable that I am very well satisfied with our acquisition," said the minister upon reentering.

"Don't you think her a little intrusive?" said des Lupeaulx with a piqued air.

The women present all exchanged expressive glances among themselves; the rivalry between the minister and his secretary-general amused them. Then there transpired one of those pretty little comedies that Parisian women play so well. The women stirred up the minister and des Lupeaulx by focusing on Madame Rabourdin: one thought her too forced and trying to appear clever; the other compared the graces of the bourgeoisie with the manners of high society in order to criticize Célestine, and des Lupeaulx defended his pretended mistress as one defends an enemy in the salons.

"Do her justice, ladies. Is it not extraordinary that the daughter of an auctioneer should be so wonderful? See where she came from and what she is. She will finish up in the Tuileries. That is her aim. She told me so."

"If she is an auctioneer's daughter," said Madame d'Espard, smiling, "how can that prevent her husband's advancement?"

"In these times, isn't that what you mean?" said the minister's wife, pursing her lips.

"Madame," said the minister sternly to the marquise, "of such talk, which the Court unfortunately spares no one, are revolutions made. You cannot imagine how indiscreet conduct on the part of the aristocracy displeases certain clear-sighted personages at the Château. If I were a great lord, rather than a mere country gentleman who seems to be placed where I am to transact your business, the monarchy would not be in as poor a position as it presently is. What becomes of a throne that is unable to pass on its brilliance to its representatives? We are far from the days when the king made great men at his pleasure—the Louvois, Colberts, Richelieus, Jeannins, Villeroys, Sullys. . . . Yes, Sully, at first, was no greater than I. I am telling you this because we are here in private among ourselves, and I would indeed be small if I were myself shocked at a similar trifle. It is up to us and not others to make ourselves great."

"You are appointed, dear," said Célestine, squeezing her husband's hand. "If it had not been for that des Lupeaulx, I would have explained your plan to the minister; but that will be for next Tuesday, and so you will be Master of Petitions all the sooner."

In the life of every woman there comes a day when she shines in all her glory, giving her an eternal memory to which she refers with happiness all her life. As Madame Rabourdin undid, one by one, the intricacies of her ornaments, she mulled over the evening, counting it among the triumphs and glories of her life: all her charms had been jealously envied; she had been flattered by the minister's wife, who was delighted to pit her against her friends. But, above all, all her vanities had radiated for the benefit of conjugal love. Rabourdin was appointed.

"Didn't I look good tonight?" she said to her husband, as though she had the need to animate him.

At that very moment Mitral, who was waiting at the Café Thémis for the two usurers, saw them come in and did not discern anything on those two impassive faces.

"Where do we stand?" he said to them once they were seated.

"Well, same as always," said Gigonnet, rubbing his hands. "Victory to the cash."

"True," replied Gobseck.

Mitral took a carriage and went straight to the Saillards' and Baudoyers', where Boston had drawn on late; but only the Abbé Gaudron was still there. Falleix, half dead with fatigue, had gone to bed.

"You'll be appointed, my nephew, and there's a surprise in store for you."

"What?" asked Saillard.

"The Cross!" cried Mitral.

"God protects those who guard His altars!" said Gaudron.

And thus the Te Deum was sung in both camps with equal joy.

»»» IX «««

Forward, Mollusks!

The next day, Wednesday, Monsieur Rabourdin was to work with the minister, for he had been the interim chief since the onset of the late La Billardière's illness. On those days, the employees were very punctual; the office boys were especially on the ball, because on signature days everything was up in the air in the bureaus. And why is that? No one knows. And so the three boys were at their posts and flattering themselves that they would get some sort of bonus, for the rumor of Rabourdin's nomination had spread the night before, thanks to des Lupeaulx. Uncle Antoine, the bailiff, and Laurent were in full uniform when, at a quarter to eight, the secretary's boy came to ask Antoine to secretly give Dutocq a letter the secretary-general had told him to deliver to the chief clerk at seven o'clock.

"I'm sure I don't know how it happened, my friend; I slept on and on and only just woke up. He would read me the riot act if he knew it hadn't gotten to his place; instead, I'll just tell him that I myself took it to Monsieur Dutocq's. It's a big secret, Père Antoine; don't say a word to the employees, promise! He would get rid of me, I'd be out for one single word; that's what he said."

"What's in it?" asked Antoine.

"Nothing. I saw it. Here, it looked like this." He opened the letter only to reveal a blank page.

"Today's your big day, Laurent," said the secretary's boy. "You are to have a new director. Surely they're making budget cuts, the two divisions are being put under one director. Boys beware!"

"Yes, nine employees pensioned off," said Dutocq, who had just come in. "How did you guys find that out?"

Antoine gave the letter to Dutocq, who tore down the staircase to the secretariat after having opened it.

Since the day of Monsieur de La Billardière's death, after having gossiped their way through the issue, the Rabourdin and Baudoyer bureaus ended up resuming their usual appearance, their administrative dolce far niente. Nevertheless, the impending end of the year did evoke in the offices a sort of studious industry, in the same way that it makes servants more unctuously servile. Everyone came in on time and more people were to be seen around after four o'clock—all because the distribution of bonuses depends upon the final impression one leaves on the chiefs' minds. The day before, the news of the uniting of the two divisions, La Billardière's and Clergeot's, under one head with a new title had stirred up the two divisions. The number of employees to be retired was known, but not their names. It was assumed that Poiret would not be replaced; his post would be eliminated. La Billardière, Jr., had left. Two new supernumeraries had been taken on; and—alarming circumstance!—they were both sons of deputies. The news that broke the day before, just as the employees were leaving, impressed terror on their minds. Furthermore, during the half-hour when people arrived, there was a lot of talk around the stoves. Before anybody had gotten there, Dutocq had spotted des Lupeaulx washing up, and, without putting down his razor, the secretary-general threw him the glance of a general issuing an order.

"Are we alone?" he asked.

"Yes, Monsieur."

"Very good. March on Rabourdin. Forward and steady! You must have kept a copy of his paper?"

"Yes."

"Do you understand? *Inde irae*! There must be a general out-cry. Find some way to start a clamor. . . ."

"I can have a caricature made, but I don't have five hundred francs to pay. . . ."

"Who would make it?"

"Bixiou."

"He shall have a thousand and be deputy chief under Colleville, who will get along with him."

"But he won't believe me."

"By any chance, do you want me to compromise my position? Get going or no dice. Do you understand?"

"If Monsieur Baudoyer were director, he could advance the amount. . . ."

"Yes, he will be. Now get going and hurry up. And don't let people know you've seen me; go down the back stairs."

While Dutocq was returning to the office, his heart was pounding with joy and he was asking himself how he could best incite a clamor against his chief without compromising himself too much. Bixiou had gone in to the Rabourdins to say hello. Thinking he had lost, the joker amusingly made out as if he had won.

Bixiou (mimicking Phellion's voice): "Gentlemen, I congratulate you and extend to you a collective 'Good morning!' I designate next Sunday for a dinner at the Rocher de Cancale. But a serious dilemma presents itself: are the dismissed employees included?"

Poiret: "Even those who are retiring?"

Bixiou: "I don't care, it's not me who's paying. (General amazement.) Baudoyer is appointed. I believe I can already hear him calling Laurent! (He mimics Baudoyer.) 'Laurent! lock up my hairshirt, and my scourge.' (They all roar with laughter.) 'Ris d'aboyeur d'oie!' Colleville is right about his anagram, because you know the anagram of *Xavier Rabourdin, Chef de Bureau* is

D'abord rêva bureaux, e, u, fin riche. If I were named *Charles X, par la grâce de Dieu roi de France et de Navarre*, I would tremble at the thought of the fate prophesied in my anagram coming true."

Thuillier: "What! Are you making fun?"

Bixiou (laughing in his face): "*Ris au laid [riz au lait]*! That's a good one there, Papa Thuillier, that is, since you're not good-looking. Rabourdin resigns in a rage when he finds out Baudoyer is director."

Vimeux (entering): "What a joke! Antoine, whom I have just repaid forty francs, told me that Monsieur and Madame Rabourdin were received yesterday at the minister's intimate soirée and stayed until a quarter to midnight. His Excellency escorted Madame Rabourdin to the staircase; it seems she was divinely dressed. In short, he is surely director. Riffé, the personnel copy clerk, was up all night to speed up the papers; it's no longer a mystery. Monsieur Clergeot has retired. After thirty years' service that's no disgrace. Monsieur Cochin, who is rich . . ."

Bixiou: "According to Colleville, he makes *cochenille*."

Vimeux: "Yes, but he's actually in the cochineal business; he's a partner in the Matifat concern, rue des Lombards. Anyway, he's retired; Poiret's retired. Neither is going to be replaced. That much is for sure. The rest isn't known. The appointment of Monsieur Rabourdin is set for this morning; they're afraid of intrigues."

Bixiou: "What sort of intrigues?"

Fleury: "Baudoyer of course! The clerical parties are backing him, and here's another article in the Liberal paper, only half a dozen lines, but it's funny (he reads):

Certain persons spoke last night in the foyer of Les Italiens of the return of Monsieur de Chateaubriand to the Ministry, basing their opinion on the choice of Monsieur Rabourdin (the protégé of the friends of the noble Vicomte) to fill the office initially slated for Monsieur Baudoyer. The Clerical party would not have been able to back down, except in deference to the great writer.

"Dirty bunch of rats!"

Dutocq (entering, having heard the whole discussion): "Dirty rat, who? Rabourdin. Then you know the news?"

Fleury (rolling his eyes savagely): "Rabourdin? . . . a dirty rat! You're crazy, Dutocq. Do you want a bullet to give your brain ballast?"

Dutocq: "I said nothing against Monsieur Rabourdin, only I have just secretly been told in the courtyard that he denounced many employees, graded them, so that, in fact, the reason for his favor is due to a study of the ministries in which every one of us is sunk. . . ."

Phellion (in a loud voice): "Monsieur Rabourdin is incapable of . . ."

Bixiou: "Isn't that just great! Indeed, Dutocq?" (They whisper together and then go out into the corridor.) "What's going on?"

Dutocq: "Do you remember that caricature?"

Bixiou. "Yes, so what?"

Dutocq: "Make it and you will be deputy chief and get a great compensation. You see, my friend, there's dissension among the higher powers. The minister is pledged to Rabourdin, but if he doesn't appoint Baudoyer he is in trouble with the clergy. Don't you know, the king, the Dauphin and Dauphine, the Grand Almonry, and even the Court, all want Baudoyer; the minister wants Rabourdin."

Bixiou: "Great!"

Dutocq: "In order to resolve this, for the minister recognizes that he must give in, he wants to eliminate the problem. There has to be a good reason for getting rid of Rabourdin. So an old study of his on the administrations and how to clean them up has been dug up, and parts of it are being circulated. At least, this is how I understand the matter. Make the drawing; you are playing in the big leagues, you are at the service of the minister, the Court, everyone, and you will be appointed. Do you understand?"

Bixiou: "I don't understand how you can know all this; or you're making it up."

Dutocq: "Do you want me to let you see the article on you?"

Bixiou. "Yes."

Dutocq: "Okay. Then come to my place, because I want to put this document into safe hands."

Bixiou: "You go on alone." (He enters Rabourdin's bureau.) "What Dutocq told you is really all true, word of honor! It seems that Monsieur Rabourdin has written very unflattering reports on the employees to be 'reformed.' That's the real secret to his promotion. We live in a day and age when nothing is surprising anymore." (He cloaks himself like Talma.) "'Ye have seen illustrious heads fall before thine eyes. / And yet, oh senseless man, ye show surprise!' at finding such reasons behind a single man's favor? Our Baudoyer is too stupid to get ahead by those means! Accept my congratulations, gentlemen; either way you are under a most illustrious chief." (He leaves.)

Poiret: "I'll leave this ministry without ever having understood a single sentence that man has said. What does he mean with his 'heads that fall'?"

Fleury: "Why! the four sergeants of La Rochelle, Berton, Ney, Caron, the Faucher brothers, and all the massacres!"

Phellion: "He flippantly announces things he's only guessing about."

Fleury: "Say he's lying, or he's kidding! and that in his own mouth it turns into verdigris."

Phellion: "Your language transgresses the laws of courtesy and the consideration due among colleagues."

Vimeux: "It seems to me that if what he says is false, the proper name for it is slander, defamation of character; and such a slanderer deserves a thrashing."

Phellion (hoping to avoid a quarrel, tries to turn the conversation): "Gentlemen, calm down. I am writing a new little treatise on morality, and I am about to address the topic of the soul."

Fleury (interrupting): "What are you saying, Monsieur Phellion?"

Phellion (reading):

Q: What is the soul of man?
A: A spiritual substance that thinks and reasons.

Thuillier: "A spiritual substance, that's like saying an immaterial stone."

Poiret: "Let him continue . . ."

Phellion (continuing):

Q: Whence comes the soul?
A: It comes from God, who created it of a nature simple and indivisible and wherefore one consequently cannot conceive its destructibility, and He hath said . . .

Poiret (amazed): "God?"

Phellion: "Yes, Monsieur. The tradition supports it."

Fleury (to Poiret): "Don't interrupt!"

Phellion (resuming):

. . . and He hath said that He created it immortal; that is, that it shall never die.

Q: What is the soul for?

A: To comprehend, to will, to remember; these constitute understanding, volition, memory.

Q: What is understanding for?

A: To know. It is the eye of the soul.

Fleury: "And the soul is the eye of what?"

Phellion (continuing):

Q: What is understanding?

A: The truth.

Q: Why does man possess will?

A: To love good and hate evil.

Q: What is good?

A: That which leads to happiness.

Vimeux: "Are you writing this for demoiselles?"

Phellion: "Yes" (continuing):

Q: How many kinds of good are there?

Fleury: "It's prodigiously flimsy!"

Phellion (indignant): "Oh, Monsieur!" (Calming down.) "Here is the answer anyhow. I've got it." (He reads):

A: There are two kinds of good: eternal good and temporal good.

Poiret (with a contemptuous look): "And will that sell for much?"

Phellion: "I hope it will. It requires great application of the mind to establish a system of questions and answers; that is why I ask you to let me think, for the answers . . ."

Thuillier (interrupting): "The answers could be sold separately . . ."

Poiret: "Is that a pun?"

Thuillier: "Yes, we'll make a tossed salad out of it, a rampion salad."

Phellion: "I was wrong to interrupt you." (He buries himself in his boxes.) "But (to himself) they aren't thinking about Monsieur Rabourdin anymore."

Meanwhile, a scene was taking place between the minister and des Lupeaulx that would decide Rabourdin's fate. Before breakfast, the secretary-general had gone to find His Excellency in his private study to make sure that La Brière could not overhear anything.

"His Excellency is not being frank with me . . ."

"He wants to argue," thought the minister, "because his mistress flirted with me last night."

"I thought you less juvenile, my dear friend," he said aloud.

"Friend," said the secretary-general, "that is what I mean to find out."

The minister looked haughtily at des Lupeaulx.

"We are alone, and we can come to an understanding. The deputy of the arrondissement in which my des Lupeaulx estate is situated . . ."

"So there really is an estate?" said the minister, laughing to hide his surprise.

"Enlarged by two hundred thousand francs'-worth of acquisitions," replied des Lupeaulx carelessly. "You have known of this deputy's resignation for ten days, and you said nothing to me of it;

you did not have to. But you knew very well that I wish to take a seat in the Center. Had you thought that I might join the Doctrine party, which will swallow up both you and the monarchy if it is allowed to continue recruiting men of a, shall we say, 'disgruntled talent'? Don't you know that in a country there are not more than fifty or sixty dangerous minds, whose cunning is in proportion to their ambition? Knowing how to govern is to know those minds well, and either to chop them off or buy them off. I do not know whether I have the skill, but I do have the ambition, and you are committing the error of not getting along with a man who only wishes you well. The coronation dazzles for but an instant, and then what? . . . Then, the war of words and arguments will spring up once more; it becomes acrimonious. And so, as far as you are concerned, do not expect to find me in the Center-Left, believe me! In spite of the maneuvers of your prefect, to whom secret instructions against me were no doubt given, I will have a majority. After a little coup de Jarnac, one sometimes ends up as friends. I will be made count and will not be denied the grand cordon of the Legion for my services. However, I care less for those two things than I do for something in which only your best interest is involved. . . . You have not yet appointed Rabourdin; I have received news this morning that you would satisfy many by choosing Baudoyer over him. . . ."

"Appoint Baudoyer!" exclaimed the minister. "You know what he's like."

"Yes," said des Lupeaulx. "But once his utter incompetence is proven, you will get rid of him by asking his protectors to take him in their employ. Thus, you will have an important directorship to bestow upon your friends, which will facilitate some sort of deal to rid yourself of someone ambitious."

"His resignation?"

"Yes."

"Why. . . ?"

"He is the tool of a secret power for whom he does extensive espionage throughout all the ministries, which has only inadvertently been discovered. So, please do not work with him today, let me find some excuse to get you out of it. Go see the king. I am sure you will find some people very pleased with your concession in regard to Baudoyer; you will even receive something in return. Then, later on, you will be in a position of strength to get rid of that fool, since they will see that he was, shall we say, forced upon you."

"What has made you change your mind about Rabourdin?"

"Would you help Monsieur de Chateaubriand write an article against the Ministry? Well, here is how Rabourdin has treated me in his report," he said, handing the note on himself to the minister. "He is reorganizing the whole government, no doubt for the benefit of some secret society of which we are not aware. I shall continue to be his friend for the sake of watching him; I will be rendering a great service that will earn me a peerage, for the peerage is the sole object of my desires. Let it be understood, I seek neither a ministry nor anything else that would stand in your way; I am aiming for peerage, which will enable me to marry some banker's daughter with two hundred thousand francs in income. And so, allow me to render you a few great services that will let it be said to the king that I have saved the throne. I have been saying it for some time: liberalism will no longer lead us to pitched battle; it has renounced conspiracies, Carbonarism, armed sieges; it is burrowing under and is readying a full-fledged, 'Get thee hence that I may take thy place!' Did you believe that I have been courting Rabourdin's wife for my own pleasure? No! I had leads! So now, two things for today: the postponement of the appointment, and your *sincere* support of my election. You shall see at the end of the session whether I have not amply paid my debt."

To say it all, the minister took the personnel papers and handed them to des Lupeaulx.

"I will go and tell Rabourdin," added des Lupeaulx, "that you must put off the business until Saturday."

The minister consented with a nod. The office boy of the Secretariat shortly crossed the courtyard and went to Rabourdin to tell him the minister could not work with him until Saturday, the day on which the Chamber only concerned itself with petitions and the minister had the whole day to himself.

At the same time, Saillard slipped in his word to the minister's wife, who replied with dignity that she hardly was one to meddle in affairs of state and that, moreover, she had heard that Monsieur Rabourdin had been named. Saillard, terrified, rushed up to Baudoyer's office and found Dutocq, Godard, and Bixiou in a state of exasperation difficult to describe, for they were reading Rabourdin's terrible paper on the employees.

Bixiou (with his finger on a paragraph): "Here *you* are, Père Saillard. 'Saillard: The office of cashier to be eliminated in all ministries, which in turn should have their current accounts at the Treasury. Saillard is rich and has no need for a pension.' Would you like to see about your son-in-law?" (He leafs through.) "Here we go: 'Baudoyer: Utterly incapable. Dismissed without a pension; he is rich.' And as for our friend Godard?" (He leafs on.) "'Godard: Should be dismissed; pension one-third of his present salary.' In short, we all are in here. I am, 'an artist to be employed by the Civil List, at the Opéra, at the Menus-Plaisirs, at the Museum. Plenty of ability, poor manners, incapable of application, a restless disposition.' Ha! *I'll* give you an artist!"

Saillard: "Eliminate cashiers! . . . Why, he's a monster!"

Bixiou: "What does he say about our mysterious Desroys?" (He leafs on and reads.) "'Desroys: A dangerous man in that he is unshakable in principles that are opposed to any monarchial power. Son of a Conventionel, he admires the Convention, and may become a very pernicious publicist.'"

Baudoyer: "Even the police aren't that sneaky!"

Godard: "I'm going to the secretary-general to lodge a formal complaint; we'll all have to resign en masse if a man like that is named."

Dutocq: "Listen to me, gentlemen! A little sense. If you rise up right away, we'll be accused of revenge and personal interest! No, let the rumor spread slowly. When the whole Administration is aroused, your protests will have unanimous support."

Bixiou: "Dutocq is wrapped up in the mood of the great aria invented by the sublime Rossini for Don Basilio, which proves that this great composer is a politician! That seems fair and reasonable. I'm planning on dropping off my card at Monsieur Rabourdin's tomorrow morning, and I'm going to have it inscribed: BIXIOU, and for titles underneath: *Ill-mannered, incapable of application, and restless disposition.*"

Godard: "Great idea, gentlemen. Let's go have our cards made up so that Rabourdin has them all tomorrow."

Baudoyer: "Monsieur Bixiou, you take charge of that little detail, and see to it that the plates are destroyed after one single print has been made."

Dutocq (taking Bixiou aside): "Well, would you like to draw the caricature now?"

Bixiou: "I see, my friend, that you've been in on this secret for ten days." (He looks him in the eye.) "Am I going to be deputy chief?"

Dutocq: "Word of honor, and a thousand-franc bonus too, just like I told you. You don't know what a service you're rendering to powerful people."

Bixiou: "You know who they are?"

Dutocq: "Yes."

Bixiou: "Well, I want to talk to them."

Dutocq (dryly): "You can make the caricature or not, you'll either be deputy chief or not."

Bixiou: "Well then, let's see the thousand francs."

Dutocq: "I'll have it for you in return for the drawing."

Bixiou: "Forward march! The lampoon will make the rounds of the bureaus tomorrow. Then let's go pester the Rabourdins." (Talking to Saillard, Godard, and Baudoyer, who were quietly chatting among themselves.) "We're going to work the neighbors over." (Leaves with Dutocq and goes into the Rabourdin office. At the sight of him, Fleury, Thuillier, and Vimeux rouse themselves.) "Well, what's with you all, gentlemen? What I told you is so true that you can go see for yourselves the proof of the most infamous denouncement of the virtuous, honest, upstanding, upright, and pious Baudoyer, who is utterly incapable, he is! at least of *this* sort of work. Your chief has invented some sort of guillotine for the employees, that's for sure, go see! Follow the crowd: refunds provided if you're not satisfied; complete satisfaction for your calamity *guaranteed*, *gratis*. Furthermore, all nominations are postponed. The bureaus are up in arms and Rabourdin has just been informed that the minister will not work with him today. So get a move on!"

Phellion and Poiret are left alone. The former loved Rabourdin too much to seek out proof that could destroy a man he did not wish to pass judgment on; the other had only five more days to go in the bureau. Just then Sébastien came down to look for the papers included among the documents for signature. He certainly was surprised, though without letting it show, to find the office deserted.

Phellion: "My young friend" (he rose, a rare event), "do you know what's going on? What rumors are circulating about Monsieur Rabourdin, whom you like so much and" (he lowers his voice and leans over toward Sébastien's ear) "for whom my esteem is as great as my respect? They say he has committed the imprudence of leaving a paper on the employees lying about. . . ." (With this,

Phellion stopped short; he had to support in his own fidgety arms the young Sébastien, who turned pale as a white rose and collapsed into the chair.) "A key in his back, Monsieur Poiret, do you have a key?"

Poiret: "I have the one to my place." (Old Poiret, Jr., puts the key in Sébastien's back as Phellion gives him a glass of cold water to drink. The poor lad only opens his eyes to shed a flood of tears. He lays his head on Phellion's desk, throwing down his limp body as if struck by lightning, and his sobs are so heartrending, so genuine, so profuse, that for the first time in his life Poiret is moved by the suffering of another.)

Phellion (hardening his tone): "Come, come, my young friend, cheer up! Tough times take guts. You are a man. What's the matter? How can this upset you so?"

Sébastien: "I have ruined Monsieur Rabourdin. I left the paper I had copied lying around. I have killed my benefactor; I feel like dying. Such a great man! a man who would have been minister!"

Poiret (blowing his nose): "So it's true he wrote the report?"

Sébastien (through his sobs): "But it was to . . . Here we go, I'm going to tell his secrets now! Ah! that miserable Dutocq! who stole it. . . ."

And his tears and sobs started all over again, so much so that Rabourdin heard his sobs, recognized the voice, and went up. The chief found Sébastien on the verge of swooning like a Christ in the arms of Poiret and Phellion, who grotesquely mimicked the poses of the two Marys and whose faces were contorted with compassion.

Rabourdin: "What's the matter, gentlemen?" (Sébastien struggles to his feet and falls on his knees before Rabourdin.)

Sébastien: "I have ruined you, Monsieur. The report—Dutocq, the monster, he must have taken it."

Rabourdin (calmly): "I already knew." (He raises Sébastien up and draws him aside.) "You are a child, my friend." (He speaks to

Phellion.) "Where are those gentlemen?"

Phellion: "Monsieur, they went to Monsieur Baudoyer's bureau to see a report which is said to . . ."

Rabourdin: "Enough." (He goes out, taking Sébastien with him. Poiret and Phellion look at each other, stunned by the great shock and not knowing what to say.)

Poiret (to Phellion): "Monsieur Rabourdin . . . !"

Phellion (to Poiret): "Monsieur Rabourdin . . . !"

Poiret: "Well, I never! Monsieur Rabourdin!"

Phellion: "But did you see him, in spite of it all, calm and dignified . . . "

Poiret (with a sly look resembling a grimace): "There's something behind all this; it wouldn't surprise me at all."

Phellion: "A man of honor, pure, and without blemish."

Poiret: "And that Dutocq?"

Phellion: "Monsieur Poiret, are you thinking what I'm thinking about Dutocq? Don't you see what I mean?"

Poiret (nodding two or three times, replies with a sly look): "Yes." (The other employees return.)

Fleury: "It's very hard to swallow, and after having read it I still don't believe it. Monsieur Rabourdin, a king among men! My God! If there are spies in *his* ranks, it is enough to disgust you with virtue. I always put Rabourdin among Plutarch's heroes."

Vimeux: "Oh, it's true!"

Poiret (thinking of having only five more days left): "But gentlemen, what do you say about the man who stole the paper, who took advantage of Rabourdin?" (Dutocq leaves.)

Fleury: "He's a Judas Iscariot! Who is he?"

Phellion (with finesse): "He surely is not among us."

Vimeux (enlightened): "It's Dutocq!"

Phellion: "I have yet to see the proof, Monsieur. While you were gone, that young man, Monsieur Delaroche, looked as if he were about to die. Look, see his tears on my desk!"

Poiret: "We held him fainting in our arms. And the key to my place, well, he's still got it in his back." (Poiret goes out.)

Vimeux: "The minister did not want to work with Rabourdin today, and Monsieur Saillard, to whom the personnel chief said a few words, came to tell Monsieur Baudoyer to apply for the Cross of the Legion of Honor—there's one to be granted to the division on New Year's Day—and it's for Monsieur Baudoyer. Is everything quite clear? Monsieur Rabourdin is being sacrificed by the very persons who employ him. That's what Bixiou says. We were all to be axed, except for Phellion and Sébastien."

Du Bruel (entering): "Well, gentlemen, is it true?"

Thuillier: "To the last word."

Du Bruel (putting his hat on again): "Good-bye, gentlemen." (He leaves.)

Thuillier: "He doesn't like being on the firing line, that vaudevillist. He's off to the duc de Rhétoré and the duc de Maufrigneuse; but let him run! It's Colleville, so they say, who'll be our chief."

Phellion: "And yet he seemed to be fond of Monsieur Rabourdin."

Poiret (returning): "I've had a world of trouble getting my house key back. The little guy is in tears and Monsieur Rabourdin has completely disappeared." (Dutocq and Bixiou return.)

Bixiou: "Well, gentlemen! There are strange goings-on in your bureau! Du Bruel?" (He checks in his room.) "Gone!"

Thuillier: "At full speed!"

Bixiou: "And Rabourdin?"

Fleury: "Melted away, evaporated, gone in a puff. To say that a man, the king of men. . . ."

Poiret (to Dutocq): "In his grief, Monsieur Dutocq, the little Sébastien accuses you of having taken the paper ten days ago. . . ."

Bixiou (looking at Dutocq): "You must clear yourself of that accusation, my friend." (All the employees stare at Dutocq.)

Dutocq: "Where is he, that little viper who was copying it?"

Bixiou: "How do you know he was copying it? My friend, it takes a diamond to polish a diamond!" (Dutocq leaves.)

Poiret: "Listen, Monsieur Bixiou. I only have five and a half days left in the bureaus, and I would like—once, just once—to have the pleasure of understanding you! Do me the pleasure of explaining to me what a diamond is good for in this situation. . . . "

Bixiou: "That means, papa—since I'm willing just once to come down to your level—that, just as only a diamond can polish a diamond, so only a snoop can beat a snoop."

Fleury: "Here, 'snoop' stands for 'spy.'"

Poiret: "I do not understand . . ."

Bixiou: "Oh well, that'll be for some other time!"

Monsieur Rabourdin had run straight to the minister's. The minister was at the Chamber. Rabourdin went to the Chamber of Deputies, where he wrote a note to the minister. The minister was at the bar, engaged in a heated debate. Rabourdin waited, not even in the conference room but in the courtyard, and he resolved, in spite of the cold, to plant himself in front of His Excellency's carriage so as to talk to him as he got in. The usher had told him that the minister was in the midst of a row raised by the nineteen members of the extreme Left, and that it was a stormy session. Rabourdin paced up and down the palace courtyard, a victim of feverish anxiety; and he waited five solid hours. At six-thirty the recessional began, but the minister's messenger boy came out to find the coachman.

"Hey, Jean!" he said to him. "Monseigneur left with the minister of war; they're going to see the king, and from there they're going to dinner together. We're to pick him up at ten o'clock, there'll be a council this evening."

With slow steps Rabourdin made his way home in a state of despondency easy to imagine. It was seven o'clock. He barely had time to dress.

"Well, you're appointed," cried his wife joyously as he entered the salon.

Rabourdin raised his head with a horribly melancholy movement and replied, "I fear I shall never again set foot in the Ministry."

"What?" said his wife, stirred with a horrid anxiety.

"My memorandum on the employees is circulating in the bureaus, and it was impossible for me to meet with the minister!"
Célestine had a sudden vision whereby, with one of his infernal flashes, the Devil showed her the meaning of her last conversation with des Lupeaulx.

"If I had behaved like a common woman," she thought, "we would have had the post."

She gazed at Rabourdin with a sort of grief. A dreary silence fell, and dinner was eaten in a state of mutual meditation.

"And it's our Wednesday," she said.

"All is not lost, my dear Célestine," said Rabourdin, planting a kiss on his wife's forehead. "Perhaps tomorrow morning I'll be able to speak with the minister and everything will be cleared up. Sébastien was at it all last night: all the copies are ready and collated. I'll ask the minister for a reading by placing it all on his desk. La Brière will help me. A man is never condemned without a hearing."

"I am curious to see if Monsieur des Lupeaulx will come to see us tonight."

"He? Surely he won't miss it," said Rabourdin. "There's something of the tiger in him: he likes to lick the blood of the wound he has inflicted."

"My poor dear," said his wife, taking his hand, "I don't see how a man who could conceive so fine a reform did not also see that it ought not to be told to a soul. It is one of those ideas that a man keeps to himself, for he alone can apply it. You should have done in your domain as Napoleon did in his; he stooped, twisted, crawled! Yes, Bonaparte crawled! In order to be made commander-in-chief he married Barras's mistress. You should have waited, been made deputy, gone with the political flow, sometimes to the depths of the sea, at other times on the crest of the wave, and, like Monsieur de Villèle, followed the Italian motto *Col tempo*, in other words, 'All things come to those who wait.' That orator aimed at power for seven years, and he began in 1814 by protesting against the Charter when he was the same age you are now. There's the mistake! You have subordinated yourself when you were born to rule."

The entrance of Schinner the painter brought silence upon the wife and husband, whom these words had rendered pensive.

"Dear friend," said the painter, shaking the administrator's hand, "the support of an artist is rather useless; but under the circumstances, we are all faithful, we are! I bought the evening paper. Baudoyer is appointed director and is decorated with the Cross of the Legion of Honor. . . . "

"I've been there the longest, and I have twenty-four years of service," said Rabourdin, smiling.

"I know Monsieur le comte de Sérizy, the minister of state, pretty well. If you would like an appointment, I can go and see him," said Schinner.

The salon filled with persons who knew nothing of the administrative activities. Du Bruel did not show up. Madame Rabourdin was all the more gay and gracious, like the horse which, wounded in battle, finds the strength to bear its master.

"She is very brave," said a few women who put on the charm for her as they saw her in her misfortune.

"And yet she certainly poured it on for des Lupeaulx," said the Baronne du Châtelet to the vicomtesse de Fontaine.

"Do you think that . . . ?" asked the vicomtesse.

"But Monsieur Rabourdin would have at least gotten the Cross!" said Madame de Camps, defending her friend.

Around eleven o'clock des Lupeaulx appeared, and to depict him one can say that his spectacles were sad and his eyes merry; yet the lenses shrouded his glances so well that one would have to have been a physiognomist to discern their diabolical expression. He went up to shake Rabourdin's hand, which the latter could not help but extend to him.

"We must have a chat," he told him as he went to seat himself beside la belle Rabourdin, who received him graciously.

"Well!" he said, casting her a side glance. "You are grand, and I find you just as I might have expected, sublime in defeat. Did you know that it is very rare for a superior being to rise to one's expectations of her? Defeat does not overwhelm you? You're right, we shall triumph," he whispered in her ear. "Your fate is always in your own hands, so long as you have as your ally a man who adores you. We shall have a little meeting."

"But is Baudoyer appointed?" she asked him.

"Yes," said the secretary-general.

"Is he decorated?"

"Not yet; but he will be."

"And so?"

"You don't understand politics."

While this evening seemed eternal to Madame Rabourdin, at the Place Royale a comedy was in progress just as it is played out in the seven Parisian salons with every ministerial change. The Saillard salon was packed. Monsieur and Madame Transon arrived at eight o'clock. Madame Transon kissed Madame Baudoyer, née Saillard. Monsieur Bataille, Captain of the National Guard, came with his wife and the curate of Saint-Paul's.

"Monsieur Baudoyer," said Madame Transon, "I want to be the first to congratulate you; your talents have been done justice. Now you have certainly earned your promotion."

"Here you are, Director," said Monsieur Transon, rubbing his hands, "it speaks well for the neighborhood."

"And we can truly say it came to pass without any intrigue," exclaimed Père Saillard. "*We* are not intriguers; *we* don't go to select soirées of the minister."

Uncle Mitral rubbed his nose, grinning; he was looking at his niece Elisabeth, who was chatting with Gigonnet. Falleix could only think of the blindness of Père Saillard and Baudoyer. Messieurs Dutocq, Bixiou, du Bruel, Godard, and Colleville (named chief) entered.

"What a bunch!" said Bixiou to du Bruel. "What a wonderful caricature if they were drawn as skates, bream, claquarts—common name of a shellfish—all dancing a saraband!"

"Monsieur Director," said Colleville, "I have come to congratulate you, or rather we congratulate ourselves for having you as the head of the department, and we come together to assure you of the zeal with which we shall cooperate in your labors."

Monsieur and Madame Baudoyer, father and mother of the new director, were there to enjoy the glory of their son and daughter-in-law. Uncle Bidault, who had dined at the house, had a fidgety look in his eye that upset Bixiou.

"There's one for you," said the artist to du Bruel, pointing out Gigonnet, "who could be a character in a vaudeville! What would it fetch? An odd fish like that ought to serve as a sign at Deux-Magots. And what a coat! I thought only Poiret was capable of wearing something like that after ten years' exposure to the Parisian elements."

"Baudoyer is magnificent," said du Bruel.

"Stunning!" replied Bixiou.

"Gentlemen," said Baudoyer, "this is my own uncle, Monsieur Mitral, and my great-uncle through my wife, Monsieur Midault."

Gigonnet and Mitral threw a glance at the three employees, one of those penetrating glances that gleamed of gold and made its impression on the two scoffers.

"Ha!" said Bixiou as he walked off under the arcades of the Place

Royale. "Did you get a good look at those two uncles? Two model Shylocks. They go, I'll bet you, to Les Halles and put their ecus down for a hundred percent. They lend against securities; they deal in clothes, galloons, cheeses, women and children; they're Arab-Jew-Genoese-Greek-Genevese-Lombard and Parisian, suckled by a wolf and born of a Turk."

"I believe Uncle Mitral used to be a bailiff," said Godard.

"You see!" said du Bruel.

"I'm going to see my proofs printed," Bixiou said, "but I'd like to study Rabourdin's salon carefully tonight. You're lucky to be going there, du Bruel."

"I!" said the vaudevillist, "what would you want me to do *there*? My face doesn't lend itself to condolences. Anyway, it's rather vulgar these days to line up to see people who have been dismissed."

By midnight Madame Rabourdin's salon was deserted; only two or three people remained, des Lupeaulx and the masters of the house. When Schinner and Madame and Monsieur de Camps had left, des Lupeaulx rose with a mysterious air, stood with his back to the clock, and looked in turn at wife and husband.

"My friends," he said, "nothing is lost, for you still have the minister and me. Between two powers, Dutocq simply preferred the one he thought the stronger. He has served the Grand Almoner and the Court; he betrayed me. It's all in a day's work: a politician never complains of a betrayal. Still, Baudoyer will be dismissed in several months and no doubt moved to the Prefecture of Police, for the Grand Almonry will not abandon him."

And he went into a long tirade about the Grand Almonry, the dangers the government ran in leaning upon the church and the Jesuits, etc. . . . Yet it is not necessary to point out that the Court and the Grand Almonry, to whom the Liberal newspapers attributed enormous influence over the Administration, actually had very little to do with one Monsieur Baudoyer. These petty intrigues died in the upper sphere before the great interests that were at stake. If a few words were obtained by the importunities of the curate of Saint-Paul's and Monsieur Gaudron, the request had been put down at the minister's first remark. Passions alone made up the police force of the Congrégation, as it put itself above whomever. . . . The occult power of this association, surely justified in the face of the brazen society whose doctrine is summed up by "Heaven helps those who help themselves," only became a factor as the subordinates freely endowed it out of selfish threats. In the end, the Liberal slanderers were only too happy to fashion the Grand Almonry into a political, administrative, civil, and military giant. Fear creates idols for itself. At this time, Baudoyer believed in the Grand Almonry, although the only almonry that had protected him was seated at the Café Thémis. There are, at certain times in history, certain names, certain institutions, certain powers to whom one attributes all misfortunes, whose talents one denies and which serve as deciding factors in folly. Just as Talleyrand was supposed to hail every event with a bon mot, so in these days of the Restoration, the Grand Almonry did and undid everything. Unfortunately, it neither did nor undid anything. Its influence was in the hands of neither a Richelieu nor a Cardinal Mazarin, but in the hands of a sort of Cardinal de Fleury who, timid for over five years, acted only on one day—and poorly at that. Later on, the "Doctrine" did more, with impunity, at Saint-Merri, than Charles X pretended to do in July 1830. Without the article on censorship so foolishly introduced into the new Charter, journalism would have had its Saint-Merri too. The younger branch could have legally carried out the plan of Charles X.

"Remain bureau chief under Baudoyer," continued des Lupeaulx, "be a true politician; put generous thoughts and impulses aside. Retreat to your duties; don't say a word to your director;

don't give him advice; and don't do anything without orders. In three months Baudoyer will be out of the Ministry, either dismissed or deported to some other administrative shore. Perhaps he'll go to the Royal Household. It's happened to me twice in my life to be buried under an avalanche of folly. I let it pass."

"Yes," said Rabourdin, "but you were not slandered, your honor impugned, compromised. . . ."

"Ha, ha, ha!" cried des Lupeaulx, interrupting the bureau chief with a burst of Homeric laughter. "Why, that's the daily bread of every great man in this glorious realm of France! There are two ways to take it: either buckle under—that is, pack your bags and go plant cabbages; or else rise above it, and walk on, unfazed, without so much as turning your head."

"I have only one way of untying the noose that espionage and treachery have slipped around my neck," replied Rabourdin, "and that is immediately to explain myself to the minister, and if you are as sincerely devoted as you say, you can bring me face to face with him tomorrow."

"You mean to explain your administrative plan to him . . . ?"

Rabourdin nodded.

"Well then, entrust me with your plans, your memos, and I swear to you he shall be at it all night."

"Then let's be off!" said Rabourdin eagerly, "for at least after six years of work I should have the pleasure of two or three hours during which the king's minister will be forced to applaud such perseverance."

Compelled by Rabourdin's tenacity to take the path without camouflage for his ruse, des Lupeaulx hesitated for a moment and looked at Madame Rabourdin, asking himself, "Which shall triumph, my hatred for him or my feeling for her?"

"You don't trust me," he said to the bureau chief after a pause. "I see that to me you will always be the man of the 'secret note.' Adieu, Madame."

Madame Rabourdin bowed coldly. Célestine and Xavier retreated to their respective corners without a word, so overcome were they by their misfortune. The wife thought of the dreadful position in which she stood toward her husband. The bureau chief, who was resolving never again to set foot in the ministry and to hand in his resignation, was lost in the vastness of his thoughts: for him it was a matter of a complete change of life and the necessity to start off on a new track. All night he sat in front of his fire, taking no notice of Célestine, who several times came in on tiptoe in her nightgown.

"Since I have to go to the ministry one last time to collect my papers and put Baudoyer in charge of business, let's try to imagine the effect of my resignation," he said to himself.

He drafted his resignation, thinking over the phrasing of the letter, which he wrote as follows:

Monseigneur, I have the honor of addressing my resignation to His Excellency in this envelope; yet I venture to hope that he will recall hearing me say that I had entrusted my honor to his hands, and that it was a matter of an immediate explanation. This explanation, which I earnestly besought, and which today would perhaps be useless since a portion of my work on the Administration, prematurely disclosed and distorted, is circulating in the bureaus, is being misinterpreted out of spite, and forces me to resign before the tacit reprobation of those in power. Your Excellency, the morning on which I sought to speak with him, may have thought that it was a question of promotion, when I was thinking solely of the glory of his ministry and of the public good; it was necessary for me to redirect his thinking in this regard.

There followed the usual respectful closing remarks.

It was seven-thirty when this man consummated the sacrifice of his ideas, for he burned his work. Worn-out by his thoughts and overcome by his moral suffering, he dozed off, his head resting on his armchair. He was wakened by a strange sensation and found his hands covered with his wife's tears and saw her kneeling before him. Célestine had come in to read the resignation. She could fathom the depth of the fall. She and Rabourdin were now to be reduced to living on four thousand francs a year. She had added up her debts; they amounted to thirty-two thousand francs! That was the most ignoble of all miseries. And this man, so noble and trusting, overlooked her abuse of the fortune entrusted to her care. She was sobbing at his feet, as beautiful as Magdalene.

"My cup is full," cried Xavier in his state of terror. "I am dishonored at the Ministry, and dishonored . . ."

The flash of her pure honor emanated from Célestine's eyes and she sprang up like a startled horse and cast a terrifying glance at Rabourdin.

"I! *I!*" she said, on two sublime notes. "Am I a base wife? If I were, you would have been appointed. And yet," she added, "it's easier to believe that than to believe the truth."

"Then what is it?" said Rabourdin.

"In few words," she said, "we owe thirty thousand francs."

Rabourdin grabbed his wife with a wild gesture and sat her down on his knee with joy.

"Take heart, dear," he said in a tone of such adorable kindness that the bitterness of her tears was transformed into something inexpressibly tender. "I too have made mistakes! I've worked uselessly for my country, or at least I thought I could be useful to her. . . . But now I mean to tread another path. If I had sold groceries, we'd be millionaires. Well, so let's be grocers. You're only twenty-eight, my angel! And so, in ten years, hard work will have won the luxury you love, and which we'll have to renounce for a short time. I too, dear child, am not a base husband. We'll sell our farm; in seven years it has appreciated. That added value and our furniture will pay *my* debts. . . ."

She kissed her husband a thousand times in a single kiss for those generous words.

"We'll have," he added, "a hundred thousand francs to put into some sort of business. Within a month, I'll have chosen some sort of venture. The luck that made a Falleix run into a Saillard won't pass us by. Hold breakfast for me. I'll return from the Ministry free of my yoke of misery."

Célestine held her husband in her arms with a strength men do not possess even in their most passionate moments, for women are stronger through emotion than men are through power. She wept, and laughed, and sobbed, and spoke all at once.

When Rabourdin left the house at eight o'clock, the porter handed him the scathing cards from Baudoyer, Bixiou, Godard, and the others. Nevertheless, he went to the Ministry and found Sébastien waiting at the door to entreat him not to enter the bureaus, through which an infamous caricature of Rabourdin was making the rounds.

"If you wish to cushion the bitterness of the fall, bring me that drawing," he said, "for I am taking my resignation to Ernest de la Brière personally, so that it won't be perverted in passing through administrative channels. I have my reasons for asking you for the caricature."

After having assured himself that his letter was in the hands of the minister, Rabourdin entered the courtyard to find Sébastien in tears as he handed him the lithograph.

"It's very clever," said Rabourdin, showing a serene mien to the supernumerary even as the Saviour did when he was crowned with thorns.

He entered the bureaus with a calm air and went at once to Baudoyer to ask him to come to the division office to receive instructions from him as to the business which this incompetent was henceforth to direct.

"Tell Monsieur Baudoyer that this matter cannot wait," he added in front of Godard and the employees. "My resignation is in the minister's hands, and I do not want to stay in the bureaus a minute longer than I have to!"

Seeing Bixiou, Rabourdin went straight up to him, showed him the lithograph, and to everyone's great astonishment said to him: "Was I not right in saying you are an artist? It's just a shame you directed the point of your pencil against a man who cannot be judged in this way, nor by the bureaus. But everything is a laughing matter in France, even God!"

Then he took Baudoyer into the office of the late La Billardière. At the door he found Phellion and Sébastien, the only two who, in this great disaster, dared remain openly faithful to this accused man. Rabourdin, noticing that Phellion's eyes were moist, could not refrain from clasping his hand.

"Monsieur," said the good man, "if we can serve you in any way, we are at your service. . . ."

"Well, come in, my friends," said Rabourdin with noble grace. "Sébastien, my lad, write your resignation and submit it through Laurent, you're sure to be wrapped up in the calumny that brought me down. I'll see to your future: from now on, we'll always stick together."

Sébastien burst into tears.

Monsieur Rabourdin shut himself up in the late La Billardière's office with Monsieur Baudoyer, and Phellion helped him explain all the administrative difficulties to the new division chief. With every dossier Rabourdin explained, with every box he opened, Baudoyer's little eyes grew as big as saucers.

"Adieu, monsieur," said Rabourdin at last, in a manner that was both solemn and scoffing.

Meanwhile Sébastien had put together a stack of the documents belonging to the bureau chief and carried them off in a coach. Rabourdin walked through the Ministry's grand courtyard with all the employees watching from the windows and waited there a moment for the minister's orders. The minister did not make a move. Phellion and Sébastien stuck by Rabourdin. Phellion courageously escorted the fallen man to the rue Duphot while he expressed his respectful admiration. He returned, satisfied with himself, to take up his work, after having paid the funeral honors to that misunderstood administrative talent.

Bixiou (seeing Phellion come in): "*Victrix causa diis placuit, sed victa Catoni.*"

Phellion: "Yes, Monsieur!"

Poiret: "What's that supposed to mean?"

Fleury: "That the clerical party is rejoicing, and that Monsieur Rabourdin has the respect of men of honor."

Dutocq (annoyed): "You weren't saying that yesterday."

Fleury: "If you speak to me one more time, you'll have my fist in your face, you! It's a sure thing that you *pinched* Monsieur Rabourdin's papers." (Dutocq leaves the office.) "Go and complain to your Monsieur des Lupeaulx, spy!"

Bixiou (laughing and making faces like a monkey): "I'm curious to know how the division will get along. Monsieur Rabourdin was such a remarkable man that he must have had *some* purpose in writing that work of his. The minister is losing a fine mind." (He rubs his hands together.)

Laurent: "Monsieur Fleury is summoned to the Secretariat."

The employees of both bureaus: "Done for!"

Fleury (leaving the room): "I don't care. I have a responsible editorial postion. I shall have all my time to myself to lounge about or do amusing work in the newspaper office."

Bixiou: "Dutocq has gotten that poor Desroy fired; he's accused of wanting to chop off the heads . . ."

Thuillier: ". . . of kings? . . ."

Bixiou: "My compliments! That's a good one!"

Colleville (entering joyously): "Gentlemen, I am your chief. . . ."

Thuillier (he embraces Colleville): "Ah, my friend, if it were me myself, I would not be so pleased."

Bixiou: "It's his wife's work, but it's not a masterpiece! . . ." (Bursts of laughter.)

Poiret: "Can anyone tell me the moral of what is happening here today?"

Bixiou: "Do you really want to know? The antechamber to the Administration is henceforth the Chamber, the Court is the boudoir, the main entrance is though the cellar, and the bed is more than ever the beaten path."

Poiret: "Monsieur Bixiou, may I ask, would you explain?"

Bixiou: "I shall paraphrase my opinion. To be anything, you must begin by being everything. Obviously, an administrative reform is needed. For, on my word of honor, the state robs its employees as much as the employees rob the state of time due it. But we don't work much because we receive next to nothing in return, we are far too numerous for the task at hand, and my virtuous Rabourdin saw all that! Gentlemen, that great administrator foresaw what must happen, what fools call the 'games of our admirable liberal institutions.' The Chamber will want to administrate, and the administrators will want to be legislators. The government will try to administrate, and the Administration will want to govern. Even the laws will be mere regulations, and ordinances will become laws. God made this epoch for those who like to laugh. I live in a state of jovial admiration for the spectacle the greatest joker of modern times, Louis XVIII, bequeathed us." (General amazement.) "Gentlemen, if France, the best-administered nation of Europe, is in this condition, imagine what other countries are like? Poor nations! I ask myself how they can possibly get along without two Chambers, without freedom of the press, without reports, without memoranda, without an army of bureaucrats? How, how can they have armies and navies? How can they survive without debating every breath they take and every bite they eat? Can that be called a government, a nation? I've been told (a traveler's tale) that these people act as if they have a policy and that they enjoy a certain influence; but I pity them! They are in the dark as to the *progress of the Enlightenment*, they can't stir up new ideas, they don't have independent tribunals, they're living in a state of barbarism. Only the French people understand the realm of ideas. Do you understand, Monsieur Poiret" (Poiret jumped as if jolted), "how a nation can do without division chiefs, director-generals, this splendid corp of officials, the glory of France and of the Emperor Napoleon, who had his own good reasons for creating offices? Think about it, how these countries have the audacity to exist; and how in Vienna there are about one hundred employees in the war ministry, whereas, for us, salaries and pensions amount to a third of the whole budget, something they never dreamed of before the Revolution. I'll sum it up by saying that the Academy of Inscriptions and Belles-Lettres, which has very little work to do, might well offer a prize for the answer to this question: Which state is better organized, one that does a lot with a few employees, or one that does little with many employees?"

Poiret: "Is that your last word?"

Bixiou: "Oui, Monsieur! . . . Ja, mein Herr! . . . Sì, Signor! Da! . . . I'll spare you other languages. . . ."

Poiret (lifting his hands to heaven): "My God! . . . and they call you clever!"

Bixiou: "Then you didn't understand me?"

Phellion: "Although your last remark made a good deal of sense. . . ."

Bixiou: "Like the budget, complex as it seems simple, I've set it as a beacon on the edge of this cliff, this pit, this abyss, this volcano, called, in the language of the Constitutionnel, 'the political horizon.'"

Poiret: "I would very much like any explanation that I could understand. . . ."

Bixiou: "Long live Rabourdin! . . . That's my opinion. Are you satisfied?"

Colleville (gravely): "Monsieur Rabourdin had only one fault."

Poiret: "What?"

Colleville: "Being a statesman instead of a bureau chief."

Phellion (standing in front of Bixiou): "Why, Monsieur, did you, who understand Monsieur Rabourdin so well, make that disgus——, that inf——, that horrible caricature?"

Bixiou: "And what about our bet? Did you forget I was playing the devil's advocate, and that your bureau owes me a dinner at the Rocher de Cancale?"

Poiret (very put out): "Then let it be said that I will leave the bureau without ever having understood a sentence, a word, a single thought of Monsieur Bixiou's."

Bixiou: "It's your own fault! Ask these gentlemen. Gentlemen, did you understand the meaning of my observations? Are they true?—revealing? . . ."

All: "Alas, yes!"

Minard: "And the proof is that I just wrote my resignation. Adieu, gentlemen, I'm going to forge into industry. . . ."

Bixiou: "Have you invented the mechanical corset or baby bottle, a fire engine or overshoes, a stove that burns no wood or an oven that can cook cutlets with three sheets of paper?"

Minard (leaving): "I'll keep my secret to myself."

Bixiou: "Well, young Poiret junior, you see, all these gentlemen understand me."

Poiret (humiliated): "Monsieur Bixiou, would you just once do me the honor of coming down to my level and speaking to me in a language I can understand?"

Bixiou (winking at the employees): "By all means." (He grabs Poiret by the button of his frock coat.) "Before you leave here, perhaps you would care to know what you are. . . ."

Poiret (quickly): "An honest man, monsieur . . ."

Bixiou (shrugging his shoulders): ". . . to be able to define, explain, fathom, and analyze precisely what a bureaucrat is? Do you know what he is?"

Poiret: "I think I do."

Bixiou (twisting the button): "I doubt it."

Poiret: "It's someone paid by the government to do a job."

Bixiou: "Well then, a soldier is a bureaucrat."

Poiret (puzzled): "Why, no."

Bixiou: "But he is paid by the state to do work, to go on guard and pass in review. You'll tell me he's too anxious to leave his post, that his rank is too low, that he works too hard and touches metal too little—except for his gun, of course."

Poiret (his eyes wide): "Well then, Monsieur, a bureaucrat is, logically speaking, a man who needs his salary to live, is not free to quit his post, and cannot do anything except push papers."

Bixiou: "Ah! Now we're getting at a solution. . . . So the bureau is the state employee's shell. No employee without a bureau, no bureau without an employee. But what, then, of a customs officer?" (Poiret tries to slip away; he gets away from Bixiou, who has snapped one button off but pulls him back by grabbing another.) "Bah! In the bureaucratic order, he would be neuter. The customs officer is only half civil servant; in the confines of the bureau or the service it is just as if he were on the borderline—not altogether soldier nor altogether civil servant. But, Papa, where are we going?" (Twists the button.) "Where does the state employee end up?

That's a serious question. Is a prefect a state employee?"

Poiret (timidly): "He's a functionary."

Bixiou: "Ah! You are implying the contradiction that a functionary is not a civil servant!"

Poiret (weary, looks over at the employees): "Monsieur Godard looks like he wants to say something."

Godard: "The civil servant is the order, the functionary the genus."

Bixiou (smirking): " I didn't think you were capable of such an ingenious distinction, you clever subordinate."

Poiret: "Where's this leading? . . ."

Bixiou: "La, la, Papa, let's not step on our leash. . . . Just listen, and we'll come to an understanding. Look, let's assume an axiom which I shall dedicate to all bureaus! Where the civil servant ends, the functionary begins; where the functionary leaves off, the statesman begins. However, there are very few statesmen among the prefects. The prefect is therefore a neutral pawn to the higher genus. He comes between the statesman and the state employee, just as the customs officer stands between the civil and the military. Let's continue to clear up these important points." (Poiret turns crimson.) "This can be stated in a theorem worthy of La Rochefoucault: above salaries of twenty thousand francs, there are no more civil servants. Mathematically, we may deduce this first corollary: directors-general may be statesmen. Perhaps it's in this sense that more than one deputy says to himself, 'It is a fine thing to be a director-general.' Yet, in the interests of the French language and of the Academy . . ."

Poiret (completely fascinated by the fixity of Bixiou's gaze): "The French language! The Academy!"

Bixiou (twisting off the second button and grabbing the next one up): "Yes, in the interests of our noble language, one must observe that if the bureau chief can, strictly speaking, be a civil servant, then the division chief must be a bureaucrat. These gentlemen" (turning to the employees and showing them a third button off Poiret's coat), "these gentlemen appreciate this delicate nuance. And so, Papa Poiret, the employee absolutely ends with the division chief. So there, the question is settled: there is no room for doubt: the employee who seemed undefinable is defined."

Poiret: "That seems beyond a shadow of a doubt."

Bixiou: "Nevertheless, do me the kindness of resolving the following question: a judge, being irremovable, and therefore, according to your subtle distinction, unable to be a functionary, and receiving a salary not in proportion to his work, is he to be included in the class of state employees . . . ?"

Poiret (gazing at the cornices): "Monsieur, I don't follow . . ."

Bixiou (snapping off a fourth button): "I wanted to prove to you, monsieur, that nothing is simple, and what I am going to say is intended for philosophers (if you will allow me to misquote a saying of Louis XVIII): I wish to point out that, 'Right alongside the need to define lies the danger of getting stuck.'"

Poiret (wiping his forehead): "Excuse me, monsieur, I feel queasy." (He tries to to button his coat.) "Ah! you've cut off all my buttons!"

Bixiou: "Well, *now* do you understand me? "

Poiret (upset): "Yes, monsieur. I understand that you wanted to play a very dirty trick by twisting off my buttons without my noticing! . . . "

Bixiou (solemnly): "Old man, you're mistaken! I wanted to stamp on your mind the clearest possible image of a constitutional government" (all the employees look at Bixiou; Poiret, stupefied, gazes at him uneasily) "and so keep my word to you. I used the parabolic method of the Savages. Listen! While the ministers engage in discussions in the Chambers that are just about as conclusive and useful as ours, the Administration is cutting the buttons off the tax-payers."

All: "Bravo, Bixiou!"

Poiret (who understands): "I don't feel bad about my buttons anymore."

Bixiou: "I shall do as Minard. I don't want to keep accounts for such paltry sums any longer; and so I shall deprive the Ministry of my cooperation." (Departs amid general laughter.)

Meanwhile, another more insightful scene was taking place in the minister's receiving room, for it reveals how great ideas die in the higher sphere, and how they rise above misfortune.

At that moment, des Lupeaulx was presenting the new director, Monsieur Baudoyer, to the minister. Two or three ministerial deputies and Monsieur Clergeot, to whom His Excellency assured a respectable pension, were gathered there. After a few banal remarks, the event of the day was brought up.

A deputy: "Then you've lost Rabourdin?"

Des Lupeaulx: "He handed in his resignation."

Clergeot: "He wanted, so they say, to reform the Administration."

The minister (looking at the deputies): "Salaries are perhaps not in proportion to the demands of the civil service."

De La Brière: "According to Monsieur Rabourdin, one hundred employees paid twelve thousand francs would do better and quicker work than a thousand employees paid twelve hundred."

Clergeot: "Perhaps he is right."

The minister: "But what can you do? The machine is built that way; you'd have to take it all apart and then put it back together again. Who would have the courage before the Chamber, under the heat of the foolish cries of the Opposition or the terrible articles in the press? So someday there will be some disastrous link-up between the Government and the Administration."

A deputy: "What will happen?"

The minister: "A minister wants to serve the public good yet doesn't have the power to do so. You'll create endless delays between things and their results. If you've actually made the theft of even a single ecu impossible, you still can't prevent collusion in the realm of private interests. Some things can only get done after secret stipulations, difficult to uncover, have been put forth. Moreover, the civil servants, from the least up to the bureau chief, will have opinions of their own; they'll no longer be the hands of one mind, they'll no longer represent the ideas of the government, the Opposition is giving them the right to speak out against the government, to vote against it, and to judge it."

Baudoyer (in a low voice, but meaning to be heard): "Monseigneur is sublime."

Des Lupeaulx: "Certainly, the bureaucracy has its faults: I myself find it slow and insolent; it hampers ministerial action, stifles projects, and prevents progress. But the French administration is amazingly useful. . . ."

Baudoyer: "Certainly!"

Des Lupeaulx: " . . . if only to maintain the paper and stamp industries! If, just like a good housekeeper, it is at times a little fussy, it can, at any time, account for each and every expense. Show me the businessman who wouldn't gladly give five percent of his earnings, of his turnover, if there were some sort of insurance against 'leakage'!"

The deputy (a manufacturer): "Industrialists of both worlds would gladly strike a deal with that evil genius called 'leakage.'"

Des Lupeaulx: "Well then, although statistics are the childish foible of modern statesmen, who take figures for calculations, we must make use of figures to calculate. Shall we, then? Figures are, moreover, the convincing argument of societies based on self-interest and money, and that is the sort of society the Charter has given us, at least in my opinion. Nothing convinces the 'intelligent masses' more than a few figures. Everything certain, so say our statesmen of the Left, can be resolved in figures. So let's figure." (The minister takes one deputy aside and talks with him in a low voice.) "There are about forty thousand civil servants, a deduction based on their salaries, not counting roadmen, street sweepers, and cigarette rollers, all of whom are not civil servants. The average salary is fifteen hundred francs. Multiply forty thousand by fifteen hundred and you have sixty million. Now, in the first place, a publicist could point out to China and Russia, where all the civil servants steal, to Austria, the American republics—indeed, to the whole world—the fact that for this price France possesses the most ferreting, meticulous, scribbling, paper-pushing, inventory-keeping, auditing, cross-checking, tidy set of bureaucrats—in fact, the famed housekeeper of administrations! Not one payment, not one centime, is on account in France which has no written order, is not backed by currency, is not produced and reproduced on balance sheets and paid out with a receipt; then, orders and receipts are logged in and checked by men with glasses. At the slightest error in format, the civil servant is shocked, for he lives by his scruples.

"Plenty of nations would be satisfied with this, but Napoleon didn't stop there. That great organizer reappointed the supreme magistrates of a court which is unique in the world. These magistrates spend their days verifying the money orders, documents, registers, payments, accounts received, accounts paid, etc., which the civil servants write up. These stern judges push the gift of exactitude, the genius for enquiry, the sharp-sightedness of lynxes, the shrewdness of accounting, to the point of going over all the credits in search of debits. These sublime martyrs to figures sent back, two years after the fact, to a military intendant, an account in which there was an error of two centimes. This is why the French Administration, the purest of those on the planet which pushes paper, has made theft, as His Excellency has just said, next to impossible. In France, misappropriation is a myth. And so who's to complain? France has revenues of twelve hundred million and she spends it, that's all there is to it. Twelve hundred million come into her coffers, and twelve hundred million go out. Therefore, she handles two billion, four hundred million and pays only sixty million—that is, two and a half percent—for the reassurance that there is no 'leakage.' Our political kitchen costs us sixty million, but the gendarmerie, the tribunals, the galleys, and the police cost just as much, and give no return. And believe you me, we find work for people who couldn't do anything else. Waste, if there is any, can only be moral or legislative, and the Chambers are therefore the accomplice, for waste becomes legal. 'Leakage' consists of: works that are neither urgent nor necessary; outfitting and reoutfitting troops; ordering ships regardless of the availability of timber, and then paying too much; preparing for war; paying the debts of a state without requiring reimbursement or insisting on security, etc., etc."

Baudoyer: "But this 'leakage' in the higher ranks has nothing to do with the state employees. This bad management of national affairs concerns the statesmen who guide the ship."

The minister (who has finished his conversation): "There is truth in what des Lupeaulx has just said; but bear in mind" (to Baudoyer), "Monsieur le Directeur, that no one sees things from a statesman's point of view. Ordering expenditures of all kinds, even useless ones, does not constitute bad management. Doesn't it stir up the circulation of money, the stagnation of which, especially in France, becomes dangerous by reason of the miserly and profoundly illogical habits of the provinces that hoard so much gold . . . ?"

The deputy (who had listened to des Lupeaulx): "But it seems to me that if His Excellency was right just now, and if our clever friend here" (takes des Lupeaulx by the arm) "is not wrong, what can we conclude?"

Des Lupeaulx (after looking at the minister): "Of course, something must be done. . . ."

De La Brière (timidly): "Then Monsieur Rabourdin is right?"

The minister: "I'm going to see Rabourdin. . . ."

Des Lupeaulx: "That poor man made the blunder of setting himself up as supreme judge of the Administration and the men who comprise it; he wants only three ministries. . . ."

The minister (interrupting): "He's crazy!"

The deputy: "How could you, in three ministries, represent the party chiefs in the Chamber?"

Baudoyer (with an air he imagines to be shrewd): "Perhaps Monsieur Rabourdin would also change the Constitution of our legislator king?"

The minister (grown thoughtful, takes La Brière's arm and leads him aside): "I want to see Rabourdin's work, and since you know about it . . ."

De La Brière (in the study): "He has burned it; you allowed him to be disgraced and he is resigning from the Ministry. Don't think for a moment, Monseigneur, that he had the absurd thought, as des Lupeaulx tries to make it seem, of changing things for the better in the centralization of power."

The Minister (to himself): "I made a mistake." (He is silent for a moment.) "Bah! We'll never be short of plans for reform."

De La Brière: "It's not ideas, but men to carry them out that we lack."

Des Lupeaulx, that adroit advocate of abuses, entered the minister's study. "Monseigneur, I'm off to my election."

"Wait," said His Excellency, leaving his personal secretary and guiding des Lupeaulx by the arm into the recess of the window.

"My dear friend, let me have that arrondissement; you'll be made count and I'll pay your debts. . . . Then, if I'm still in after the Chamber's reelection, I'll find a way to submit your name in a group to be named for the peerage."

"You are a man of honor. I accept."

And this is how it came to pass that Clément Chardin des Lupeaulx, whose father was ennobled under Louis XV, who quartered bore a ravishing silver sable wolf carrying a lamb in its mouth; second, in purple, three silver clasps, two and one; third, play of twelve, gules and silver; fourth, gold on a pale endorsed, three batons fleur-de-lisés gules; supported by four movable griffon's claws from the sides of the coin, with the motto *En lupus in historia*, was able to surmount these rather satirical arms with a count's coronet.

In 1830, around the end of December, Monsieur Rabourdin had some business that took him to his old ministry, where the bureaus had all been shaken up by dismissals from the highest down to the lowest. This revolution bore heaviest on the office boys, who were not fond of new faces. Rabourdin came early to the Ministry as he knew his way around, and he overheard the following conversation between Laurent's two nephews, as the uncle had received his pension.

"Well, how's your division chief doing?"

"Don't mention him to me. I can't do a thing with him. He rings me to ask if I've seen his handkerchief or his snuffbox. He receives people without making them wait; in short, he hasn't the least bit of dignity. Me, I often have to tell him, 'But, Monsieur, Monsieur le Comte your predecessor, in the interest of authority, whittled away at his armchair with his penknife to make believe he was working.' In fact, he makes a mess of everything! I find everything topsy-turvy. He's very uninspired. How about yours?"

"Mine? Oh, I ended up training him. He knows exactly where his stationery is, his envelopes, his wood, and all his stuff. My other one used to swear, this one is a softie—but he still isn't big on style. On top of that, he isn't decorated, and I don't like a chief without medals: he could be taken for one of us, and that's humiliating. He takes his papers home and asked me if I couldn't come over and wait table at receptions."

"Hey! What a government, my dear fellow!"

"Yes, indeed; everybody plays the game these days."

"I hope they won't cut our piddling wages."

"I'm afraid they will. The Chambers are prying into everything. Why they even count the sticks of firewood."

"Well, it can't last long if they go on that way."

"Hush, we're in for it! Somebody's listening."

"Hey! It's the late Monsieur Rabourdin. Ah, Monsieur, I recognized you by your walk. If you're here on business, no one knows the respect due you, since we're the only ones left from your day. . . . Messieurs Colleville and Baudoyer didn't wear out the morocco on the armchairs after you left. Heavens, no! Six months later they were made Collectors of Paris."